THE UNDROWNED

THE
UNDROWNED

Toby Vieira

WEATHERGLASS BOOKS

We have lingered in the chambers of the sea
By sea-girls wreathed with seaweed red and brown
Till human voices wake us, and we drown.

Prologue

In The Land Of

I.

'I've just remembered,' Ricardo said. 'This weird thing that happened in Bamako.'

'Sure,' I said. 'When we were sitting on that rooftop terrace. Mirages taking off all through the night. Sonic booms, fiery trails. The beer was good.'

'Not that,' Ricardo said.

'Don't tell me,' David said. 'You got lucky when the rest of us went to bed. That girl from France Inter. Bloody like you.'

'No,' Ricardo said. 'Not that. Something knocked on my window at four in the morning.'

'Sure,' David said. 'The girl from France Inter.'

Nikki squirmed, but she put up with it. Pretended to be one of the boys.

'Fuck off,' Ricardo said. 'Like this.' He knocked on the glass table in the departure lounge, once, twice, three times.

'You had a garden room, right?' I said.

'No I didn't,' Ricardo said. 'We were all on the fifth floor, remember. I was sleeping, and then I heard it.'

'If you were sleeping, how could you have heard it?' Nikki said.

'It woke me up, and then I was awake, and I heard it.'

'So then what?'

'I went to the window and checked. Nothing there. A ledge, right, about this wide.' Ricardo held up a spare battery pack.

'So she had a sideline in acrobatics,' David said.

Nikki made a face. 'How old are you anyway?'

'Yeah,' Ricardo said to David. 'Fuck off.'

'But what's the big deal?' Nikki said. 'You woke up in the middle of the night. So what.'

'There was a knock,' Ricardo said, 'and no one was there. I looked outside, in the corridor. No one there.'

'Maybe it was Guy Money,' David said, or at least that's what I thought he said, and the others looked at each other.

'That's not funny,' Ricardo said, and Nikki said something about how some things were better left unspoken. I asked who Guy Money was, but all of a sudden there was a lot of noise, like a storm bearing down angrily on the terminal building, and the roof began to shudder, the tables started to vibrate, and no one answered my question.

A C-17 was coming in, a big black shadow over the small airfield, and everyone got excited and took out their camera phones. There were Ospreys, too, a whole pack of cartoon gull-wings sitting fat on the tarmac further down.

And a Hercules, and a Transall, and a couple of Antonovs, and a big Boeing disgorging an airborne company or two. We took pictures of them all, and worried, and pretended not to.

'Three down, one to go,' Ricardo said, and popped open a can of Coke. 'Nothing gets between me and my Coke,' he said to no one in particular, rubbing the can down with a squidge of disinfectant.

The C-17 had parked opposite the departure lounge now, and they were unloading pallet after pallet of stuff wrapped in flags. PPE most likely, or bits of labs, or body bags.

None of us really wanted to go, and none of us really wanted to stay. There wasn't much fun to be had in these parts any more. The beaches were deserted, the bars empty at nine in the evening. There were people who travelled round with their cabin cases crammed full of bags of dried fruit and little plastic cups and who'd drink nothing but Coke from screw-top bottles they'd insist on opening themselves. None of us was given to squeamishness, but we'd look closely every time a waiter opened the bottle, make sure he didn't touch too far up its neck, and we wondered where the glasses had been, out back in some dark unseen place. You could be sure there were no thermometers at the back entrance, no one to shine a torch into your eyeballs. Not that the thermometers told you much. That same morning I'd gone from 37.9 to 35.2 in the space of a couple of hours.

Our plane was late. Some kind of a scare in Brazza had messed up the whole schedule. The guy had got taken off at the last minute, beeped and maybe more.

'Oh shit,' David said. 'Hope they managed to clean up the plane.'

'Not likely,' Nikki said. 'They're on a tight schedule.'

It was getting dark. I went to the gents. The toilets were all blocked and there was no water in the taps. Yellow impasto splashes on the walls. You could only catch it from live bodily fluids, from what anyone knew, but I didn't linger. I almost emptied the whole bottle of disinfectant on to my hands as I walked back to the departure lounge. When I got back, the others seemed to be arguing. I thought I heard that name again, Guy Money, but they stopped as soon as they saw me.

'What are you lot talking about?' I asked.

'Bloody food on that bloody island,' Nikki said. She didn't sound very convincing.

'So what's it like then, the island?' I asked.

David screwed up his eyes.

'Imagine an island—' Nikki said.

'Imagine a dump,' David said before she could finish.

Our plane came in to land. It looked normal enough, a worn-out UN Dash with a Kenyan crew who weren't letting anything on. 'You scrubbed this thing down yet?' David barked at the pilot, and the rest of us cringed, and the pilot shrugged and said, 'All done by the book, mate.' We belted up and tried not to think about who'd sat in the seats before us.

The flight was short and hot. When we landed there were some people from the health inspectorate on the tarmac with torches and thermometers. Thirty-six point seven. None of us beeped.

'*Blanc,*' they said, after shining the torch in our eyes, and filled in some perfunctory form. *Blanc, blanc, blanc.*

'Egg yolk,' David said.

'*Quoi, comment?*' one of the health inspectors said.

'*Jaune d'oeuf,*' David said.

'You'll get yourself arrested,' Nikki said.

'Anything to get out of here,' David said. 'Coming here once is bad enough. Twice is carelessness.'

'*Allez-y, vite,*' the health inspector said.

'For fuck's sake go,' Nikki said, and we did.

We got our passports stamped, found the driver organized by head office, and drove off in a little convoy with the handful of other passengers who'd got off the plane. After twenty minutes the cars stopped, and we had to get out to take the ferry across to the capital. 'It's dark,' someone said. 'They've been having power cuts,' Nikki replied. 'Same the last time we came.'

Nikki and Ricardo and David were on their second rotation. You could tell. Knowing glances, the desperate humour an attempt to steady the nerves. They'd spent a month on the island last time round, and they'd seen things they wouldn't talk about. I'd joined them in Bamako. First stop on the Grand Tour, with a little counter-insurgency thrown in for good measure. It was my first time. To these parts at any rate. I wondered how Nikki put up with the other two and their blokeish banter. David's in particular. But somehow she'd decided not to give a toss. There was a bit of light from the car headlights, and a shimmer over the water further on. '*Par ici, par ici*,' the driver said. We walked over sand that gave way to wooden planks, a jetty, and a boat called *Lumumba*.

'*Lumumba*,' David said. 'Not sure that's very reassuring.' Nor did it look reassuring, a little inshore launch with a torn tarp for a roof. We couldn't see the sea, but the white hull of the launch was bobbing vigorously. 'On the other hand,' he said, 'the alternative sucks. Stay overnight in a shack somewhere, at the heart of the district with the highest case rate in the country. In the country with the highest case rate in the world.'

We dropped our bags in the open bow of the launch and squeezed onto the low wooden bench under the tarp. There was a man at the wheel, in a uniform of sorts, and a boy in a T-shirt, taking in the painter. 'How long?' I asked the man at the wheel. 'Fifteen minutes,' he said. We didn't see the sea as the launch got under way, but we felt the swell and our trousers got wet from the spray. Fifteen minutes passed. The engine noise changed from a steady chugging to a feverish cough.

'What's going on?' David shouted at the man standing at the wheel.

'Problem,' he said.

'What do you mean, problem?' David shouted, standing up shakily. I guessed he'd been taking slugs from his hip flask on the car ride over from the airport.

'Easy now,' Nikki said, and tried to pull David back down on the bench.

'I'm trying to sort this out,' David shouted.

The engine's cough sputtered out, and the only noises now were the wind and the waves battering the hull of the launch.

'We're drifting,' Nikki said.

'This is not a good place to be drifting,' I said.

'What place is this anyway?' Ricardo said.

We peered out through a gap in the tarp. Not a light to be seen. Fifteen minutes, the guy at the wheel had said when we set off. The island should have been right there opposite us.

'There should be villages all along the coast of the island,' I said.

'So where does that leave us? Nikki said.

'Drifting out into the Atlantic,' I said. 'Next stop São Tomé.'

'Fuck,' David shouted, and grabbed the man at the wheel by his shoulders.

'You're mad,' someone said, but it didn't matter, because the launch hit something, and everyone fell over, and David tumbled headlong over the side of the boat, and something heavy smashed into the back of my knee, and all the little lights by the wheel went off, and then there was just the wind battering the tarp and a creaking sound from the hull of the launch.

Someone turned on their phone torch. The boat was listing heavily, with water coming in over the gunwale on one side. David was hanging onto the side of the boat with one hand, and holding his head with the other and moaning. The others had been thrown on top of each other on the low side of the bench. Someone was swearing. The man in the uniform who had been at the wheel staggered past us to the back of the launch and threw back the tarp. 'Got to get out, this way, *faut sortir*,' he shouted, and without thinking we all scrambled to our feet and clambered over the side of the launch and into the water. This is it, I thought. But I came down hard on the bottom, with the water only up to my chest, and something pointy scraped my face, like thorns or the outgrowth of a wreck.

II.

When I awoke, the wind had let up but was still buffeting the tarp. At least I thought it was the tarp, but it wasn't; it was a length of white canvas stretched over a rough wooden structure of pillars and crossbeams and rafters. The light was mottled and grey, and there were camp beds all down the length of the structure and big blue plastic vats at intervals. There was an opening at one end, and I could make out an open space, and another tented structure a little further on. I knew where we'd landed even before the nurse came in, and I did what anyone would have done: I panicked. The nurse was wearing full PPE, and it was only when he took off his face mask and goggles that I relaxed a bit.

'What am I doing here?' I asked, and my throat hurt as I spoke.

'Found you in the mangrove last night,' the nurse said. He had an Australian accent.

'Oh,' I said. 'But,' I said, pointing at the canvas roof and walls. 'This. Am I.'

'Don't worry,' the nurse said. 'No cases in right now. Only beds we could find.'

'Oh. What about the others?'

'They're fine. Outside, having breakfast.'

I felt hot, so I asked the nurse for a thermometer. But it only said 36.4, and we went outside, and there were more tented structures, all identical, long and white, with an entrance at one end and an exit at the other.

The nurse led me out past the tents, through an enclosure made with bright orange plastic net fencing. There were mud huts visible in the distance, set amid the usual mess of dust and scrub. Nikki and David were sitting on a couple of upside-down crates. Nikki was going through one of her bags, checking her gear. David was sipping coffee from a plastic cup and eating what looked like a pancake. He had a bandage round the top of his head.

'Bugger,' I said. 'What happened to you?'

'I went over the side,' David said. 'But then I got stitched up by a friendly man in a spacesuit.'

'Thank goodness.'

Another figure in PPE walked past a couple of tented rows further along, pushing a wheelbarrow.

'Is Ricardo with you?' I asked.

'No,' Nikki said. 'We thought he was with you. Having a lie-in.'

I swore, and went looking for the nurse with the Australian accent. Behind the tents, at the end of a narrow alleyway, I thought I could make out a red T-shirt, of the kind I'd once seen Ricardo wearing, with a charging elephant on it and the name of a Kenyan brewery. I ran down the alleyway between the tents, calling Ricardo's name, but the T-shirt was gone. At the end of the alleyway was a metal cylinder with a short chimney on top, and black smoke coming out of the chimney. It reminded me of driving past a similar place, late at night, a couple of weeks earlier, in another country, and seeing the orange glow in the dark, and occasional sparks coming out of the chimney, hard and yellow. I found the Australian nurse taping down the sides of one of the tents.

'Here's the thing,' I said. 'We had another colleague with us, guy called Ricardo. We're really worried about him.'

The Australian put down the tape. 'There's only the three of you we found last night, and the boatman and the kid who was crewing.'

'Could he have come ashore somewhere else?'

'Not likely. This is the only village for miles. And the mangrove's pretty much impenetrable. Pure stroke of luck one of the villagers heard you lot shouting last night.'

I didn't remember anything about anyone shouting, but then I didn't remember much. Only the cold water and the mangrove and then lights and noise and stretchers and being given some sort of a jab in the arm, and waking up under the rafters with the white canvas.

'Are you sure you didn't find anyone else where the boat went down?' I asked.

'Positive, mate. We had a good poke around in the mangrove. Nothing there. I'm so sorry.' He said it with such a matter-of-fact tone that it took a while to sink in.

'But what you're saying is—'

'Afraid so. The currents are really strong round the coast here. Would have taken him right out into the Atlantic.' A wailing sound came from the entrance to the treatment unit. 'Sorry, mate, we've got new patients coming in, got to go. We'll give you a lift to the ferry later, right.' And with that he suited up and put on his goggles and was gone.

I walked along the gravel paths between the tents once more and peeked in through the little squares cut into the canvas. A mother with sweat running down her forehead was nursing a baby, and a little boy was playing with a plastic plane that had a wing missing. One of the tents had red-and-white tape across the opening, and a little red pennant suspended from the tape; inside, two figures in full PPE were standing over an inert body on a camp bed. They were attaching transparent rubber tubes to a little machine on a tripod that looked like a Geiger counter; one of them seemed to be handling a blade. They must have seen me, because they started gesticulating in my direction, and I heard muffled sounds from inside the suits. It was obvious I wasn't supposed to be there, and I wasn't supposed to be looking.

'No sign of Ricardo,' I said when I got back to where Nikki and David were sitting.

'That's not good,' David said.

Nikki swore but didn't look up from her gear, which she was carefully dabbing with a lens cloth. 'Do you know I've got salt water in the bayonet?'

'Yeah, but head office will pay,' David said.

'Not on the shit contracts they've put us on,' Nikki said.

'I think we should stay here and get head office to send over a team,' I said.

David looked up from his pancake. 'Look, I get that you're worried about Ricardo, we all are, but staying here won't help us find him. Assuming he's still alive.'

I looked at Nikki, who shrugged and put down her lens. 'I think David's right. Not much we can do here. We'll go and talk to the Spanish consul when we get to the island, and we'll make some noise so the authorities do a proper search.'

David took a big bite out of his pancake. 'I'd say you're outvoted two to one.'

At lunchtime we got a lift back to the ferry landing, an hour through the bush over muddy winding tracks. We had called in Ricardo's disappearance to head office, to the insurance company contracted by head office to deal with emergencies, and to the local police, and nothing had come back. Filing a missing person report in a place like this would do about as much good as putting up posters in the mangrove.

It had been raining overnight. Some of the villages along the way to the ferry were under quarantine. Nikki had her window down, one of her cameras out, her lens trained on soldiers with paper face masks by the roadside, houses with white PVC sheets draped across the doors and windows. The wooden decks outside the shacks had a thick white patina from the chlorine, like the salt crust on the deck of an old ferry. Every once in a while, when the car had to slow down for a chicken or a goat, someone would come up, a child or an old woman, curious or defensive, and some of them shouted at Nikki when they saw her camera pointing from the window.

'Well, that's for pinching their soul,' David said. 'You know what these people are like.'

Nikki didn't even put down her camera. 'That's a complete myth and you know it. They just want to be paid for the picture.'

In one of the villages the driver had to stop when a couple of kids stretched a length of rope across the track in front of the car. One of the children came to the driver's door to ask for money. The driver gave him a few tattered notes. Nikki got out and asked the kids to stretch out their rope once more so she could take a picture. She gave them five dollars and they stepped back with sullen faces.

'What do you want people back home to think,' David asked when Nikki was back in the car. 'Folks will think they're a bunch of *coupeurs de route*.'

'I don't care what people think,' Nikki said. 'I just record.'

When we got to the jetty, everything looked different from the night before. There was a busy traffic of lighters and old landing craft ferrying cars and trucks, with wooden cranes unloading crates and barrels, goats and sheep swaying in the air in makeshift hoists. The boat we took over to the island was called *President Lakamba*, and it tore across the gentle swell like a playful dolphin. A Land Cruiser with a driver was waiting by the ramshackle terminal at the other end, and after getting in we inched along the potholed highway into town in a thick scrum of banged-up old vans with crude round windows cut out of the side panels. It was strange to see so much traffic on an island a few miles across. 'I don't get it,' Nikki said. 'Why would they put the airport on the mainland and the capital on an island?'

'It's a dump,' David said, and I got the impression it was what he said on arriving somewhere, anywhere, but here he had a point. Little mounds of garbage lay all along the side of the road like heaps of manure in a farmyard, layer upon sedimented layer of crap. We crept along until the highway came to an abrupt end, with a few big lumps of concrete strewn across the carriageway, and all the traffic had to take a sharp left turn, then you knew you were in the city centre, and it was not much to look at, random shacks and the occasional office building encircled by fences topped with razor wire.

The car dropped us off outside the hotel head office had booked for us, a seven-storey marble mirage overlooking the Gulf of Guinea. There were no temperature controls or eyeball checks at the entrance, just the manager with a smile that was a little too friendly and a glass of champagne.

We understood why when we checked in. Head office had made an open-ended reservation for us. We'd only been supposed to stay a few days, do a few interviews, get some good pictures, et cetera. Not stay forever. No wonder the manager was rubbing his hands, what with all the usual customers keeping away, the oil wells slowed to a trickle.

They gave us rooms on the top floor; it said PRESIDENTS CLUB next to the lift button; there was a big welcome hamper in each of the rooms, with a bottle of claret *avec les compliments de la direction*, and that cheered us up a bit.

'Beats the shithole we stayed in last time,' David said.

We went to the Spanish consulate to get something done about Ricardo, but it was a waste of time. 'He probably went off to do filming,' the consul said. 'You know, get the best picture, and in some days he will come back with the best pictures, ho ho, he will get all the prizes.' I didn't think so, but beyond putting another piece of paper in to some part or other of the local administration, there wasn't anything the consul would do. We did some shopping, bought new clothes and phones and thermometers and gloves, and went back to the hotel. We had sandwiches and a few drinks at the bar, talked about Ricardo. I didn't know much about him, and neither did Nikki or David, even though they'd been working as a team when they got assigned to cover The Land Of. They'd worked together quite a bit. I'd only met them when it all started for real and head office wanted a writer to work alongside the AV team for their second rotation.

Until then I'd covered a shitty little war on the other side of the continent. I'd overlapped briefly with Ricardo when I arrived. But not enough to get to know him properly.

Nikki and David didn't even know if Ricardo had a family, but thought he didn't, or else he would have talked about it. He was from Cordoba, but he'd lived in London for years; he'd done Mali and Nigeria and Chad and Afghanistan, then he'd spent some time on the other side of the continent covering the shitty little war, and that was about it. We didn't have a plan; not for the pictures and the interviews we were supposed to do, and certainly not for finding Ricardo. It was about eleven when we went to our rooms, and we vaguely agreed to meet for breakfast in the morning and take it from there.

I stayed up with the bottle of claret, flicking through the TV channels. There were only two channels, and neither seemed too worried about what was going on out in the villages. One had an endless loop of speeches by the president, interspersed with footage of the president opening a highway, reviewing the presidential guard, getting out of a helicopter somewhere in the jungle in his immaculate suit. We needed to get a bit of face time with him, a couple of soundbites, to make our stay worthwhile; but it wouldn't be easy. The president did not like foreigners, and he certainly did not like journalists. David had mentioned knowing someone who knew someone at the palace. For whatever that was worth. I didn't know David well, but I knew enough to have my doubts.

Sometime after midnight, I turned off the TV. It took me a while to fall asleep. The air con was noisy but ineffective, and I kept thinking about the treatment centre when I'd been wandering among the tents looking for Ricardo. I didn't think I had touched anything I shouldn't have. I got up once or twice. The thermometer said 38, and that gave me a fright, and then it said 38.5, and I started to panic, and then it said 37.0 and I calmed down a bit. I looked at my eyeballs in the bathroom mirror. Nothing, just porcelain-white with red streaks. As far as anyone knew – and they didn't – the incubation period could be anything between a day and two weeks. The yellow in the eyes came after the temperature went up, except when it came before the temperature went up, and the next thing you knew there was a chill rising up through your legs, your knees were going wobbly, and then it started cooking your innards and then your brain and by the time you put two and two together it was too late anyway.

I was woken by my mobile ringing. I thought I'd overslept, but it was pitch-black outside and the time on my phone said 4 a.m. It was Nikki.

'Can you come over to my room?'

'Why?'

I could hear her breathing impatiently. 'It's important,' she said, so I got dressed and went out into the corridor. It was warm outside, and one of the lights was flickering.

Nikki's room was a couple of doors further down. I don't

know what I was expecting to find. An enormous green snake in the bathtub, perhaps.

Something heavy was being moved behind the door. 'You all right in there?' I shouted.

Nikki opened the door. She was in shorts and a T-shirt. She looked even smaller than usual. She had moved an armchair and a small table into the narrow corridor leading into her room, which I guessed she had put up against the door from the inside. She looked pale, the freckles around her nose standing out urgently like warning signs. Did you beep? I wanted to say, but she put a finger to her lips then took the key card out of the slot by the door. All the lights went out.

'What on earth?' I whispered, but Nikki went to the windows and pulled the curtains back. The room was cast in a yellow glow from the lights outside. 'So,' I said, 'what's this about?'

'Someone knocked on the window. When I was sleeping.'

'That's impossible. It's seven floors up.'

I walked to the window, which was the width of the room, from floor to ceiling, with a waist-high railing outside. It looked out over the back of the hotel, the swimming pool, a bar, some palm trees, a short strip of rocky beach, the lagoon that curved into the side of the island. Nothing stirred around the pool. The bar was deserted, and everything beyond the palm trees was dark.

'Impossible.'

'There's a ledge.'

I opened the window a few inches and peered out. 'There's a ledge,' I said, 'but it's too narrow for a person. You were dreaming.'

'No I wasn't. I'd know if I'd been dreaming. I heard it, it woke me up, and it came from the window. Remember what Ricardo was telling us about Bamako.'

'Well, that's just it. You dreamed it because you remembered Ricardo's story.'

'Like I keep telling you,' Nikki said, 'I wasn't dreaming.'

'Number one, you were dreaming it. And number two, if they'd come in, they at least had the decency to knock first.'

'Not funny.'

'Maybe someone in one of the other rooms was moving stuff around,' I ventured.

'The hotel's virtually empty,' Nikki said, and I knew she was right. 'Anyway, do you want a drink?' I was tired and my brain was foggy from the claret and we had work to do the next day, but there was something imploring in her voice, and it wouldn't have done to leave her on her own when she was worried about cat burglars creeping up the walls of the hotel.

'OK, sure.'

She switched the lights back on and poured out a whisky miniature from the minibar. Her hands were shaking. 'We're all a bit on edge,' she said, and walked over to the window. Nobody was out, the pool and the rocks were dimly lit for no one to see by a few dirty globe lights; and beyond that was the lagoon, darkness layered upon darkness. 'It's all a bit too much,' she said. 'Ricardo vanishing, the knocking. The odds are against it.' She was staring straight ahead, past the sad pale shimmer of the lights into the black heart of nothing, as if scanning for something out there among the invisible waves. I didn't follow.

'What do you mean, the odds? Is this something to do with that Guy Money character you were talking about yesterday?'

Nikki gave a start. 'Khai Manni,' she said. 'K-H-A-I M-A-N-N-I. At least that's what people assume.' She emptied her glass in one go and poured another miniature. 'But it's all just talk anyway. Probably.' From the way she was staring into the jet-black night I could tell she wasn't sure.

'I'd still like to hear it.'

So Nikki got talking. Nervously, as though she was afraid something out there in the Gulf might hear her.

They'd first come across the name Khai Manni in Bamako, or perhaps in Ouaga: listening nervously by the hotel pool for distant gunshots, the first ripples of revolution, already picturing beds and deckchairs afloat in the deep end among empty bottles of Havana Club; or was it when they'd been doing their hostile environment training together before deployment: waiting in the forest for the next checkpoint to cross with a mad captain ready to pop paintballs at everyone, and some loquacious instructor telling them what he shouldn't have, a former para in between stints of close protection in Bangui or Agadez. Or was it on their previous tour, when David and Ricardo had been covering the war in Mali: horned vipers and pyramids in the sands and grass like razor wire, humming to itself, something or somebody in white fleeting from point to point, the name on people's lips when anything and everything went belly up, except it wasn't, because you weren't supposed to say the name, so people didn't, except they did: no one ever talked, until somebody did. Was there any pattern behind it? Perhaps there was and perhaps there wasn't, a pattern like the wind, like the dusty harmattan, mayhem in a zigzag line: is there one, or a multitude, a swarm even? Funny thing was, no one had ever seen his face; distinguishing features: bugger all, a bloody gash across the continent, crawling. And the name not much to go on: Khai Manni, some delta dialect, river wolf, which probably meant crocodile. Nikki seemed to be in a trance, eyes fixed on some spot beyond the surf silently curdling in the feeble radius of the globe lights.

'But there must be a footprint,' I said. 'Everybody's got a footprint.'

Nikki wasn't listening. She seemed to be talking to herself. Mumbling something about villages where people had built pre-emptive shrines to Khai Manni: speculative offerings to stave him off. Pascal's wager, Sahel-style.

Fascinating though not conclusive, I wanted to say. But then came a hard knocking on the door, thud-thud-thud. And David's voice like a megaphone, loud enough to wake whoever else was staying in the Presidents Club, or on any other floor for that matter.

'So what's this? You're partying behind my back?'

Nikki turned around with a start. 'Don't say a word about any of this.' I nodded and went to the door.

David came in, dishevelled, wide awake, wearing jeans and an old, torn Chili Peppers T-shirt. 'I heard the doors going,' he said. 'I want in on the fun.' He helped himself to a beer from the minibar and threw himself into one of the chintzy armchairs. 'What, why the glum faces? You don't think that's going to bring Ricky back any faster?'

'Someone knocked on the window,' Nikki said, looking outside again.

'Oh no, you're not going to start with all that again,' David said. 'Unless I finally get to meet her,' he added.

'Meet who?' Nikki said, and I could see where this was heading.

'Well, the girl from France Inter, who else?'

Nikki made a face. 'Tosser,' she said. 'It's not funny.'

'It's hilarious though.'

'*This* window,' Nikki said. 'And it's seven floors down to the garden and no one could walk along the ledge and there's nothing funny about it.'

David looked out into the night for a few moments, then turned around and looked at both of us and said, 'I'll tell you what else is hilarious though. Two worldly-wise grown-ups with a few decades of field experience between them thinking that something or someone could glide up seven floors and knock on your window in the middle of the night and then vanish again.' He laughed. 'I mean, seriously? The folks at head office will love this.'

Nikki looked at David as if she was about to punch him.

'I think it's best we all go to bed,' I said. 'Long day tomorrow.'

David put his feet up on the glass coffee table. 'Suit yourself,' he said.

Nikki shrugged and turned on the TV. The endless loop of the president's speeches was spliced with stills of a beach, coconut trees, turquoise waters probably in another hemisphere, but what did the president care? Nikki was sulking and David was noisily sucking on his bottle, like a big, boisterous baby. I left them to it and went back to my room.

I tried to sleep but couldn't. Thirty-seven point four, rising, and was that a bit of jaundice spreading in my eyes?

III.

'Knock knock,' David said when he arrived for breakfast in the hotel restaurant the next morning.

'Ha ha,' Nikki said. She looked tired. Her freckles had subsided to a pale pink shimmer. I had a hangover like a bass drum being kicked about inside my skull. 'I asked the manager just now. There's no access to the roof. And no one's ever climbed the facade.'

'Of course they haven't,' I said. 'Because you were dreaming.' I wasn't sure myself, but it seemed the right thing to say.

David started joking about the girl from France Inter. We didn't laugh. Ricardo was still gone. No one mentioned Khai Manni.

We didn't have much of a schedule. We more or less knew what head office wanted, a mix of the gory and the political, and that was what we had given them, more or less, on the previous legs of our trip. 'Instead of pissing our time away in the hotel, let's give it a shot,' David said. We couldn't argue with that.

Giving it a shot meant turning up unannounced at the presidency, then going round town so he could talk into the camera and Nikki could get some pictures. The gorier the better. People having seizures in the street, patients getting scooped up by one of the makeshift ambulances cruising the streets, clean-up teams with flamethrowers. But first we'd go to the palace.

The palace stood on a narrow isthmus, a couple of hundred metres over a causeway in the lagoon. The easier to secure when things got a bit rough about town. We had no idea how we'd get across. We hit a succession of checkpoints as we got closer. We got through the first with a haughty '*On a rendez-vous à la Présidence de la République*'. The second one had a medical tent, and we had to get out of the car for a temperature and eyeball check. The third was on the lagoon. A couple of tanks and a prefab. But we only had to part with two fifty-dollar bills and then we were in, driving over the smooth empty tarmac of the causeway, occasional tufts of spray splashing up against the rocks on either side, gilt street lights at regular intervals with flags. There was no way of telling that in the city behind us, people were dropping like flies. You might as well have been cruising down the Mall on a festive Sunday morning.

No one seemed particularly interested in us when we reached the palace grounds. There were palm trees, unnaturally neat and tall, the leaves so bright they seemed sprayed in the dull white glare, and hedges, and walls. You couldn't see the palace itself. The driver stopped.

'Now what?' I said to David.

'Now we follow my lead.'

'What lead?'

'We ask for Albert.'

'How do you know Albert?'

'I don't.'

David walked up to a big flat building that looked like it might have been part of the presidential administration. A man in a dark suit came out of the building, frowning.

'We've got an appointment with Monsieur Albert,' David said.

'*Ah bon*,' the man said. 'Wait here.' He disappeared.

We waited. David started whistling to himself. Nikki got out one of her cameras and started taking pictures.

The man in the dark suit came back out of the building. 'Maybe tomorrow,' he said. '*On vous appelle.*' David tried to argue with him, but that was that. Nikki got out of the car to film a quick take of David talking, with the palm trees on the approach to the palace in the background: A country in a state of siege; here in the streets of the capital fear is palpable; and so on and so forth.

'Let's hope it doesn't look like it was filmed by a fifteen-year-old doing a school project,' David said as he got back in the car.

'I'm a photographer,' Nikki said, 'not a camera operator.

You'll have to make do with me. Or fish Ricardo out of the bloody mangrove.'

No one stopped us driving back out through the check-points over the causeway. The soldiers looked nervous and out of their depth. An AK didn't do you much good with what was going on here. Even a tank wasn't much use.

'At least we got a tour of the palace,' David said. 'Let's think of a way of working that into the story.'

'We didn't get a tour of the palace,' I said.

'Whatever,' he said. 'Let's go find that place we went to last time around.'

'What, you don't mean the actual place?' Nikki said. She looked nervous.

'No, don't be daft,' David said. 'I mean the shanty town, the big one. The one with the amputees.'

We drove for another ten, fifteen minutes, and the potholes got bigger and the tarmac patchier till we were skidding on sand sifted through with bits of junk, plastic bags and bicycle wheels and old engine oil canisters. The washed-out cement apartment blocks gave way to corrugat-ed iron shacks, and the corrugated iron shacks gave way to shacks made of any old crap, sheets of plywood and woven straw and plastic sheeting.

'*Pas bien de venir ici,*' the driver said.

'*Parfait ici,*' David replied, making it clear he was in charge.

An amputee came up to the side of the car in a make-shift wheelchair. He had stumps for arms and a spoon in his mouth with a paper cup attached. It was beyond me how he managed to move the chair through the mounds of dirty sand. I put my window down and a ten-dollar note in the cup.

'What did you do that for?' David said.

'I don't know.'

'There's thousands like that from the war. Why this one?'

'Why not this one?'

'Let's go,' Nikki said.

We got out of the car. Nikki looked like a little drummer boy with his drum kit around his neck, tramping through the junk, weighed down by her cameras and bags. 'Do you need a hand?' I asked.

'I can look after myself, thank you very much,' she said, and she started snapping away, shacks white with chlorine from preventive spraying and shacks that were burnt-out shells, black from being done over with flamethrowers when the inhabitants had been taken away, and groups of kids with nowhere and no one to go to.

A crowd had formed a bit further on, and I could hear shouting. People were gathering outside a hut. A truck was parked outside, a police pickup behind it. A woman was standing in the porch, gesticulating, her face in a furious grimace. Three or four men in PPE were arguing with her. One had a rolled-up stretcher. Nikki was snapping away, focused entirely on the scene in front of her. Another woman came running down the track, yelling. I couldn't make out what she was shouting, it must have been Creole, but it did something to the crowd. The men in PPE beat a hasty retreat to their truck. A policeman started shooting in the air, and that really got the crowd worked up.

Nikki kept pointing her camera, standing right in front of the officer who was shooting in the air. She looked as if she was taking snaps of a guardsman in Whitehall. Not bored, but nonchalant. From where I was standing behind Nikki I could see big globules of sweat running down the officer's face, and I thought I saw yellow in his eyes. He looked nervous and scared and was lowering his gun ready to shoot.

There was a movement at the back of the crowd, like the onset of a wave some way out at sea before it picks up momentum, gently rising before it turns vicious. Nikki held her camera above her head, scanning the crowd. I suppose she was getting the drama we'd all been waiting for on this trip: contorted faces, fists waving, the anger visible. Just then the ripple reached the front of the crowd. It's possible the officer fired his gun, but the crowd surged in on him and collapsed on itself and its roar was so deafening you wouldn't have heard a gunshot anyway.

Nikki had been standing right at the front facing the mass of angry people, at the point where the wave came in to break. I don't know if she got any photos, because everyone who hadn't been trampled underfoot when the crowd collapsed upon itself was running and rushing and scrambling. I couldn't see her anywhere as the crowd spun itself out. There were things on the ground in the mud, bits of clothing and maybe more, it was hard to tell. The heat was biting into my eyes. Things went fuzzy like binoculars shifting in and out of focus. I went up and down the track among the huts, looking for Nikki. I went back to the hut with the truck parked outside, but there was no sign of her. I walked up to the entrance of the hut and looked inside.

It was completely dark inside the hut and my eyes were watering from the heat. I turned on the light on my phone. Someone or something was lying in a heap on the floor in the corner. It wasn't Nikki.

There was more agitation outside. The woman who'd been arguing with the men in PPE was running towards me, shouting in a language that wasn't French. I walked as fast as I could to the police pickup that was still parked across the muddy track leading back out of the shanty town, went up to one of the officers climbing back on the pickup, tried to tell him about Nikki – '*Il y a une collègue à nous là-bas, il faut la retrouver*' – but he took his baton with both hands and shoved me back so hard I almost fell over.

People in the crowd were starting to look at me now. I could see the sweat on their foreheads and the yellow in their eyes. 'Nikki,' I shouted, again and again, and I called her on her mobile but she didn't pick up and the men in PPE had jumped on the back of the police pickup and it was turning around and went quickly back down the track and the crowd needed someone or something else to focus on and they started coming at me, and then I turned and ran, and when I got to the car I yanked open the door and jumped in.

David was having a nap on the back seat. 'Where's Nikki?' he asked, looking at me like a sleepy old bloodhound.

'I don't know. There's a riot, and Nikki's gone.'

'What do you mean, gone?'

By now the crowd had surrounded the car, and some of them were waving sticks and there were shots ringing out, and the driver started driving, the crowd only just parting, banging on the bonnet and the doors, and one of the windows shattered but somehow the driver managed to reverse back out of the shanty town, and I kept calling Nikki's number, and there was nothing, nothing at all.

'We've got to go back and find Nikki,' I kept shouting as the car crept down the road back to the centre of town.

David was looking stoically out of the window. There were stalls selling drinks in bags, there were stalls selling glutinous pastes wrapped in palm leaves, and there were stalls selling what looked like grilled rats on sticks. 'She's probably having a mojito on the terrace of the hotel right now,' David said. 'Sending her lovely pics back to London. For all I know she's back on that *Colonel Lakamba* or whatever it was called, getting the hell out of here. Don't bloody blame her.'

I didn't think so, but there was no turning around now. The traffic was solid and a ravine of sorts ran along the middle of the highway, with dark pointy trunks growing spearlike out of the thin strip of wasteland. We got back to the hotel, eventually.

'Tomorrow we'll get that exclusive at the palace,' David said as he got out of the car.

'Tomorrow we'll keep looking for Nikki and Ricardo.'

'Whatever. I need a drink.' And with that he disappeared into the air-conditioned lobby.

I told the driver to turn around and go back to the shanty town.

It was early afternoon when we arrived. The crowd had dispersed by now. I got out, took out my phone, with a picture of Nikki on a previous leg of the trip, in Monrovia or in Conakry maybe or in Freetown, and went from shack to shack showing it to people.

'*Excusez-moi, vous l'avez vue celle-ci, elle est passée aujourd'hui?*'

'*Non, jamais vu,*' they all said.

I asked the driver to take me to the *commissariat central*. A big cream colonial-style building with a grand portico in the shape of a Moorish arch and the national tricolour painted across a large part of the facade. The cream had curdled a little around the edges but it looked grand enough. I had to wait for half an hour for the officer on duty to see me. He had an impressive-looking uniform with extravagant lapels like a general in a Tintin story, and a peaked blue cap, proud and tall as a racing yacht. I said I wanted to file a missing person report.

He didn't seem particularly interested in a missing reporter. 'You know there are dozens of people dying every day,' he said. He scrawled something on a crumpled form and dropped it onto a tall pile of papers on his desk.

'What are you going to do to find her?'

'Everything,' the officer said. 'Everything.'

'Have you filed a report?'

'Filed and witnessed.' He pointed at the pile of papers on his desk.

I walked out of the station. The cream colour on the corners of the building looked even more curdled than before. Even from behind its veil of haze the sun was starting to throw dirty shadows everywhere. The green goo on the apartment blocks next to the commissariat had begun to grow a third dimension.

I called head office.

'What do you mean, Nikki's gone?' they said. 'You know Nikki, she's got a mind of her own.'

'There was a riot. She wouldn't just have walked away.'

'Have you told the police?'

'The police,' I said. 'Ha ha.'

'Don't worry,' they said. 'Keep us posted.'

I asked the driver to take me back to the other side of the island and criss-cross the knotty tangle of streets around the shanty town. I didn't think I'd spot Nikki, but I couldn't sit on my hands doing nothing. We kept going in circles till nightfall. There were people everywhere, walking and sitting by the side of the road among the mounds of rubbish, staring into the hazy evening sky. Once or twice when we passed a policeman I got out of the car and showed them Nikki's picture. '*OK, c'est bon on va rentrer*,' I said at long last to the driver, as the sky went from mushy sepia to grainy black.

David wasn't in the bar when I got back to the hotel, and I didn't text him. I asked about for Nikki. The receptionist, the bartender, the manager, the lift boy, no one had seen her. I went up to my room and had a whisky miniature and a beer, and I kept calling Nikki's mobile number and sending her WhatsApps that didn't get read, and somehow I managed to fall asleep.

IV.

When I heard the knocking I was gliding like a very big bird over a city that looked like Bamako, with a long white bridge over a shallow river and a palace on a hill and a teeming market and endless furniture sellers by the roadside. I was gliding over the city, and I was lying in a hotel bed, and then came a knock on the window. It wasn't a knock on the window. It was a knock on the door, and it was insistent, and when I got up and put on my bathrobe, there was another knock, even louder. Daylight was coming in through the gaps between the curtains and my neck ached. I put the chain on and opened the door. It was David. He was dressed and looked excited.

'What?' I said. 'What time is it?'

'Get dressed. I got a call from the palace.'

'Yeah, sure.'

David pushed past me into my room, grabbed the clothes I'd left over an armchair and threw them at me.

'What about Nikki? And what about Ricardo?'

'This is our chance,' David said. 'Don't spoil it.'

I checked my temperature. Thirty-seven point five, edging upwards. My eyeballs remained white. We called the driver, then we almost had a fight to decide where we'd go.

'We've got to go back to the shanty town,' I said.

'To do what?' David said. '*On va au palais,*' he told the driver, and he got in the passenger seat and closed the door.

I was still standing next to the car. '*Non, on va d'abord retourner à l'endroit où on a perdu notre collègue hier,*' I said to the driver through the open window.

David looked at me with disdain. 'This is our only fucking window,' he snarled. 'You don't want to blow it.'

'They're our fucking colleagues. For them, the window's closing.'

'We've got nothing so far. Two days in this place and fuck all to show for it. We haven't even got Nikki's photos.'

'All the more reason to go and look for her,' I said. '*On va aller chercher notre collègue,*' I told the driver once more.

'*On va au palais, et maintenant,*' David said to the driver, raising his voice. '*C'est moi le chef de cette équipe.*'

Finally, David took a banknote from his pocket and passed it to the driver and at the same time the window on the passenger side went up and with a jump the car started moving and it almost ran over my foot, and I was left standing on the patchy tarmac outside the hotel as the car went with a screech round the little roundabout outside the hotel and disappeared in the mad swirl of island traffic.

I tried to call David but he didn't pick up, and he wasn't reading the WhatsApps I kept sending him. I called head office again, and this time they got a fright: 'What do you mean, she hasn't come back yet?' They told me to get the next plane out. 'Yes,' I said, 'but I can't just leave, I need to keep looking, there's no one here to keep looking for them,' and they said, 'Don't worry, we'll send out a team.' It was the first I'd heard of head office being able to send out search teams, and I suspected they were making it up as they went along. But I said OK and put the phone down.

There wasn't much else I could do to try and find Nikki. I could already picture David's gloating I-told-you-so face, but I flagged down a taxi and asked the driver to go to the palace.

We crept along, wedged between a lorry and a makeshift bus, so close I could see the eyes of the woman sitting behind the cut-out porthole window, its metal edges frazzled and raw, and I thought I could make out a bit of yellow in their whites, but there was no way of being sure, and anyway I had a bad headache. In between the rows of shacks, in the distance, I could make out the sea now and again. An oddly shaped hut stood on the pavement, like a bulky newspaper kiosk but as tall as a house. It was covered in old plastic sheeting and there were sticks leaning against one side, with rags thrown over them. Something like a chimney stuck out at the far end, or a funnel; and as we crept past, I saw it was not a hut but an ancient steam engine, beached on the pavement.

'What's a steam engine doing here, in the centre of town, on an island?' I asked the taxi driver.

'*Ben quelqu'un a volé les rails quoi*', the driver said. Someone had stolen the rails. I couldn't tell if he was taking the mickey.

I felt a sharp pain in my temples, then there was a knock on the car window. I didn't see who was knocking because I had been looking out of the other window at the locomotive, and when I turned around, no one was there. The bus with the cut-out windows had fallen behind and a lorry was next to us now, an old removal van with a Dutch inscription, Verhuizingen Altremont. I couldn't see anyone in the driver's cab; old, tinted foil was stuck to the panes, peeling at the edges, a dark silvery mirror reflecting the pale grey sun.

My phone rang. It said *Unknown number*. There was nothing at the other end, not even a busy signal. I wanted to say something to the taxi driver, but it was too late, and suddenly I felt very weak. There was a yellow flash, and I took out my thermometer and did a forehead scan, and the red light came on and the beeping started and the driver must have seen something in the rear-view mirror because he panicked and then was gone and the door was open and the engine was still running and everyone was hooting their horns and I could feel a riot brewing.

Gone, they were all gone. But people were kind to me. I never got round to asking how I got to the airport, but behind their breathing apparatus and their goggles, I could feel their kindness. It was something to hang on to. My bones were burning, but I managed to get a flight out, and I had it all to myself.

One

Hope and Glory

V.

The first thing I did when I got back from the Very Dark Place was pick Wystan up. I'd left him with my mother months earlier and I wasn't even sure he'd recognize me. The leaves were coming off the trees, there was no traffic on the road from Goring, and the river that kept coming in and out of view looked oily and black. The track leading from the road to Palavers End was muddy and the old Golf kept skidding.

Wystan ran yapping towards the car when I got within a couple of hundred metres of the cottage. 'Hey, boy,' I said when I got out of the car, and he jumped up at me, leaving a big black print on my trousers. He seemed a little apprehensive. As if he could smell something, the smell of the Very Dark Place perhaps clinging to me like the wrong kind of perfume, metallic and putrid at once, disinfectant and blades and catheters and balanced crystalloids and electrolytes pumping non-stop for weeks on end though I had no memory of any of it: then one morning they'd brought me gently back up from the Deep and said, 'You can go home now, Mr de Souza.' As a souvenir they'd given me a hospital badge that said DR DE SOUZA on a nice blue NHS lanyard, these friendly folks in green and blue smocks who'd taken off their goggles and their breathing apparatus, and there were windows behind the bubble and the screens and all the machines measuring and pumping; and a world, leaves and brickwork and ambulances coming and going and a sullen brown river lethargically going nowhere.

My mother hugged me and made me a cup of tea and gave me a piece of a carrot cake she'd made the day before, and looked worried. 'Any news?' she asked.

'No, nothing.'

'But everybody's been so nice to you.'

'Yes,' I said, 'everyone's been incredibly nice to me.' Even the arseholes have been nice to me on the whole, I thought, but I didn't say it out loud.

'What about those friends of yours, the ones who didn't make it?'

'We can't say they didn't make it,' I said, 'but yes, they're still missing.'

I hadn't been able to follow things the four weeks I was in the Very Dark Place. But I'd read up on it all once I'd come up from the deep and they'd started disconnecting the wires and the drips and the probes and given me an iPad to reconnect with the world. Ricardo had been declared drowned, though no body had ever been found. The police investigation into Nikki's disappearance had concluded that she'd got caught up in '*un movement de foule irrégulier*', though it didn't bother to explain why hers was not among the dozen or so trampled bodies brought to the morgue after the stampede. As for David, the police hadn't done much investigating, simply informing the British consul that they were not in a position to account for his movements in The Land Of, and that his visa had expired without any border crossing being registered. I didn't even know whether he'd ever made it to the presidential palace after he'd got the driver to speed away without me, outside the hotel. And the driver couldn't be found anywhere, so there were no witnesses.

'What are you going to do all day long?' my mother asked.

'I'll be walking Wystan. Or maybe I'll take up pottery.' I looked at the shelves and the sideboards and the mantelpiece, the speckled vases and roughly indented globes and plates shiny with metal gleam.

'Don't. I barely know where to put the stuff.'

Wystan put his snout in my lap.

'What are the doctors saying?' my mother asked.

'They're reserving judgement.'

'Is that good or bad?'

It was neither good nor bad, and it was neither true nor untrue. It was hard to know what Dr Bicknell really thought. When I'd got out, I was given to understand that she'd been hovering around my bed all that time I was in the Very Dark Place. Like a benevolent sorceress in a hazmat suit. I didn't remember much, a vague delirium of polished steel and chemical flavours, but I'd have flashbacks now and then and in that uncertain miasma I'd see things: big yellow blobs busying themselves with monitors and needles and tubes, shapes shifting in and out of the blur; and maybe, watching, this: long leather coat and wide-brimmed hat, and a beak like a curlew's and eyes of frosted glass darkly staring. 'Simply some random image stored away in your brain,' Dr Bicknell said, when I told her. She didn't talk much; she listened and observed and plotted data on her PC and jotted stuff down in a bland little notebook. She wore thick black cat-eye glasses and sensible suits and kept whoever she was behind those glasses well out of her consulting room. She was a fellow of this and professor of that and I'd lost count; she was the pre-eminent consultant virologist in the country and I couldn't tell how much she knew about the thing. 'Do we know how it started?' I'd asked her, at the end of that first appointment, and she hadn't really answered my question, saying the jury was out or something to that effect, though I had the impression she knew more than she was letting on. 'It means they don't know,' I said to my mother.

'Well, none of us can be sure we won't be hit by a comet tomorrow morning, so that's all right,' my mother said, and gave me a vase to take home.

I went out to the car and opened the back door and beckoned Wystan to get in – 'Come on, boy,' and again, 'Come on, boy, it's all right' – but he turned around and trotted back to my mother and looked at me, doubtful. 'Come on, boy,' I said again, and he dug in his paws and my mother had to get in the back of the car herself to lure him in and he whined when she got out at the gate. I drove back to the road and he kept turning and pawing at the doors.

Just outside Reading I stopped by a little park on the river and took Wystan for a walk, and I made sure I had the lead wrapped tightly around my wrist because I knew he'd try to run straight back to Palavers End. Everything looked soggy and sad, wet leaves in the long wet grass and empty beer cans spilling from the bins and down by the river a couple of old canoes in a rusty old rack. The smell vaguely amphibian, leaf mulch and compost and slimy things on riverbanks. It made me think of another place, up the river, boathouses and bumps and blades and pints and cheering from a bridge; I don't know what I'd been thinking, back then, about where I'd end up, but this would not have been it, a mottled mongrel with wonky ears straining against my leash and peeing against a pile of old beer cans and wet leaves in the wet grass, alone, on the outskirts of Reading. And it made me think of a certain bend in the White River, and the phone call I'd got from Jonathan, my editor, one evening as I was sitting in the compound on the riverbank listening to the house band, drinking a warm trucked-in Tusker and thinking If there is a worse place in the world I have yet to hear of it, and What am I doing here? and thinking of a particular spot on the Thames, the willows and the grebes and horses in the background, random thoughts, and then my phone went off and Jonathan asked me to go to The Land Of and I thought What the heck, it can't be worse than this place. I'd seen some of the headlines, but right there on the White River no one much cared or worried about The Land Of, what people cared about was getting decent pictures from the swamps upcountry and surviving if ever the compound got raided again, remembering the basics from pre-deployment training, down on the floor or behind a thick wall, tourniquet at the ready, don't look them in the eyes, and wondering if any of it would ever be of use.

Jonathan hadn't come to see me on the special ward. He'd never even sent me a text to ask how I was doing. I called on him, at head office, the day after I picked up Wystan from my mother's, and he was friendly enough, but he didn't shake my hand and he didn't offer me an assignment.

'It'd be a little difficult, you know,' Jonathan said. 'Everything we do is about talking to people, direct contact, all the time.'

'Gosh,' I said, 'this is a little unexpected. I was in there all that time, and what kept me going was the idea that when I'd come out there'd be a job waiting for me. You know no one from the agency even came to tell me, when I was in there, so this is a bit of a shock.'

'I didn't have a pass,' he said, and it wasn't an embarrassed mumble, it was a brazen outright lie, and he said it with a straight face and his usual smug smile. 'I'll let you know if anything comes up. I'm sure it's only a temporary thing.

Why don't you use the time to do stuff, catch up with old friends, make up for it all with a bit of partying.' He paused, as if he'd realized he had said something monstrous, but I thought he was just trying to gauge my reaction.

'Make up for it,' I said. 'Partying.' I got up. 'By the way,' I asked, 'can I see the report from that team you sent, on Ricardo and David and Nikki?'

'No.'

'Why not?'

'It doesn't concern you.'

'But it does,' I said. 'I almost didn't make it back. And now I'm back I can't even get an assignment.'

'Look, I'm really sorry you had to go through all that. But digging away at whatever happened on that island won't bring them back.' He got up and put on his jacket.

'So you're saying something happened on that island,' I said, walking with Jonathan to the door.

'Well, yes,' he said. There was an edge to his voice, annoyed and embarrassed at once. 'We lost three of our best frontline staff, that's what happened.'

You know that's not what I meant, I wanted to say; or perhaps I wanted to say that I knew it wasn't what he had meant. But Jonathan was already in the lift and the doors closed on him giving me a condescending little wave as he checked his phone for whatever ambassadorial power lunch or background briefing with a Foreign Office bigwig he was heading to.

When I got home a little white van was waiting outside my block of flats, the sort you'd normally expect to see going round delivering meals on wheels, but this one had an NHS logo on the side. I thought I caught a whiff of something medicinal in the air. Eucalyptus perhaps, or camphor. I had no idea what camphor smelled like, but I was sure it was camphor. As I walked up the steps to the front door, someone got out of the van, calling out to me, 'Mr de Souza, Sebastian de Souza?' It was a woman with a baritone voice, a Falstaffian boom, short grey hair and glasses, and she was wearing an anorak over what looked like a nurse's outfit, baggy blue trousers and blue smock, and she had a clipboard in one hand and a little black suitcase, like a clarinet case, in the other.

'Yes,' I said, and I paused.

'Just a routine check-up, sir.' Her voice like a PE teacher or a Scoutmaster or rotund bishops speaking from a pulpit high above a dark and cavernous cathedral.

'Oh really? I don't remember Dr Bicknell telling me about this.'

'We're regional public health,' the woman bellowed back at me. 'Our responsibilities are set out in the Public Health Amendment Act. We are required to check on you. Everybody who's on the database needs to be checked.'

'Well, you could have called,' I said, but I opened the door and asked her in. 'First floor, on the right.'

She went up the stairs, and Wystan growled and strained hard at his leash as he bounded up the steps.

'Anyone living with you, sir?' she asked as she caught her breath on the first-floor landing.

'No, just Wystan and me.'

'Wystan. Is that your, like, boyfriend?'

I was about to say no and point at Wystan but then I got to the landing and saw that the door to my flat was open.

'Because I'll need to put them in the database as well,' she was saying. 'It's a standard precaution.'

I rushed past her into the hall and then the living room, thinking there'd been a burglary, but everything was in its place, the TV, the DVD player, the stereo. I went to the bedroom and everything looked fine, no drawers yanked out, no pillows knifed.

'I'm sorry,' I said. 'It's strange that the door should have been open.' I pulled the door shut. The lock seemed to be working normally.

'You must have forgotten to close it properly. Gust of wind blew it open.'

'Yes. Gust of wind, no doubt.'

The nurse put her little black case on the kitchen table and snapped open the latches. I noticed she'd put on surgical gloves. 'You've been checking your temperature regularly, have you?' she asked.

'Every day,' I said. 'Morning and evening.'

'Let's see your charts then.'

I showed her the pad of graph paper on which I'd been plotting my temperature as they'd shown me, 36.4, 35.2, 38.1, hang on, what's that it can't be, heart racing, temples pounding, phone at the ready on speed dial for the number I'd been given on a little laminated card, but then it was fine, 37.2, I must have pointed the wrong way and anyway I'm feeling just fine thank you.

'All right,' she said. 'Sit down for me, won't you?'

She took a thermometer from her case, the big type with a separate pointing thing and a flex leading to a box like a Geiger counter, and she pointed it at my forehead, and for a moment there was nothing and then came a beep, a friendly sort of beep, from the box.

'That's one bit done.' She took a pen torch from her case. 'I'd like you to look up at the ceiling now, sir.' She shone the torch in my eyeballs. 'Right. Another box we can tick.' She sounded relieved as she yanked off her gloves and put her torch and thermometer back in the little black case.

'When will you be back?'

'Not my call, sir. These parameters are determined at a higher level.' She gave me a card. BRIDGET MERSEY, it said, CASE OFFICER, REGIONAL PUBLIC HEALTH (EMERGENCIES) DIVISION.

'So I'm an emergency.'

'No, it's all just routine, sir.'

'Perhaps you'll want to call in advance, to make sure I'm in.'

'Sorry, sir,' she said, 'that's not part of the protocol.'

'All right,' I replied, and I guessed it had something to do with not allowing people to stuff themselves with parac-etamol to get round the temperature check if they were feeling hot, though who those people might be I had no idea, since I knew of no one else in my situation.

When she had left I made myself a cup of tea and turned on the TV. There was a report from The Land Of, case numbers were going up, footage from a shanty town, the kind of scene Nikki was supposed to have been shooting when she disappeared, funerals. You could tell they were using a local crew; the pictures were all shaky, the framing random. There weren't any expat crews left. The big US and European networks had pulled out their correspondents long ago, and the agencies no longer sent any crews in after what had happened to Ricardo and Nikki and David, whatever that was, and the way I'd come back in a bubble had put their risk ratings up to a point where no one could go any more anyway. So they relied on lousy footage from local agencies or even lousier footage from local government-run stations, and occasionally they'd blend in an interview with an NGO worker or UN official who'd just returned. It didn't make for very compelling TV, and anyway no one was that interested any more, now the initial exotic excitement of all those people in bright-yellow PPE and ski goggles had worn off.

I recognized the highway where I'd come across the lorry that said VERHUIZINGEN ALTREMONT, and I began to feel nauseous. My neck went, my heartbeat palpitated in my ears and the joints in my fingers itched. If I'd followed the protocol I would have called the number on the little laminated card there and then, but I reckoned it must have been some sort of stress reaction, and I didn't want an ambulance with police escort tearing down my peaceful suburban street. I spent the rest of the day lying on the sofa, waiting for the pain in my neck to go away, and Wystan sat on his haunches on the other side of the living room with a sad face. But then again he always had a sad face. Every day was a dog day, lucky bastard. I took him for a walk in the evening, still groggy; the few people I met going round the block must have thought I was drunk, and even Wystan must have felt embarrassed because he was rushing ahead, pulling me along as if he couldn't wait to get back home.

When I got ready for bed I couldn't find my toothbrush, and I thought that was strange, but then my neck pain got worse again and I took my pills and went to bed and turned out the lights and hoped I'd be better in the morning.

VI.

I dreamed that someone was in my flat. A burglar all in black with a blur where his face should have been, and my flat wasn't a flat but a hotel room in a sprawling white city by a river, the whiteness of the city lighting up my room even though it was four in the morning and the curtains were closed, and I could hear the tidal murmur of the lagoon outside. The burglar was looking for something, not the usual bric-a-brac, money gold diamonds, he was looking for something special and sooner or later he'd turn to me and that wouldn't be pleasant, but for now he was going through my suitcase while I was stuck in my bed and I couldn't move and I knew how he'd got in the window even though it was four floors up and at least he'd had the decency to knock, vintage Khai Manni, and if I cared to check the ledge outside my window I'd find the Gulf of Guinea at my disposal all tepid and black. The water was rising, wet and warm and a little rough against my hand, and then I woke up and Wystan was licking my hand asking for his walk.

It was ten in the morning and the air was pregnant with rain and complications: not a smell exactly, but something tight and tense brewing. There was just enough time to take Wystan for his walk before I had to go into town for an appointment with Dr Bicknell. I'd only met her once, when I got out. And she'd told me I'd be seeing a lot of her: 'You're quite a subject,' she'd said, or quite a case. I shouldn't have made it, in other words, and I had, and she certainly wasn't going to pass up the chance to find out why. I put on my jeans and a jacket and went down to the river with Wystan and sat on a bench watching him run up and down the towpath while sculls pulled past on the moss-green water. I still had the image of Khai Manni in my mind, a blank where the face should be, robes flowing in the hot Saharan wind. Or was it jet-black ninja garb? It wasn't the first time I'd dreamed of Khai Manni since getting back from The Land Of. I did a quick google on my phone, not for the first time: all that ever came back was pictures of Khao Manee cats and videos of obscure Thai or Indonesian pop stars. Or maybe they were Kyrgyz. I tried every spelling imaginable: Ky, Kai, Khy. Mani, Munny, Mhanee, et cetera.

Nothing, but a ping told me I had mail. In the days since my release from the Very Dark Place I'd only been getting junk mail and checklists and guidelines from public health people and reminders for medical appointments. The message was from someone called Will Farrar. I didn't know any

Will Farrars. His email address had the extension of one of the big Sunday papers. It had run a couple of nasty leaders when things first got bad in The Land Of. Anybody going to The Land Of knew what they were letting themselves in for and shouldn't expect to be let back into the country until science had firmly established that they did not constitute any risk of contagion, et cetera. I didn't know what they had written when I got back from The Land Of. I couldn't read anything when I was in the Very Dark Place, and I never read the clippings head office sent me afterwards. I knew there had been some unpleasant stuff in there. But I opened the mail from Will Farrar. *Dear Sebastian*, it said, *we realize how busy you must be. I'm writing to you as special assistant to Helen Beaumont, lead features writer on the People and Lives supplement.* I thought that was a bit pretentious; no journalist I knew had ever had an assistant. If I wanted to talk to someone I'd pick up my phone and call them, not send an email through a secretary. The email went on to say that Helen Beaumont wanted to do a profile of me for 'People and Lives'.

I knew a Helen who wrote for the paper Helen Beaumont worked for, but her name wasn't Beaumont. I put my phone in my pocket and looked out at the river and the sculls and the swans cruising and the barges moored alongside the sliver of island in the middle of the river. Wystan was chasing after an elegant-looking Dalmatian bitch. He looked ridiculous, hobbling along on his short legs trying to get close to her, streaks of mud up his backside and slimy froth on his muzzle, his sad face pulled into a desperate grin, to love is to hope and all that, the Dalmatian bounding effortlessly away down the towpath. An old ferryboat had been stuck in the mud among the sandbanks of the White River, opposite the compound, it must have been stuck there for decades, its white hull turned a messy patchwork of rust brown and gooey algae green, and every time I'd come I'd thought the angle at which it was stuck in the mud had changed, and I'd take another photograph even though taking photographs anywhere in town was illegal, and even more so on the White River than anywhere else in town. They'd shot a guy once for taking pictures of some crocodiles. The river was strategic. It was just as bad as taking pictures of the guys in the technicals who went cruising round town taking petrol without paying. But I'd had to compare the angle at which the steamer was listing, its bow pointing proudly at the pallid moon, its stern embedded deep in the alluvial slime. And when I'd compared my pictures, the angle had always been the same. The food had been good at the camp: nasi goreng and chicken curry and samosas, even though everything had to be trucked in. You didn't want to think about what the chicken in the curry had been through, frozen and unfrozen and refrozen a dozen times over, but the curry tasted good, and the Tusker was cold, most of the time, and what else could you have asked for?

Wystan was starting to molest the Dalmatian. I had to go after him and take him by the neck and pull him off, and he snarled at me and started shaking off the black mud and left my trousers speckled like a magpie's egg, and I knew he'd done it on purpose, and perhaps he even knew I wouldn't have time to change my trousers before going into town for my appointment. The rain had stopped but whatever was brewing was still brewing, and I thought of stuff I'd read about animals acting funny before an earthquake, and I shuddered.

'How very interesting,' Dr Bicknell said. 'Do tell me more.' She wore a neatly ironed white collar and a workaday suit in low-key beige and most of our appointment consisted of going over temperature charts and checklists of possible late-onset complications, but I could tell she was intrigued. She asked me how I was feeling, always the first question in the standard protocol, and I told her I was OK, albeit with the occasional headache, then I told her I'd started smelling things, things that were probably not there. 'Oh really,' she said. 'And how do you know they're not there?'

'Because no one else can smell them. Flowers, offal, burnt things.'

'There's huge variability in olfactory acuity among humans.' She liked her big words, but I didn't hold it against her.

I tried to explain. 'It's not like that. It's not just smells. It's as if I can smell colours. Moods, even. Vibes, if you like.'

'Vibes,' she repeated, and she raised her eyebrows slightly. I could see her trying to work out how to present a vibe in a peer-reviewed article in the *Lancet*. I didn't mind being a research subject, potential or actual. She'd saved my life after all. But it made for some subliminal awkwardness when I came in for my check-ups. 'Perhaps you could keep a journal of sorts,' she said. 'Make a note when you notice these unusual sensations. Describe them.'

'OK.' I asked her if she'd come across similar phenomena with her other patients.

'You do know you're the only case in this situation,' she said sternly. 'So far.'

'Yes, I know. I'm special.'

She prescribed me some pills, to make sure things didn't get out of hand. 'And try to keep that diary.'

A slow drizzle started when I was back in the street, the kind that sticks to you like mist from an atomiser bottle, oily and dank. I walked down Lambeth Palace Road towards Waterloo. There was no one about except for a guy in a hoodie and a baseball cap across the road, talking into his phone. I stopped to tie my shoelaces. The guy with the cap stopped and looked at his phone. I walked on. The guy with the cap walked on. When I got to the station he was still there, standing by one of the bus stops at the bottom of the stairs going up to the main entrance.

I went into a newsagent's on the station concourse and got a copy of the paper Helen Beaumont wrote for. I could have looked it up on the internet but they had a paywall and anyway I liked the feel of a real paper, even if it wasn't a paper I'd ever read or was ever likely to read, though a million people did. A thing somewhere between a broadsheet and a tabloid, gardening features wall-to-wall and Support our boys and smiling royals on their way to church. Helen Beaumont's name plastered above the banner of the fattest supplement. And her picture next to it, the usual bland Photoshopped job, ivory-smooth skin and perfectly sculpted blondish hair and no way of knowing if it was real. I knew it wasn't: when I knew her she'd had dark hair and glasses and her name wasn't Beaumont. She worked harder than any of us, late nights and early mornings in a dingy office down a little alleyway off Cornmarket, piles of old newspapers up against the wall and front-page mock-ups spread across the worktops, a darkroom at the back, a kettle and dirty mugs and spoons and a jar of Nescafe; and even on Sunday afternoons in the meadow by the river there'd be a pile of books by her side and she'd be thinking about the front page for the following week's edition. I was supposed to be revising for prelims, Begg Dornbusch Fischer and Hume's billiard balls, but there were too many distractions, and Helen accounted for most of them though she never got distracted herself. *OK*, I wrote back to Will Farrar. *Whatever.*

When I came out of the newsagent's the man in the baseball cap was standing in the middle of the station concourse looking up at the departures board. I decided on a whim to take the Tube and go back to head office.

At least my lanyard hadn't stopped working

'Hello, Carol,' I said to Jonathan's secretary. 'Is he in?'

'No, afraid not,' she said, even though I could see his legs below the frosted bit of the glass partition around his office. So I walked among the desks of the international department, and people greeted me politely but I could feel them shrinking from me and I didn't offer any handshakes. When I arrived at my desk it was obvious they'd reassigned it. Where I'd once sat on my occasional passages through London, a former intern called Doug now spread his stuff: a Slavic languages graduate in his twenties, covered most of Eastern Europe. It had been a while since I'd spent any length of time at a desk in London. I knew Doug by sight only.

'Oh hi, you're Sebastian, right?' he said now, folding his hands behind his head, legs crossed, sliding a long way down the office chair that used to be mine.

'And you must be Doug.'

'Missing the blood and gore?' he asked. He checked himself. 'Sorry, I meant your reporting, not, like, you know.'

'It's all right.' I didn't expect anyone who hadn't been to the Very Dark Place to understand, ever. It just washed over me.

'There's an empty desk somewhere behind here,' he said, trying to be helpful and pointing vaguely down the aisle of open-plan desks. '

'All right,' I said, and I wandered along the desks till I came to the empty one.

The empty desk looked like someone had gone off for a long holiday, pencils and pads and notebooks neatly tidied, a pile of documents in a corner. I didn't know what I was looking for, or if I was looking for anything. I leafed through one of the notebooks. There were scribbles in a hand I couldn't read and doodles, big sprawling chequerboard growths filled in with black ink so thick it had bled through the paper, and twirly Mandelbrot spirals and dragon's teeth and little islands perched on stems like flowers. Whoever sat at this desk spent a lot of time being bored, or worried. I should have felt bad about looking through somebody else's things, but I didn't. I looked at the first page of the notebook. It had the initials D and W, and the W was a rough sketch of two fingers stuck up, and it wasn't a victory sign. I pulled at the drawer under the desk. It wasn't locked. There were paper clips and a pack of playing cards with Japanese girls on the back and a KitKat long past its sell-by date and a raspberry-flavoured condom and a bunch of keys, and a stack of passport photos in a little transparent pouch, the kind you'd have if you were constantly having to do visa applications. The face in the passport photos was David's, of course.

'I'm told you were looking for me.'

I hadn't seen Jonathan coming up from behind among the partitions between the desks. His voice had an impatient edge to it.

'I just dropped by to check if there was any work for me.'

'I thought we'd discussed that. I'll let you know if anything comes up.'

'And has it?'

'No.'

'There's something else,' I said.

'What?'

'That report on Ricardo and David and Nikki, did it find anything?'

'I thought we'd discussed that too,' Jonathan said. 'It's very restricted circulation.'

'Maybe I should write my own report.'

I meant it flippantly, but it got Jonathan even more annoyed. 'I think you should drop this thing before it bites you,' he said.

'I think it already has.'

'You know what I mean.' He sounded a little less belligerent now. 'I'm sure Carol can show you out.'

I didn't know what Jonathan meant, and it bugged me. I showed myself out, and I put two fingers up to head office when I was out in the street and went to a cafe round the corner and sat down and tried not to think about the agency, then I pulled the keys I'd taken from David's desk out of my pocket and put them on the table in front of me. There were a couple of small ones, like locker keys, and a big old-fashioned one of the sort they no longer make, long and rounded and slightly rusted. I remembered David talking about a cottage. Ricardo had been going on about some place he had in the hills near Ronda, his 'pile of beautiful stones' he called it, and how he'd be doing it up once we all got back, then David had mentioned his place. 'Isle of Sheppey,' he'd said. 'Arse of the world, just a shack, but right on the beach. Not another house for miles. Looking right out into the North Sea, only me and the birds.' I think that was supposed to be some sort of double entendre.

When I'd finished my coffee I went home. Wystan was scratching at the door from the inside when I reached the door to my flat. I put his lead on and took him for a walk round the block, then I had a frozen pizza and kicked off my shoes and lay on the sofa and turned on the news. There were more reports from The Land Of. The usual archive pictures overlaid with the usual bar chart, up up up, then a report from some teaching hospital out in the Fens, for some reason they had a research programme going, the science editor all springy and excited as if they'd discovered a new planet, and then the factlet, a bit silly in the circumstances. 'We're only beginning to understand the full impact on the organism,' a young-looking professor was saying. 'The fatality rates are very high of course, blah blah blah,' and I drifted off and felt Wystan licking my hand. I brushed my teeth with a worn old toothbrush and went to bed and lay awake wondering whether Helen had married someone called Beaumont or had simply decided it sounded better than Porlock and in the middle of the night I thought I was smelling things, trouble mostly and something that might have been death but just turned out to be a long and dank tunnel, then I woke up and Wystan was at the door. It was 4 a.m. according to my alarm, the shadows of the trees outside like troubled scarecrows against the curtains in the living room. He was growling softly but fiercely, which wasn't his style at all. I couldn't see anything through the frosted glass panes in the door, but he continued snarling and scratching.

I opened the door and stepped onto the landing. The lights in the staircase should have come on but didn't. Wystan stood on the threshold. 'Go,' I said. 'Find.' I had no idea what I wanted him to find, and anyway he wasn't about to. He stood on the threshold with his head cocked and wouldn't go forward. I went down the stairs. There was nothing, but I could feel a draught on my skin. A car started outside. I ran out of the door just in time to see brake lights, a dark shape going round the corner. Wystan was sitting on the threshold. 'You didn't step up,' I said. He trotted back to the kitchen and I closed the door. I'd need to get the lights in the staircase looked at. I had a wooden wedge to shove under the door from the inside, brought back after travelling in some of the dodgier places, so I kicked that firmly into place and went back to bed, but I didn't sleep much. I didn't know who or what I was afraid of. Somehow I didn't think Khai Manni would come for me by car at 4 a.m.

In the morning I took out an old exercise book and jotted down everything the way Dr Bicknell had told me to, smells and dreams and stuff, then I turned on my PC and started looking at maps of the Isle of Sheppey. I'd never been to the Isle of Sheppey. It looked like a pudgy baby hippo burrowing down into a silty river, with a big blob of snot dripping from the tip of its nose into the North Sea. There were a couple of villages, a road and car parks up towards the top end. 'Not another house for miles,' David had said, and that meant his place must have been somewhere around the south-eastern tip. And then I got another email from Will Farrar, asking if I'd meet Helen Beaumont for lunch today. *I realize it's a bit short notice*, the message said, *but Helen is really keen to meet; she could still do the piece for this weekend's edition.* It did seem a bit short notice, but I called Will Farrar on the number he'd given in his email.

'She must be very busy, Helen,' I said to Will Farrar.

'I beg your pardon,' Will Farrar said.

'Too busy to call me herself.'

There was a pause and I was tempted to drop the whole thing, tell Will Farrar I was suffering from impossible migraines ever since I'd got back from The Land Of, and good bloody riddance.

'We'll send a car,' Will Farrar said, before I got a chance. 'Helen suggests the restaurant in Kew Gardens, that way you don't have a long way to go.'

I didn't know I'd given Will Farrar my address, but I said OK. I took Wystan for a walk. The sky looked tight and bunched-up as if trussed and cut by invisible wires and there was something in the air, something straining to get out. But the air by the river smelled of vanilla and hibiscus, like a box of expensive macarons. The elegant-looking Dalmatian was there, too, by the river, so I kept Wystan on his lead. The Dalmatian's owner, a blonde woman in a Barbour jacket, must have recognized Wystan because she gave me a mocking smile when she walked past, and the Dalmatian danced past on her dainty legs like a stuck-up gazelle.

When I got back home a little white van with an NHS

logo on the side was waiting outside again, and I thought this was getting boring, or perhaps something was messing with my mind and taking me through some twisted tunnel back in time. The door of the van opened and someone in a blue nurse's outfit got out. But it wasn't Nurse Mersey; it was a skinny dark-haired man with a tattoo on his wrist, and he was carrying a black case like Nurse Mersey's.

'It's not long since you lot were last here to check me out,' I said.

'The intervals aren't regular,' the man said. He had a high-pitched voice and a funny accent, something about the Rs, vaguely Irish but not really. 'It's a random algorithm.'

'I see. What happened to Nurse Mersey?'

'She's on sick leave.'

'On sick leave, is she? Isn't that ironic.'

The dark-haired man didn't smile. 'Shall we go upstairs?' he said.

I led him upstairs to the flat, but he seemed to know the way already. I showed him into the kitchen; he put his little black case on the kitchen table and took out a thermometer, the kind Nurse Mersey had used.

'Heard from your mates yet?'

I wasn't sure if he was trying to be chatty or fishing for information. 'What mates?'

'That lot you left behind in The Land Of.' He put on surgical gloves and held the pointy bit of the thermometer against my forehead.

I thought there was something funny about his questions.

'They're still missing.'

'Not what we've been hearing.' The main unit of his thermometer started beeping and a red light started flashing. 'Oh dear,' he said. 'How are you feeling today?'

'Absolutely fine,' I said, and it wasn't a lie.

'Roll up your sleeve.'

The more he talked, the more his accent sounded like something he was putting on. I rolled up my sleeve, and I was expecting him to try another reading somewhere on my arm, or measure my blood pressure, but he took a syringe and what looked like a vacuum tube or a vial from his black case and started feeling for the vein in the hollow of my elbow.

'What are you doing?'

'Routine procedure. It's what we always do when people beep.'

'What do you mean, routine procedure? There's no one else in my situation,' I said. 'No one else has come back from The Land Of, so how can it be routine procedure?'

'Hold still now, sir, won't you.'

And that's when I pulled my arm away, and as he tried to grab hold of my shoulder with one hand, syringe in the other, the sleeve of his blue nurse's smock rolled up, I saw the rest of his tattoo, a flower with daggers for petals and teardrops for leaves, probably based on a regimental badge, and I thought that was a bit unusual for a nurse. He kept trying to grab hold of my arm. I stood behind the table and took a bread knife from the sink, though I had no idea what

I planned to do with it. Wystan came bounding up behind the man, snarling and jumping up his legs; perhaps he felt bad about letting me down the night before.

Right then the doorbell rang, and the dark-haired man paused. Someone knocked on the front door, which I hadn't closed, and I could see a man in a grey suit on the landing.

'Mr de Souza. Come to pick you up for your lunch with Ms Beaumont.'

The dark-haired man put the syringe and the vacuum tube and the thermometer back in his case. 'You're not doing yourself any favours,' he said. 'We could have done this the easy way.' Then he flicked shut the metal catches on his case and walked out.

The smell that hit me when I went through the gates at Kew wasn't the smell of flowers or leaf mulch. It was the colours themselves I could smell, even without looking at the flowers, a light pastelly pink spangled with purple and a bright waspish yellow with dark brown filaments. It gave me goosebumps, and the smell only got stronger as I walked along the neatly raked paths among the flower beds and ponds and alpine rockeries. There weren't a lot of people about, tourists and retired folks in the midweek doldrums and mothers pushing prams. Helen Beaumont was sitting at one of the cast-iron tables outside the restaurant looking at her phone. She was wearing a pale blue suit and a white blouse and looked tidy and businesslike. When she got up I leaned in to kiss her on the cheek but she just put out her hand, and her handshake was brisk and efficient and if there was any awkwardness on her part she didn't show it. 'Hello, Sebastian,' she said, and I noticed the dark brown roots in her hair.

'I wasn't sure it was you at first when I got that email from your charming assistant.'

'Oh gosh. I thought you'd kept up.'

'I've been away. It's been a bit difficult to keep up.'

She looked a little embarrassed.

The waitress brought the menus, natural healthy stuff with husks and grains and chlorophyll.

'When did you get married?'

'Last month.'

No wonder I'd missed it. I would have struggled to keep up with society columns on the isolation ward.

'Quite unusual, though, the name change and all that,' I said. 'Particularly when people know your byline.'

'That depends on whom you're marrying.' It was clear she didn't want to elaborate.

'Amazing, this flowery smell, don't you think?'

'Flowery smell? What flowery smell?'

She ordered a goat's cheese salad and a glass of Chablis, and I ordered a plate of vegetable fritters with dips, fennel and knobbly carrots and things pulled from the flower beds, and I thought of the samosas by the White River, miraculously crisp and dripping with oil after a week of overland from Port Sudan.

'Do you remember how we lived on crisps and Walton Street burgers?' I said, but she only smiled politely.

'How long has it been?'

'Seventeen years and four months.' For some reason I had the answer at my fingertips, down to the month.

'You've been around, I see,' she said, and I knew she didn't mean to sound patronizing, but she did. 'Do you mind if I record this?' She'd already got out her little sticklike thing, and a notebook, Japanese paper covers with some tasteful purple flower design. Foxglove or something of the sort.

'There's not a lot of things I mind these days,' I said.

'It's really too good of you to have agreed to this.'

'It beats walking the dog,' I said. 'I hope you didn't take that the wrong way.'

'Why did you go down there in the first place?'

'Why do you only ever do these interview things?'

She ignored my question. 'I thought you did wars,' she said. 'Why The Land Of?'

I didn't like her questions, but I shrugged. 'People have been going off wars,' I said. 'At least the kind I used to do.' The shitty little ones, I wanted to say, but I knew that was the one thing she'd put in her piece, a thirty-two point pull quote, and I'd be done for, Callous Bastard, I'd spend the rest of my days in hiding, and the doctors wouldn't even tell me if that was fifty years or two months. I could have talked about squalid little wars instead, but that wouldn't have done justice to things. 'The Land Of or the dole,' I added, simply.

She did the shocked thing very credibly. 'What do you mean, The Land Of or the dole? They can't force people to go down there.' She winced.

'It didn't seem such a bad deal at the time.' I wanted to tell her about the swamps up the river, the things I'd seen. Anything seemed better than that. But somehow I didn't think she'd get it. 'But honestly,' I heard myself asking, 'how can you write for that thing?'

'That thing,' she said, and she sounded more disappointed than upset, 'has a million readers every weekend.' She looked at her watch. It was a nice watch. 'It also pays the bills.'

I was starting to regret having come. The waitress brought my fritters, but there was a strange scent in the air, flowers going off or compost. It had nothing to do with the fritters, but somehow my appetite was gone.

'Can you smell that?' I said.

'Smell what?'

'Nothing.'

'Interesting.' She jotted something down in her notebook. 'You know a lot of people are wondering how it started.'

'How what started?'

'The outbreak, of course. Isn't that something you were looking for in The Land Of?'

We were looking for blood and gore, I wanted to say. Bodies sticking feet first out of pickup trucks. We were looking for chaos. 'Not really,' I said. 'I don't think anyone was thinking about how it started at that point. Everybody was just afraid it would come here.'

Helen looked a little disappointed. 'So there's nothing you saw, or heard, in The Land Of. Nothing that might have pointed in a certain direction?'

'Look,' I said, a little brusquely, 'I was there for a couple of days. Things didn't exactly go as planned.'

'Fair enough,' she said. 'I'm sorry.' She looked at her phone. 'Tell me about Nikki.'

I hadn't been expecting that. 'Does someone send you these questions over your phone,' I asked, 'like that bloke Will or Willy or whatever his name is?'

She seemed briefly taken aback by my unpleasantness. 'No, actually,' she said coolly, then she came back to her question. 'Do you mind if I ask about Nikki? Was it painful for you when Nikki disappeared?'

I thought about it. It wasn't an unreasonable question. Of course it had felt awful when Nikki disappeared. There one moment and gone the next, and yes, I'd been beating myself up over it ever since. But I didn't think there was anything personal to that. I didn't think I particularly had feelings for Nikki in that sense.

'Yes, it was painful,' I said at last.

'Did you feel guilty?'

'I suppose I did.' I immediately wished I hadn't said that. 'I mean, it's normal that you wonder if we could have done anything differently that day. I don't know.' I kept replaying the scene in my mind: Nikki weighed down by her bagfuls of kit, pointing her Nikon, the last time I had seen her, shots ringing out over the shanty town.

'What do you make of the rumours, though?'

'Rumours? What rumours?'

'Well, you know,' she said, and she looked surprised. 'That

the whole thing was staged, the three of them disappearing.'

'With all due respect, that's completely crazy. I was there when they disappeared, so I would know.'

Helen looked at me with something like pity. 'I'm sorry I brought that up,' she said. 'Let's move on. Do you remember what happened when you came back from The Land Of?'

'If I did, I wouldn't want to talk about it.'

'Right.' Again she glanced at her phone. It was obvious she wasn't enjoying the interview. I wondered why she'd got back in touch with me. 'So if you can't work, what do you do all day long?'

'I walk the dog,' I said, and I knew it sounded like I was taking the piss.

Helen poked at her goat's cheese. 'I could ask you all the obvious questions,' she said after a while, 'but somehow I don't think it's going to lead anywhere.'

'I wouldn't know. I've never written for a million readers before.'

We didn't have coffee. I told her I was thinking of going to the Isle of Sheppey, and I asked her if she wanted to come along, to wind her up. Do you remember, I wanted to ask her, how we went to Paris once, in our last year, La Courneuve, the Fête de l'Humanité, and at first you thought it was the weirdest thing to do, the Communist Party having a party, who'd be in the least bit interested, and then we had a great time, dancing in the Cuban tent and drinking cheap red wine from some cooperative in Faugères and doing a full-page feature about it together for the student paper when we got back? Her byline had been above mine, but I didn't mind. I'd always kept that number in a box somewhere at the bottom of a wardrobe at Palavers End. But I didn't ask her, and I was sure the Isle of Sheppey was the last place she'd go now, with her pale blue suit and her blonde hair and chic new surname. But she wasn't even listening. When she said goodbye there was another short and frosty handshake, and she said 'Thanks for your time' as if I was a random witness at the scene of an accident who'd just answered a question and a half. I watched her walk off towards the main gate with quick, determined steps. She looked small and fragile from a distance, and she made me think of Nikki, going into the shanty town. I walked off among the flower beds and thought I detected a slight whiff of charcoal in the air.

They didn't run me home afterwards. Instead I took the bus back and checked my emails. I didn't think it likely they'd run the piece, but I thought about sending her an email, to be on the safe side. I regretted not talking about the shitty little wars. And I should have asked her more about the rumours about Nikki and David and Ricardo. Although I wasn't interested in whatever nutty theory was trending on social media, it was peculiar to hear the same weird comment twice in a day.

There was a soapy smell about when I walked the couple of blocks to my street from the bus stop, and a little white van parked outside my block of flats. I thought about running, but then the door opened and Nurse Mersey got out.

'Which one of you is it?' I asked, and she looked at me with stern incomprehension. 'The bloke who came this morning tried to take a blood sample.'

'What bloke? What blood sample? We don't require blood samples.' Nurse Mersey went inside shaking her head. 'Wouldn't be much point taking a blood sample in your case anyway. I think we know what's in there.' She came upstairs with me and opened her little black case. 'So what was he like, this gentleman who wanted to take a blood sample?'

'Well, he was one of yours. Same van as yours, and he had a tattoo.'

'We don't have anyone with a tattoo on the team,' Nurse Mersey said as she scanned my forehead.

'A plant with daggers growing out of it.'

But Nurse Mersey had already packed up and walked back down the stairs.

I called the police, not 999, since it wasn't exactly an emergency, but the local nick.

'Excuse me, sir, but could you repeat that?' the duty sergeant said, and I could hear a racket in the background, some drunks brought in on a public order charge probably; there was a big rugby match on across the river.

'Someone came pretending to be an NHS public health person to try and take a blood sample,' I said again.

'Sorry, sir, we've got a bit of a situation here. You'll have to come down to the station, and if I were you I'd choose a quiet moment.' With that he rang off.

I put the wooden wedge back under the front door and turned on the TV. Another case had arrived in the US. They kept playing the same images from a news chopper over and over again, lights flashing blue and red in the darkness, police cars in front and behind, and you never saw a person or even a picture, only the big, boxy back of the ambulance, then a blurry shot from before, taken through the airport perimeter, the Learjet on the tarmac and something being manoeuvred out of the plane in the floodlights. A guy stood in a studio in London with a screen behind him, graphs and pictures, and he swiped up a timeline going a few months back, and my name flashed up briefly with a date, each case coming in still newsworthy, but the curves were all exponential and soon no one would care. I took out my little exercise book and jotted down the latest curiosity: colours, smelling of themselves.

VII.

I'd only just got out of bed when my phone rang early the next afternoon. *Unknown number.* I thought it was one of the public health people, so I sent it to voicemail. But it rang again and again. I picked it up. It was David, gruff and impatient.

'What's been keeping you?' he said.

'Bloody hell. Where are you?'

'You know the place, don't you?' David said. 'Better be quick, they're after me.'

I had to drag Wystan into the car on his leash, and even then he kept doing circles on the back seat as if he thought I was taking him to the kennels or the vet. I knew he was going to be a pain, but somehow I felt better having him with me. The traffic on the M25 crept along like a funeral procession, and it brought back flashes of that last drive to the palace in The Land Of, eyeballs shot through with yellow in frazzled cut-out porthole windows, the removals van with mirror foil against the cab windows, and I started feeling an ache in the back of my neck. I pulled over at a services and had a double espresso. The air around the forecourt had a foul smell to it, benzene and some burnt thing and something putrid and organic like a compost heap. I yanked Wystan's lead to get him back in the car.

The traffic got worse the further east I went. It was almost five when I finally approached the bridge over to the Isle of Sheppey. I took a wrong turning when I got off the bridge and ended up driving round a caravan park on the outskirts of Sheerness, half the caravans boarded up, rusting old shopping trolleys and bicycles upended in the little canals criss-crossing the marshland all around. I got back onto the main road and drove east and then south across the island, past more caravans and a cluster of shacks set among dunes, Nissen huts and prefabs and torn-looking sheets and superhero T-shirts swaying on a washing line in the breeze.

I parked next to an old blue Transit van with a missing headlight. There was no one outside, though you could hear a faint bass thudding from one of the shacks. A red-and-white kite was flying behind a dune in the distance. I didn't have a map and I didn't even have an address and it was starting to get dark, but there weren't too many options for where the cottage might be. I walked along the beach past the last hut. The tide was out. Oystercatchers poking about in the mud. Further out on the flats something bigger and darker was walking ponderously along the water's edge; I thought it might be a black stork, but it was probably just a heron. The light was draining out to sea, the birds and rotting wooden planks stuck in the mud and the decomposing wooden spine of what might have been a fishing boat turning grey and sepia. The beach curved into a boomerang-shaped bend. An old bunker was crumbling into the sea a little further along, one side sprayed with a rough image of what looked like a greyhound or a jackal. Something that could have passed for a storm was gathering on the horizon, an angry black curdling, patches of tarnished silver flitting among the oystercatchers, curlews, whimbrels, avocets or whatever was out there. I thought the wind had a hint of something foul in it like offal, and Wystan had his nose up on alert seaward, but it was probably random particles borne on the breeze from across the estuary, a landfill or an abattoir.

I turned another jagged corner and a hut was sitting in the dunes, blue paint peeling from the rough planks, white paint peeling from the window frames, a little porch with a wooden railing. I knew immediately it was David's from that passing mention over a beer by the Gulf of Guinea, with its sands stretching and the mangrove, the bloody mangrove curving into pallor along the lagoon. I stepped onto the wooden platform under the porch. I knocked on the door and tried the handle. It was locked. Perhaps I'd misunderstood what David had been trying to tell me. Or perhaps he'd been pulling my leg. Or perhaps they'd already got to him, whoever they were.

Wystan wasn't happy; he sat in the dirty sand a bit further down, among torn bits of netting and tossed-up milk bottles, and looked at me – So you think you're a burglar now? – but I took out the key I'd fished from the drawer in David's desk and it turned with a heavy rusty clunk. I pushed down the latch, the old-fashioned kind that's got a rough bronze lever on the other side falling into a slotted catch, and I went in.

I was hit by a smell of rancid butter and burnt toast. I groped for a light switch next to the door, but there was nothing. I turned on the torch on my phone. I wasn't sure what I was seeing. At first I thought the place had been ransacked: books and old newspapers in what looked like random heaps on the rough floorboards; a wooden desk facing one of the windows, covered in dirty old mugs and cereal packets and plates and bowls and empty bottles, gin and scotch, and things I couldn't identify at first. Clippings and things were pinned to a large bulletin board on one of the side walls, and there was a couch at the back with a crumpled sheet on it and a dirty old pillow without a pillowcase. It all made me think of the crime scene in a gory movie, but there was no body, just stuff. I thought of turning around and locking up, and I felt bad, briefly, at having walked in on something so private, even if it was a dump. But then, as I turned to go back out of the door, I shone the light from my phone at the clippings on the bulletin board. They were taken from old magazines and news-sheets, *Jeune Afrique*, *Africa Confidential*, pretty recherché stuff to be hanging from an IKEA pinboard on the wall of a tumbledown hut on the Isle of Sheppey. There didn't seem to be much of a theme to the clippings. A lot of stuff about The Land Of, maps of the outbreak spreading like an oil slick across borders and rivers and estuaries. But also reports of army posts raided in Niger, munitions dump explosions in Djibouti, cattle raids in Dar Sila. And more random stuff: a government minister disappearing off the street in Kampala, a measles outbreak in Ituri. Arrows were drawn in thick red marker across the cuttings, crudely and in a rush; some of the paper was torn, with ink marks across the cheap cork surface; and there were pictures pinned across the cuttings, rough printouts done on a bad printer with some of the cartridges low: landscape shots, spikes of karst rising from the desert, dusty riverbeds like arteries bled dry. I took a picture of the whole messy thing with my phone. It didn't feel right, like crossing a line, but then again I'd already crossed some thick lines. It wasn't exactly breaking and entering, but it came close. I went over to the desk, and still I didn't know what I was looking for. The mess was at least three layers thick, the dirty plates and empty cereal packets and bottles sitting on more old papers and magazines, hotel receipts, mail order catalogues, maps partly unfolded, bits of Africa, coastlines and savannahs and mires, and they looked old, and must have been, because they were full of white patches, and a book, stained brown wrappers and old-fashioned typeface, *Ethnologie du Soudan français*. And a notebook, the covers bound in scarlet, the edges mottled, the corners covered in black cloth. I opened it at random; it looked like a diary or a travel log, barely legible jottings in black ink alternating with roughly outlined maps and sketches of bits of landscape, dragon-tooth mountains and zigzag hills and a snaking river that must have been done in a rush from a chopper or plane. I slipped it into my pocket. It wouldn't be any use to David now, wherever he was.

The air outside the cottage had a burnt edge to it. Probably someone in the shacks along the coast having a barbecue. It was a strange time of year for a barbecue. A bunch of kids with an air rifle were shooting into the darkness by the collapsing pillbox. They looked at me, briefly, with a complete lack of curiosity. Pop, the airgun went, and the pellet tacked against the sagging concrete of the bunker.

I walked on towards the shacks and Nissen huts. The burnt smell was gone now. A few fat drops of rain started coming down. One of the kids back by the pillbox said something, and the others laughed, and I could hear the pop, then a sudden burst of sand sprayed a couple of yards further down the beach, the impact hard and sharp. It just missed Wystan, who was running with his nose down tracking something below the surface, razor clams or gastropods. But then the rain started coming down hard, and the storm swept in from the sea and the waves began whipping the sand with a mad fury that seemed poised to wash everything away, the beach and the cottage and all the junk in it and the pillbox and the air rifle, everything, and I grabbed Wystan and ran.

The rain stopped as suddenly as it had started. By the time I got back to the car the storm had swept back out to sea. The rain had drenched me to the skin and left Wystan sneezing noisily in the back of the car. It was completely dark now. I started the car and reversed out of the space next to the old Transit, but Wystan started barking. He was on his hind legs looking out of the rear windscreen. 'What, boy?' I said, then I saw little streaks of orange shooting up into the sky behind the dunes, the dark fat bulge of the clouds lit up from below.

I left Wystan in the car. It was cold outside and the tide had come almost all the way up to the dunes. When I got back to David's hut, or what was left of it, the waves were reflecting a red and yellow flicker from the flames, sparks flying in a big playful arc through the salty air and landing on the tips of my shoes and the noise one big racket, snap crackle pop, what with all the books and magazines and booze he kept in his hut.

Some of the locals from the caravans had come out and were standing there as if gathered around a bonfire, a guy in shorts with a beer in one hand, two girls in platforms, some kids who looked like they might have been the ones fooling around with the air rifle, looking and talking: 'Yeah, always thought there was something dodgy about that bloke, doesn't show up for months and then *boom*.'

'Excuse me,' I said, 'did you see the man who lives in the hut?'

'Who the fuck are you?' the man with the beer said and stepped closer to me. In the orange flicker of the fire his face looked like he meant business.

I took my phone out and called 999. 'Is there anybody

inside the building?' the operator asked. 'No,' I said, and I was hoping they wouldn't ask how I knew. I tried to get closer to the fire but it was simply too hot, a furnace in full swing, a blurry core of light too bright to look at, the sparks flying hard and yellow into the dark heart of the night. It reminded me of something, back in The Land Of, but they were burning things for a reason there, and anyway there was no time for that now and all I could do was watch.

By the time the three fire engines arrived, the fire had pretty much burnt itself out. The panels that had made up the walls were gone; some metal bits were left from the roof, twisted and collapsed, and a smoking mess was sprawled on the ground, random heaps of black goo shiny in the engines' floodlights. The firefighters sprayed it all with some foamy liquid, then the police arrived.

I started walking down the wet sand to the waterline to make my way back to the car. I didn't get far. The man with the beer can turned around as I passed him and swung his arm into my way, spilling his beer on my shoes, grunting something about where the fuck I was sneaking off to. One of the policemen came over, asking, 'What's all this about?' and then some of the teenagers who'd been messing around with the air gun chimed in: 'He was snooping around earlier, we saw him, officer,' and that was that: 'You're coming down to the station with us.'

I tried to argue with them: my dog's locked in the car, he'll be panicking, he needs to go for a pee, et cetera, but that only made it worse: 'This, sir, is a very odd place and time of day to be taking your dog for a walk.' The teenagers sneered as I walked past, their faces stark and white and mask-like in the glare of the floodlights, middle fingers erect to me behind their backs.

The two coppers didn't say much in the car on the way back to Sheerness. I heard the word 'suspect' once or twice amid the static on the radio, but it didn't click. They didn't say why they were taking me in. They hadn't cuffed me. I asked them if I was under arrest and they said I wasn't. It didn't make much sense, but I suppose they couldn't go back to the station with nothing to show for their drive across the island. I didn't think it wise to argue.

I didn't have the most comfortable of nights. The drunk a few cells down kept yelling that he was cold, his feet and knees about to fall off, and then after going quiet for a while he started moaning that he was hot and could someone come to put the fire out.

I'd just about managed to fall asleep when they came to take me up to an interview room. Grey mid-morning light lazily spilled in through the narrow window high up in the wall. I had to wait for ten minutes, then a man in a grey suit with a floral tie came in and sat down opposite me. He held a voluminous cardboard file with a purple elastic band around it, and slapped it down on the table. He switched on the heavy grey metal desk lamp screwed to the table between us. He looked bored. He didn't turn on the tape recorder at the side of the table, a big old-fashioned thing with actual tape cassettes. He made me think vaguely of some old TV detective: a less handsome Bergerac, perhaps. I wanted to ask him if that was the effect he was after, but he got straight to the point.

'DS Kennan, Kent Police. What were you doing on that beach last night?'

'Good morning,' I said. 'Before I answer that, could I ask why I'm being held?'

'You're being interviewed under caution. Purely voluntary, of course. If you want a lawyer, be my guest.'

And that's where it started to sink in, and it wasn't funny at all.

'Are you charging me with anything?'

'We'll make up our minds about that.'

I didn't think they had anything to tie me to the arson attack on David's hut. I was glad I'd left the key to the hut in my car. I thought about Wystan, who was probably getting desperate, yapping his voice out, jumping up at the windows with whatever energy he had left. But I couldn't bring that up, not now.

'So you think I'm a vandal?' I said. 'The sort who drives halfway across London in the middle of the night to burn down some shed?'

'This is not about the shed. This is a murder investigation.'

When he said it, I didn't make the connection with the burning hut. 'Murder? Whose murder?'

'Ah,' he said, and now he looked disappointed. 'I was hoping you'd tell me that.'

'I don't understand. How can you be running a murder inquiry if you don't know who's been murdered?'

He flipped open the thick cardboard file on the table in front of him. 'When this is what you're talking about.'

He took what would have been a colour photograph from the file, except it didn't have a lot of colour in it; it was shades of black mostly, charcoal black and tar black speckled with ash white, bone white, a sticky black mess with chips of burnt bone. You could just about make out the round bit at the top; it was probably a femur.

'Oh shit.'

'You might say that,' DS Kennan said, and now he seemed a little amused, though he still had a bored look.

'You want me to tell you who that was.' I pointed at the charred black mess in the photograph.

'I do.' He took a padded enveloped from in between the papers in the file and opened it. Inside the envelope was a plastic ziplock bag. He shoved the ziplock over to my side of the table. There was a watch inside. It looked distinctive: a large steel case with a polished silver face, a thick red ring around the centre, inside that the numbers, and Cyrillic lettering across. The glass was missing, the face had black streaks on it, the strap was gone. I recognized it all the same. I knew only one person who had one like it. He'd shown it round at least once on our trip to The Land Of, said he'd bought it from a Russian soldier in Grozny years ago for fifty dollars.

'David had one just like it,' I said.

'Now we're getting somewhere.'

'You don't mean to say...' I started to feel a dizziness coming on, the danger signs, the throbbing in my temples, the aching in my neck. 'I'm not feeling well.'

'Well, spare a thought for the bloke in the picture.' The DS reached inside the padded envelope once more. 'Recognize this?' He held up a little black object.

'What's that?'

'Well, I was hoping you could tell us, since you've been around and all.' DS Kennan pulled down the desk lamp that had been shining in my face and held the object in the cold white light. A carved stone animal, a couple of inches long, jagged tail, crudely chiselled jaws.

'A crocodile,' I said. 'Probably from Niger.'

DS Kennan nodded. 'You see,' he said, 'it's not that difficult, is it?' He twisted the desk lamp in my direction again. 'You've travelled a fair bit in those parts, haven't you?'

'If by those parts you mean Africa, yes, but not in Niger.'

'A minor detail. When did you last see David Weston?'

'More than a month ago. In The Land Of.'

'Ah yes,' the DS said. 'We did notice that in your file. Might come back to that. But for now, what I really want to know is, what were you doing on the beach outside Mr Weston's cottage?'

I couldn't think clearly with the throbbing and the ache. 'He called me,' I said. 'Told me they were coming for him, they were after him, something of the sort. Then he rang off.'

'I see.' The DS had picked up a pen and was taking notes

on a thick A4 pad. 'And where were you when he called?'

'I was at home.'

DS Kennan looked at his file. 'What number was he calling from?'

'It said *Number unknown.*'

'Ah. And then you decided to drive over to the Isle of Sheppey, just like that. The very night the hut burns down.'

'He did say someone was after him.'

'How convenient,' the DS said. 'How did you know where Mr Weston had his property?'

'David had talked about it. In The Land Of.'

'You think you can get away with all this In The Land Of crap.'

I didn't say anything. I wasn't sure it was a question anyway.

'And when exactly did you get to his hut?'

I could hardly tell him about how I'd been searching the hut with the light on my phone. 'Well, in the evening,' I said. 'I guess it had just started to burn.'

He looked at some notes in his file. 'We have some witnesses who say they saw you before that, walking back from the cottage along the beach.'

'Well, there were some teenagers with an airgun. They clearly had it in for me.'

'Airgun,' DS Kennan said, looking puzzled. 'In for you. What do you mean?'

'They were shooting at Wystan.'

'Wys-what?'

'My dog. I was walking Wystan. They were shooting at him.'

He shook his head. 'I'm not sure I follow. Taking medication, are you, since they discharged you?'

'Stuff for the headaches, yes.'

DS Kennan closed his file. He didn't look at me as he got up. 'We'll be in touch,' he said. He didn't say thank you and he didn't apologize for having kept me in the cells overnight. A uniformed PC made me sign a form on the way out. I wasn't offered a lift back home.

I stood on the patchy pavement outside the police station. There was a row of shops in one direction, boarded up mostly, and a sports complex in the other. KENTATHLETE, it said in huge yellow letters. SPECIAL TRYOUT OFFERS FROM £10/MTH. It was only then that it sunk in. I'd looked at the photo they showed me, in the interview room, and the watch, and even though I knew it was David's my thoughts hadn't been there, it had all seemed a bit abstract and on top of it I was chilled by the thought that they might be charging me. And now it hit me like they'd picked up the old pillbox down the coast with a crane and dropped it on me. I put two and two together, the rumours Helen had mentioned and that weird question the fake NHS bloke had asked me. So he'd made it back from The Land Of, and goodness knows what he'd had to go through in order to get out, only to be burnt to a pile of creosote in his miserable hut. 'They're after me,' he'd said over the phone, then they'd come for him, whoever they were. I wondered about the little stone crocodile the DS had shown me. Meanwhile, DS Kennan clearly thought I'd done it. But he didn't have any evidence. Other than the stupid kids with the airgun, which didn't amount to much. And my standing right there with the onlookers when the thing burnt down. Which amounted to something, but even the sergeant must have known he'd need more than that.

I walked for a mile or two till I got to a cluster of old buildings overlooking a little harbour, a red-bricked hangar-like build-ing with CUSTOMS HOUSE written over one of the arches, all the doors padlocked, a slipway green with algae, a couple of old wooden fishing boats inside the silted-up harbour, one of them half-submerged with water up to the gunwales, the other still afloat. A little grey bird with stilt-like legs was running across the mud below the harbour wall pecking at things. A hungry skua sat on the harbour wall watching. I had no idea how I'd get back to the car. I tried to look up a bus map on my phone, but the bus company's website wouldn't load the timetables and kept giving me a little rotating red serpent chasing its tail. I walked east, along the verge of the road past salt marshes and car parks and through wasteland and in the distance I thought I could see the perimeter of the prison, and for some reason it made me think of David, but it might simply have been a cash and carry.

At long last I came to a bus stop. I had to wait for an hour for a bus to Leysdown-on-Sea, and from there I walked south, past Shellness beach and through the marshy interior, picking my way across the maze of tiny stagnant channels and ponds. There was a ticket on the car when I finally got there, but Wystan was alive. The car stank of piss and wet fur. 'Wystan, you poor bugger,' I said, and he didn't seem to hold it against me: just another dog day. He'd lost his voice but he wagged his tail and I walked him along the beach, the old concrete pillbox with the image of the jackal sprayed on the side sagging a little more, the pylons across the muddy channel emitting a low, dead hum, the oystercatchers poking without conviction. There was incident tape through the dunes all the way down to the tideline long before you even got to where David's hut had stood. A police Land Rover was visible on the beach a little further down. They probably didn't get too many murders in these parts. Interesting ones, at any rate.

VIII.

I didn't see it at first. Behind the dunes the funnel of an old
steam engine stood proud like an ensign. The cries of angry
seabirds in formation sweeping the sky behind the cottage,
black curlews and rosy egrets shimmering like oxblood vases
and avocets with sabres for beaks. The mangrove went up to
my chest and someone was cursing. The water kept rising,
and the scumbags with the airgun were abroad with a nasty
little pooch the colour of excrement foaming at the muzzle.
There were five of them now, then seventeen, a battalion or
more, goose-stepping savagely round the pillbox. You look
like Johnny Foreigner, but we can fix that, they were saying
to Wystan. Wystan raised his leg, a torrent gushed forth, and
off they went. The nincompoops all departed. Whatever, I
said, and dipped my quill in the inkpot. I felt a rudeness
coming on. A joke about the girl from France Inter. A
tightness in the thighs and something about her diction,
the sheets unmade five floors up above the Gulf of Guinea,

the Bay of Pigs, the Blighted Bight. It lay on the tip of my tongue and quivered. The view meanwhile was panoptical: it ran uninterrupted to the Baltic, past oystercatchers and pickers of cockles, and though the sea had a second-hand feel to it, it was mine, its run and swish no one's to covet and trace. An Englishman's shed, his feudal redoubt and codpiece. I knew I'd be sticking one to Ricardo and Seb, and I knew what it was like, at last, looking out at David's view through David's eyes from David's desk with David's mess. The mess had a lived-in feel to it, and a died-in feel. Splinters and cartilage among the cuttings. I knew right then that there'd be no escape. Footsteps squishing in the sands at low tide. I can't see their faces but I can feel their aura, Don't try this at home, it says, and they will. Shadows on the incline of the beach. The oystercatchers scrambling kee-kee-kee, the avocets averting their sabres and their gaze. They're coming for me now, the shadows and Khai Manni and the storm, knock knock knock.

The knocking almost made me fall out of bed. Wystan sat on the carpet yapping silently, his voice not back yet. I slipped on a dressing gown and went to the front door. There was no one there. The knocking had all been in my head.

I fed Wystan and put the kettle on. I checked my inbox. Nothing much, a couple of messages from some evangelist cult telling me the end was nigh and we were all going to burn but if I cared to get out before it was too late they had a special offer, fully refundable, for £19.99. And a message from Helen: *Dear Sebastian, I thought you might want to see an advance draft of the piece which will be in next Sunday's paper. X Helen.* I opened the attachment. There was a JPEG with me staring at the bushes in Kew Gardens. And a PDF. A Man on a Mission to Find the Missing in Action, the headline said. The piece didn't talk about me much, though it said I was wracked by guilt at being the only member of the team to have got out. I thought that was funny, because I'd never said anything of the sort. But it was a nice touch of her to have shared the piece with me in advance. I sent her a reply: *Dear Helen, it was good to see you again. And really nice of you to have shared the piece with me. But did I actually say something about feeling guilt? I don't remember saying anything of the sort. Best, Seb.*

Taking out the red notebook I'd swiped from David's cottage, I tried to decipher the writing. There were dates and words that looked like place names. Arking or Anking or Auking, Saramat or Salamat or Salanat, it was hard to tell. Doodles, random-looking, zigzag mountains like fever charts, figures in what looked like Arab robes or boubous. David was not a great draughtsman but he'd captured the general idea. He clearly couldn't do faces, because the faces were either black smudges or simply left empty. There was writing next to the figures, but the script wasn't Roman. I looked again at the picture I'd taken of the pinboard in the cottage. It still didn't make any sense. The arrows between the magazine cuttings looked like they'd been drawn at random but seemed to hint at some sort of chronology. Attack on police station in Burkina followed by raid on village in Niger followed by hit-and-run on oil base in Chad. There were illegible scribbles across some of the cuttings.

I took my bowl of cornflakes to the living room and turned on the TV. Old shots from The Land Of. Things were not looking good on the island. Case numbers going through the roof. The president not seen in public for weeks. The dead lying for hours in the streets. And then they showed, as they often did, mugshots of Nikki and Ricardo and David, and some old footage of my medevac plane on the tarmac at Brize Norton, night-time telephoto shots through the perimeter and flashing lights, the usual. And yet another case arriving in the US, a motorcade fit for a president when it touched down. A patronizing-sounding man with a loud tie interviewed outside the Cabinet Office, saying, 'We're ready, we're absolutely ready. Any contingency.' He'd just come out of a Cobra meeting; the caption gave his name as Sir Jeremy Beaumont: he'd been designated the government's czar for dealing with the crisis. That's a lot of obnoxious Beaumonts for one week, I thought. I turned off the TV. It was strange there was nothing on the fire at David's cottage.

IX.

When Helen called, I thought she wanted to let me know that the piece was out there.

'I haven't got round to getting a copy yet,' I said, before she was even able to speak.

'Ah, no,' she said. 'I'm afraid I've got bad news. They've put it on hold.'

'On hold, why's that?' I didn't care. But it seemed polite to ask. 'I thought it was really well written,' I added.

'Oh, thank you.' Wherever she was calling from, her local Sainsbury's or the hairdresser's or a school fete or whatever, it sounded as if she was almost touched by the compliment.

I had no idea if Helen had kids. I don't know why the thought even crossed my mind. The last time I'd seen her, before our lunch at Kew Gardens, had been outside the ticket gates at the Eurostar terminal, just after we'd graduated, and the last thing she'd said was that she'd come out to visit, but already I could feel it all going to her head, being elected editor, getting a first, the graduate traineeship, and I didn't blame her for not visiting. And even if she had, the food and the flies would have put her off, the freelance grubbiness, Kono Kinshasa Basra, always hoping for the story that would launch me into the major league.

'Would you have time for a coffee on Monday?' Helen asked.

'I haven't got anything planned,' I said. And it was true, I had nothing planned for Monday or Tuesday or Wednesday, or any day after that.

I offered to come to her paper's offices out in Canary Wharf, but for some reason she insisted on coming into town, so we decided to meet in a cafe I used to come to in Old Compton Street, a long time ago, when I'd recently started working for the agency.

The cafe had turned into a chain and was full of tourists with National Gallery bags. I arrived too early. I smelled flowers inside, though I couldn't see any. Roses, I thought, on the cusp of wilting, and lilies. I had no idea what lilies smelled like. A sweet smell, and poignant. Helen gave me a wave when she arrived. She looked different: her hair more brown than blonde, no make-up, a few lines around her eyes.

'I knew it,' I said when she'd sat down. 'I'm too boring as a subject.'

'What are you talking about? It hasn't been dropped, it's been put on hold.'

'Same thing, isn't it?' I said. 'It's funny, isn't it? Someone must be using a really strong fragrance round here.'

'I can't smell anything. But didn't you have this thing at Kew, when we met? You kept going on about how you were smelling things.'

'It's true. My nose keeps playing tricks on me. Fragrances that aren't there. And some nasty smells too, sometimes.'

'Yes I've heard it does that sometimes, to survivors.'

I was surprised at that, because there hadn't been anything in the news or on the web. And I'd read just about everything anyone had ever written on the bloody thing.

'What exactly have you got yourself into?' she asked.

'I don't know.'

'Everybody's talking about this thing in Sheerness.'

'You're not planning to do another piece, are you?'

'I don't work in the newsroom.' A whiff of arrogance in the way she said it. 'And anyway, even if I wanted to, I couldn't.'

'How's that, you couldn't?'

'Apparently there's a D-notice on it.'

'What do you mean, a D-notice?' I said. 'They don't do those any more, do they?'

'Well, no one can go anywhere near the story. And that's why everyone's talking about it.'

'And what's that got to do with me?'

'Oh, come on, Seb,' she said impatiently. 'You went to Sheerness, didn't you, after the interview? You even asked me if I wanted to come along.'

'Ah yes.' I remembered now. It had been a joke, sort of.

'But you went, right?'

I nodded.

'And what happened?'

'When I got there it was all burning. They made me identify David's watch.'

Helen sat there, her hands cradling her latte as if she needed something to hang on to. 'His watch,' she said.

'It was all that was left.'

'Oh no. And what do the police think?'

'They seem to think I may have done it,' I said, and I watched her face as I said it. The corners of her mouth twitched slightly, and her eyes grew bigger. Her eyes were blue-green, almost turquoise, with a streak of discoloration in the iris on one side. It stood out, the little dark streak like a flare on the surface of the sun. It made her look almost human.

'And did you?'

'Did I what?' I thought she had moved her chair back an inch or two, but I was probably imagining it.

'Kill David.' She'd got a grip again now; her arms were folded, the cool professional, and she was looking at me as if gauging whether I'd be capable of murder.

'Of course not. He called me, you know, said someone was coming for him, then put the phone down. And next thing I know I'm standing on the beach and there's this big bonfire.'

Helen looked out into the street, the steady stream of cabs going past, the tourists, folks in suits, Chinese students. 'They're actually quite worried, you know.'

'Worried about what?'

She looked at me impatiently. 'People dropping like flies in the streets. Their spleens exploding as they're about to pick up the kids from school or coming out of the pub. They're saying it's all under control. But they're really worried.'

I was surprised she'd share this with me. And the spleen thing wasn't something you read about in the papers. 'You didn't hear this from your newsroom, did you?'

She shook her head. 'What do you know about this Khai Manni person?' The question threw me, and I must have shown it. Helen leaned across the table and touched my arm. 'Are you OK?' she asked.

'I didn't think anyone knew. Nikki and David and Ricardo, they thought they were on to something. But it was all very vague.'

'Well, all I've heard is that they think somehow there might be a connection with the outbreak.'

'I'm guessing you didn't hear this from your newsroom either.'

She shrugged. 'It's all very vague too.'

'How come there's nothing about this in the news?'

'You're the one who works for the wires. You should know these things.' She finished her latte and got up. 'If there's anything I can do...' she said, and I thought that was a nice touch.

'Well,' I said, 'there's the D-notice.'

'Ah yes, the D-notice. Still.'

'I'll keep you posted.'

'Do,' she said, and with that she was off.

I thought the meeting had gone better than the first. I walked down Wardour Street towards Charing Cross. A police cordon had been set up outside the station, tape and flashing lights and a couple of ambulances. Behind the crowd I could see a figure in a bright yellow hazmat suit going into the station. I went around the side of the station, but they'd also blocked the walkway across the bridge to Waterloo. I took the Tube from Embankment, and when I got home I turned on the TV. A forty-seven-year-old mother-of-two collapsing in a sweat with blood on her face as she was scanning the display boards for a train to Sevenoaks. Probably just a scare, the reporter said. A hot flush, and a faint, and a nosebleed. 'Oh really,' I said to the TV. The odds against all of those happening all at once were pretty solid. They'd kept her in for observation. But it was probably just a scare, the reporter repeated. 'Oh really,' I said. I checked for trains from Charing Cross on my phone. They'd all been cancelled. Every single one till the next morning at least. I took Wystan for a walk and hoped I wouldn't come across a little white van with an NHS logo parked outside. I didn't, but halfway down the street he started barking at something in a hedge outside a Victorian villa with a gravel driveway. I thought I saw something black and pointy like a shoe sticking out from under a hydrangea, but it was probably just a cat.

X.

They'd kept Charing Cross closed the next morning, though they'd reopened the footbridge, so I walked across from Waterloo. There was police tape across the side entrance to the station, and folks in hazmat scraping and mopping the floor, white stuff, the water heavily chlorinated, but no one seemed to care much, no one was gaping, no curiosity at all among the traipsing and stomping in their suits and frocks, all eyes averted, nothing going on here at all.

I took a bus down the Strand. The clouds were heavy like fat grey balloons waiting for a puncture to drench the Portland stone. From the top deck of the bus I saw a man from behind on Fleet Street, thinning blonde hair and rugby player's gait. It can't be, I thought, and I started knocking on the window of the bus and waving like a lunatic. Perhaps I was. People started looking at me. It wasn't David, of course, it was someone nondescript in chinos and an open-necked shirt with a lanyard dangling round his neck. An IT consultant on his lunch break.

Although I'd been expecting them to eject me as soon I set foot in the agency, the guy at reception smiled and my badge still opened the electronic gates. After all, I still worked there, sort of. Got my sick man's pay cheque on the fifteenth of each month. It turned out Jonathan was at a meeting. So I went to see the managing editor instead. He was in his office, and I could see through the frosted glass that he was on his own.

'Sebastian,' he said as I barged past his secretary. 'How long has it been? Two months? Three? How are you doing? What have you been up to?'

I tried to be polite. I answered his questions. I did two minutes of small talk, and then I got down to it. 'David,' I said.

'Ah yes. A sorry business.'

'He worked for you. Shouldn't you be doing something about it, putting someone on to it?'

'I'm not sure I understand.' Andrew's face went into stonewalling mode, his smile frozen.

'Don't tell me it's the D-notice,' I said. Something flickered across Andrew's face, fear or recognition or embarrassment.

'Ah yes. There is that small matter.'

'Is it true they've slapped a D-notice on the whole thing?'

'They don't do those any more, thank goodness.' He beckoned to the glass table in his office with a look of concern. 'But why don't you have a seat?'

I sat down and looked at him looking uncomfortable. 'Surely you must be curious about what happened to David. He worked here for, what, fifteen years?'

'I hope you don't take this the wrong way,' he said, 'but if I were you I'd get a good lawyer. You might want to have a word with Edward, he can probably recommend a couple of good barristers who specialize in that kind of stuff.' Edward was the legal correspondent. Dispatches from the latest royal divorce, et cetera. Me down by the White River knee-deep in it, and him putting away whole cases of Moët on expenses. It made the agency a lot of money, all the foreign syndication rights. I never could stand him.

'Thank you,' I said, and I got up and walked out. I was fairly sure I'd never set foot in the place again even if they threatened to cut off my pay cheques.

I passed Charing Cross, where the cordons were still up and some unmarked white vans stood outside the WHSmith, big aluminium boxes stacked on the pavement, missile-shaped containers with snout-like nozzles, over the bridge the mud-brown waters dull with the reflection of the dank umbrella sky; due south, railway arches and markets and cranes and patchy gardens trod by patchy dogs and high streets betting shops pound shops cavernous chain pubs, people drinking already. Nothing there really. Somewhere close to Clapham Junction the heavens opened, the balloons got punctured, and soon the water was up to the soft parts of my trainers. The rain didn't stop until I got to Earlsfield. I kept walking. A black broth of anger was churning my insides. Somewhere round Raynes Park the rain started again. It was late afternoon. It kept coming, black columns gushing onto the cement-coloured suburbs. There was a foot or two of dark brown water in a dip in my local high street.

Wystan looked distraught when he saw me. 'I know,' I said. I googled *Sheppey and murder*, and *Sheppey and arson*, and David's name, and sweet nothing came up, f-all.

That night I had a microwave lasagne and went to bed early. Rain showers came and went, pitter-patter against the window panes. I slept badly. I'd always slept badly, alone; and I'd mostly slept alone. The rain against the windows triggered some interesting dreams: the house underwater, a diver come looking for me, sergeant's stripes and neoprene on each of his seventeen arms, and a knock from each. But we're not charging you, he said, not yet. Just need you to look at some watches. They were nice watches, and each of them my own, sans glass sans hands sans everything except one of them was a woman's and a nice one too. Then came a gentler knock, a dream vaguely erotic that may or may not have involved Helen, I couldn't be too sure, the smell of freshly cut grass, Christ Church Meadow; no, a suburban lawn, a smell so neat and tight you could smell the imprint of the lawnmower stripes and Helen's father in shorts and sandals at the top of the hill, a chartered something or other and would I want to visit again, no way, I could feel the scrutiny from head to toe, seared like a length of dodgy tuna and thrown to the dogs. But rest assured, she said, we won't run the piece on your piece. There was more, but less interesting, and then came a knock again, no it was a beep, no a ping, a WhatsApp ping.

I woke up, looked around, remembered. The rain was striking the window, splat splat splat. I could hear Wystan shifting in the kitchen. I thought of the guy with the white NHS van who hadn't been from the NHS. Just a little sample here, just bleed into this and we'll call it quits and never mind the karma and no, I won't be showing you a badge. Sweat in the darkness, pitter-patter. I looked at my phone. A WhatsApp notification. Some dumb clown sending me useless jokes in the middle of the night, hashtag lol. Tap tap tap. It was from Ricardo. No text, only a picture, a photo of the steamer in the White River. Listing on its sandbank, rusting to oblivion. I swore so loudly it woke Wystan in the kitchen. A scratch and a snort, then he came over to the bedroom to see if I was all right. The photo was recent. I could tell it was recent because the funnel had started sagging. The funnel had only started sagging in my last month by the river. I sent a WhatsApp back to the number – *Where are you, Are you OK*, et cetera – but it didn't register as delivered. I tried to call the number but got a 'number unavailable' message. He'd probably taken out the SIM card.

The meadows around Palavers End were flooded when I dropped Wystan off. The water was almost up to the stone steps outside my mother's kitchen door.

'Maybe you should move,' I said.

'Nonsense. I survived the monsoon in Rangoon, I'll survive a bit of rain in the Thames Valley.'

'You should get some sandbags put up against the kitchen door.'

'Nonsense,' she said, and that was that. I drove back to London dogless through the sodden landscape, where I'd once known every paddock every stile every bump every squishy puddle, every black-skinned tree on the riverbank every swirling eddy in the river's flow.

I didn't get any WhatsApps that night, and no one called. The street was quiet but I barely slept. There was paranoia lurking in the shadows, the furniture billowed in the darkness, the alarm clock was stuck on 3 a.m., and I was regretting everything. I pictured Wystan sitting on the last stone step outside the kitchen door surveying an ocean of floodwater, tips of spindle trees and spires here and there and oily nothingness stretching to infinity, sad little terrier face, and he wasn't even a terrier though he had some in him.

Waking up early, I threw some clothes into a duffel bag and had some cereal in a rush and then I waited for the minicab; a strange indulgence, but I knew there wouldn't be any more indulgence after this. When the bell went I remembered I'd forgotten to call Helen. Not that I had any particular reason to call Helen; but somehow I'd said I'd keep her posted, and somehow I thought it might be useful to have her on my side, as it were. But the minicab was late and I didn't want to miss my plane.

When I opened the door there were two of them. Overalls like astronauts and respirators with tubes like a Chernobyl clean-up crew. What's with the get-up, I wanted to say, and Did Nurse Mersey send you, but before I got a chance one of them had pinned me to the wall while the other yanked open a little suitcase like Nurse Mersey's, the shape and size of a clarinet case, took out a syringe and plunged it into a little glass vial. I must have stammered something like There's no need for this really, I'm OK, I don't have a temperature, Look at my eyes not a hint of yellow, and the one who was pinning me to the wall said, 'Shut the fuck up.' It came out muffled by the respirator but I recognized the voice and the accent, hoarse and not quite Irish. The other man had put the syringe down and taken out a pair of scissors he was using to snip away at my sleeve, and that's where I saw my chance. 'Wystan, boy, come,' I shouted, in the general direction of the kitchen, and for a fragment of a second the man with the phoney accent relaxed his grip. I don't know how, but somehow I managed to wriggle out. The door was still open. I took the stairs in a single leap for each flight, coming down hard on my ankles, but for some reason I managed to stay ahead of them: the respirators and overalls probably slowed them down.

The minicab was pulling up. 'You all right, mate?' the driver asked as I sank into the back seat and slammed the door shut. I sat breathing for a few seconds, looking at the front door and listening. A couple of cars went past. An electrician's van parked outside the house opposite. The electrician started getting his gear out. The men with the respirators didn't show.

'Listen,' I said to the minicab driver, 'would you mind going round the block and then parking at the end of the street? I need to get something from my flat, but it's a bit dicey.'

The driver didn't look happy. 'I'm not paid to do that, mate,' he said. 'That's money out of my pocket.'

'I'll pay extra. Twenty quid.'

'Forty.'

A loud banging noise came from the side of the building and a volley of 'Fucks', and I figured that it must have been the two heavies descending from my bathroom window onto the bins in the alleyway next to the building.

'OK,' I said.

The car went round the block and stopped at the end of my street.

'Actually, you can drive all the way up to the door. But I wonder if you could help me with the bag.'

The driver grunted.

'Another twenty extra,' I said.

My front door was wide open, but the thugs were gone. The glass from the broken vial scrunched under my feet as I walked across the hallway. My bag was where I'd left it in the bedroom.

'Where's those big bags then?' the minicab driver asked.

'Oh,' I said. 'I've changed my mind. I'm travelling light.'

He shook his head. 'Bloody hell.'

'Spot of bother with the wife. Sorry about the drama.'

'You going far then?' he asked when we were finally on the way to the airport.

'Well, possibly. It depends how far I get.'

XI.

They'd given me a few ground rules when they discharged me from the Very Dark Place. Avoid strenuous physical effort. Keep plotting your temperature. Take your pills. Don't miss your follow-up appointments with Dr Bicknell. Avoid any long trips. And here I was a couple of weeks later, flouting at least one of the ground rules, with plenty more flouting to come. The trip would be long, and it would involve ample physical exertion. I had to go via Addis and over land from there: I'd never get in by way of the airport.

It's not that they weren't corrupt. Everyone was corrupt. The prices were higher, at the airport, and they'd be better at throwing some invented regulation at you, wrong kind of visa, two hundred; failure to register during your stay, seventy-five, et cetera. But on top of that they were under orders at the airport. Let in someone on the generals' shitlist and the guy would be sent back to fight in the marshes, or worse. Detain someone on the shitlist and the guy would get a promotion to colonel and a thousand US. Upcountry I'd get by as long as I carried enough cash around. But I'd never get in through the airport. I was sure I wasn't welcome. I'd probably got out in the nick of time when they transferred me to The Land Of.

I got in to Addis early in the morning, the sun just up in the thin crisp charcoal air, short of breath as I walked across the tarmac, brown hills in the distance and the skyscrapers starting to stir, past giant posters in the arrivals building advertising marvels zoological and architectural, trekking and Ethiopian timber wolves and rock churches and tea ceremonies, but I had no time for any of it. I never got to stop over for the fun bits. I always got straight on the connecting flight to the hardship posting when everybody else got off for a week's surfing sailing chilling with the giant sloths in the giant hammocks on the giant beach. Whatever. I'd had no more WhatsApps on my phone.

I took a taxi to the bus station in downtown Addis. In the rush hour traffic it took me three hours from the airport, but I didn't mind; I liked the slowness and the five lanes of traffic random in three directions and the constant honking and the garish shop signs and the writing puzzling and beautiful and the people tall and purposeful. I bought a length of light cotton from a stall outside the bus station, long enough to wind into a *chèche*. Then I bought a ticket to a place called Loching, on the edge of a national park, about as far as any road would take me to the border. The bus station was crawling with foreigners. No one would be asking any questions here, not yet.

On the bus I sat next to a Danish girl who kept going on about the Big Six, and every time I asked her what the sixth one was she would come up with a different list: 'elephant rhino buffalo cheetah leopard hippo no cheetah leopard croc no what's that big animal with the sideburns and the bendy horns?' I think she'd caught too much of the Ethiopian sun, crisp and unfiltered, the cool mountain air tricking you into not noticing your brains were getting grilled, but she was good company.

'And where are you going?' the Danish girl asked.

I said I was doing Africa properly, at long last, to enjoy.

'So you've been before?'

'All over,' I said, and I told her I'd worked in mining, for years, in the Congo, both Congos, all the Congos, and all the Guineas for good measure, coast and islands, and she wanted to know what I'd been mining, and I said everything, I wasn't picky as long as wars were fought over it, and she laughed and probably thought the sun had microwaved my brains.

I was almost happy, then, sitting next to the Danish girl who had a stud in her nose and told me she'd worked for a year on an ostrich farm in Georgia before starting a sociology degree in Copenhagen and now she was coming to see the Big Six, and I told her about the mines in Likuana and how everyone was in on it, the politicians in the capital rigging elections over them, the people in the sorting plant rigging the gloveboxes, the local *creuseurs* crawling through the mud with their shovels and sieves, scamming each other, and she looked at me a little surprised and a little dismayed; this wasn't what she'd come to Africa for. 'I'm not surprised you're trying to get away from all that, see another side,' she said.

'Right,' I said, and for a moment it felt like the first time I'd come, a long time ago, when everything was simple and pure and radiant with hope, not caked in the grime that comes from knowing things.

The road got smaller and windier and bumpier the further we got from Addis. At nightfall we were still driving, and it was hard to tell where we were going: no lights either side, occasional branches flitting in and out of the headlights, potholes; a sooty smell was in the air, so there must have been villages all around, but you couldn't see them. Once or twice I thought I saw an animal's eyes glowing straight ahead, then nothing, and the Danish girl had her head on my shoulder and was snoring gently; she smelled of perfume and sweat and she made me think of a puppy, a giant puppy with a diamond stud in its nose.

When I woke up the sun was rising over the savannah, a giant ball like a ripe grapefruit, the light soft and precise at once, the shadows long like charcoal sketches on the ochre soil.

The Danish girl was looking at me with something between amusement and sympathy. 'Have some breakfast,' she said, and she offered me half a crumbly pastry in a scrap of aluminium foil. 'I was thinking...'

'Oh yeah,' I said, my mouth full of the pastry, which tasted of sugar and almonds and slightly rancid butter.

'Was it for the money?'

'Was what for the money?'

'Well, you know, when you told me how you first came to work in mining.'

'Oh. I'll need to think about that.'

I looked out at the landscape, the hues all burnt, the soil and the outcrops on the hills running down into the plain like the back of some half-buried saurian, rare splashes of washed-out whitish green, the huts. There were telegraph poles now, tracks leading off from the trunk road into dusty quadrants with walled homesteads, the town approaching, motorcycles criss-crossing, people lugging stalls along the side of the road.

'No,' I said. 'The money had nothing to do with it.'

We arrived. The bus station in Loching was a shack on a rectangle of dirt the size of a football pitch and ours was the only bus.

'Well, here we are,' the Danish girl said, and it was only then I asked her name.

'Mette.'

'Well, Mette, I hope you see the Big Six.'

'I will. Why don't you come with me?'

'I'd love to, but there's some people I need to look up.'

We exchanged numbers and she gave me a little hug

and said she'd enjoyed travelling with me and then she was gone.

I walked with my duffel bag through the dusty streets looking for a likely cafe. I'd heard of people doing the crossing, but I'd never tried it myself. Traffic had slowed to a trickle since the generals had started their shitty little war, but lorries were still going across. They had to, otherwise the generals wouldn't be getting their pink champagne and the expats wouldn't be getting their apples and pineapples and defrosted chicken, and tins of corned beef and tuna for the weeks under curfew.

There was a likely cafe on the main street next to a petrol station. Inside the cafe a TV was blaring out Nigerian soaps, cases of Tusker were stacked in a corner, the tables busy with bleary-eyed single men smoking, drinking tall glasses with grainy coffee, sunglasses tucked in their sweaty shirts, exactly what I was looking for. I had a grainy coffee and it woke me up with a kick, the surge of caffeine casting everything in crisp outline: the garish twirls painted on the panels of the lorries parked across the street, the blue streak in the yellow plumage of a big finch squatting on an old red Yamaha motorbike outside. I wished I'd gone looking for the Big Six with Mette instead.

'Where are you heading?' I asked the driver sitting at the table closest to mine. He looked at me suspiciously. Some dim fear of being caught sanction-busting perhaps. For whatever he had in his lorry underneath all the plastic chairs and shelving for some new embassy building and powdered milk and bunches of bananas. But bananas grew on just about every random tree in the bush across the equatorial strip. Not bananas, then. Tinned peaches, boxes and boxes of them, and 7.62 mm rounds underneath. He wasn't very talkative. I asked the driver at the table next to him, then another one, then I found a man called Simon who also wasn't very talkative but he was heading across the border and he had a price, and the price was a thousand US.

Simon's lorry was parked round the corner. When we got to the border I'd have to get out and walk, then he'd pick me up after a mile or two. I thought a thousand dollars was steep for trafficking that didn't even involve a border crossing, but I said OK.

A rotting smell hung in the air when I got into the truck, like a steak that's been in the fridge for a couple of weeks and you've forgotten it's there and then you find it behind a stack of yoghurt and two packets of feta, and when you unwrap the neatly wrapped bundle it's all dark and gooey inside and you think there's something stirring inside the ooze more black than red now. That kind of smell. I held my nose. 'There's a meat market near here, right?' I said to Simon and he shrugged and said, 'What, nah,' and I wasn't sure if he meant he hadn't understood or that there wasn't.

The trunk road wasn't much of a trunk road any more, once we left Loching. There were tarmacked scraps here and there, the few hardy bits that hadn't been washed out by the rains, but other than that it was your average track through the savannah. It skirted the fringes of the national park for a day or two. The national park didn't look any different from the rest of the landscape, its soil a vivid carmine, its hills like crumbling sandcastles.

I wished I'd had someone to talk to when the animals showed up. It's as if they were mocking me, there were so many of them: elephants leaning into our path; white-bearded monkeys swinging across the road, so close they seemed to be grinning at me through the dirty windscreen; a family of lions, three generations, silver-haired warlord to air-punching cub; rhinos playing chicken with the truck, the driver swerving so hard he almost drove into a tree full of jeering weaver birds; a river brown with crocs pretending they weren't there at all; and in the distance the horizon a cloud of stomping buffalo. I wanted to send Mette a text message to say I'd found them, and more, but it would have been strange, a pointless message from a random stranger on a bus. I'd lied to her, but it would have been my way of atoning: *You were right.*

We drove the whole day, and when the sun went down Simon pulled into a breach between some bushes and stretched out lengthwise across the cab and I had to take my bag and go out into the braying night. I climbed up on the back of the lorry, piled high with bags of something soft and granular, and goodness knows what hard metallic things he had stashed below that. The night was warm and lit by a big red moon and a web of throbbing stars, and I lay awake listening to the humming and sawing and rasping in the bush, the occasional roar, bursts of barking, and when I sat up on my pile of bags I thought I could see shadows moving among the bushes and on the ridge of the nearest hill, and I thought about Mette in some tent a few hundred miles in behind ridges and salt licks and rivers and thorns, and it made me wonder where I'd gone wrong. I didn't get any sleep that night. There was too much going on out there.

Simon got up at seven and told me with a grunt to get back in the cab. He seemed nervous, checking the mirror all the time with a worried look.

'What are you carrying back there?' I asked him.

'Rice,' he said, and I wasn't sure I was supposed to believe that. They didn't even eat rice round here.

The road was getting worse. No more scraps of tarmac, just a broad strip of red soil stuck with splintery pebbles. After half an hour he stopped.

'Now you get out and walk. We meet in the coffee shop in Abakang.'

'That's a long way still,' I said as I got out of the cab. 'And where should I walk?' I pointed at the thorny bushes on either side of the track. But he'd already started driving off, and for a minute or two he bumped along with the door swinging open on its hinges until he leaned over and pulled it shut with a wobble that almost made the lorry keel over.

I knew Abakang was a village on the other side of the border, but that was about it. I walked for half an hour and then I heard voices and the noise of an engine, a generator perhaps, a little further ahead, so I made my way into the bushes. The soil was covered with a hard growth of some creeping succulent with spikes like toothpicks ripping into my trouser legs, but then I found a path of sorts, meandering behind the bushes in the general direction of the border. Standing behind a tree I could make out huts and a flagstaff a few hundred metres on, a tank on the Ethiopian side, ragtag this and ragtag that on the other side, men in fatigues, an old open-topped Land Rover with the windscreen missing. I kept my head down and crept along with the bushes as cover. At this rate it would take me hours to get to Abakang, supposing I found it. The whole thing was off-the-scale bonkers. I was more likely to get mauled to bits by some animal than ever to meet up with my driver again on the other side. Some animal resembling the dog-like creature that was facing me now, slunk out from behind some bush, some tamarind-like bush sleek and feathery. It was the size of an Alsatian but lighter in build, its fur sand-coloured, a black band across its eyes like a ninja mask, its teeth gleaming in the morning sun. It should have been a hyena or an African wild dog but it wasn't, it was something else. I thought of Mette again for a split second; the whole zoology was jinxed on this trip, there were seven, not six nor five, but this one didn't have a name, how was that for an ending, to get torn limb from limb by a species without a name. Then the split second was gone and I remembered this thing I'd learned about being attacked by dogs once, ages ago, from a running coach at university who'd lost an arm in the Falklands. 'Just be one,' he'd said, meaning a dog.

'But be a bigger and badder one.' So that's what I did. I snarled and barked and bared my teeth and held my hands up like claws, and the dog, if he was a dog, wasn't scared but looked at me amused, his head turned sideways, his jaws loosely open in a wolflike smile, and he seemed to be saying Go on ahead, but you do know what you're letting yourself in for, and so I walked right past him and didn't look back, and I could smell his breath foul with all the souls who'd passed by him to the other side and I never figured out what he was, because he wasn't a dog.

I made it to Abakang with the sole of my left shoe pricked right through by a thorn like a knitting needle and dragonflies that turned out to be wasps circling me with greedy curiosity, giant wings chattering like metal. There were clusters of straw-thatched huts, a shed at the centre with the corrugated iron roof half burnt-through, a few lorries parked in what must have passed for the high street. No shops. I found the cafe the driver had mentioned without difficulty. The cafe was a tree and a man selling bottles of Coke straight off the lorries.

Simon was there, impatient. 'We go now,' he said, but at least he was there. I still owed him five hundred. He didn't ask me how my walk had gone and I didn't ask him how his border crossing had gone, but the load on the back of the lorry was a bit less high now and the bags looked messed up. We drove for the rest of the day, and every couple of hours there'd be a roadblock but they weren't interested in passports or visas, it was all the same to them, no such thing as a regular army out here anyway. One of them asked me who I was and what I was doing, and I made up some spiel about working for an NGO, back from R and R, and I gave him twenty US, more than the going rate, but I noticed a captain's stars on his shoulders and he looked like he was a couple of years older than the other teenagers at the road-block and he was wearing shoes and I didn't want to risk any more questions from him.

We arrived as night was falling. Simon dropped me off at the central market and I gave him his money and he didn't say goodbye.

I waved down a motorbike to take me to the camp. The air was dirty with woodsmoke. There weren't a lot of cars on the streets. I wrapped the piece of cloth I'd bought in Addis into a simple *chèche* around my head. I didn't want to stand out in the headlights of an oncoming technical. Half the people out and about at this time of day were in some sort of uniform.

The entrance to the camp was lit with floodlights, barrels full of sand in zigzags. I paid the man with the motorbike five dollars and walked the last hundred metres past the guards dozing on plastic chairs with their feet up. A light was on in the reception booth. A small wiry man with a shadow of a goatee sat behind a PC. He looked up when I came in through the door and squinted at me, as if he couldn't make out what or who I was.

'Hello, Ahmed,' I said.

'Oh. Mr Sebastian. You're back. I thought you'd left and had trouble.'

'I'm not here as Sebastian.'

'Oh. Who then?'

'Miller,' I said. 'Jon Miller. No H in Jon.'

'I see.'

'Have you got a bungalow?'

'I have many bungalows.'

'I'd like one a bit away from the main buildings,' I said. 'Discreet.'

'Have you got a passport?'

'Mr Miller lost his passport.'

'I see,' he said. He stared at his PC before looking up at me. 'The price is different if there's no passport.'

'All right.'

Ahmed got up to take the key off a board on the wall behind him. Of the thirty or so bungalows in the camp, almost all the keys seemed to be up on the board.

'Oh, and I have a question,' I said. 'I'm looking for a friend of mine. He might have been passing through here last week.' I took out my phone and found a picture of Ricardo.

'I don't know,' Ahmed said. 'I go home to Beirut last week. But ask at the bar. Maybe he knows.'

The bungalow was set aside from the main cluster that made up the camp, hidden behind some trees, so close to the river I could hear the bullfrogs croaking on the riverbank and occasional splashes in the water made by something else. A simple prefab, but it was clean and had nets on the windows and a shower.

I looked at myself in the mirror. I had a week's worth of beard. It was OK for Ahmed to have recognized me, I'd spent a lot of time at the camp back then, but it was unlikely anybody else would. I put on an old baseball cap. I had the look, I'd blend right in. I'd pass for a security consultant working for one of the few humanitarian NGOs who'd stayed, a little washed-out and not bothered.

Later, I walked out along the river to the camp's restaurant. The hulk of the old steamer sat stuck in the mud halfway across the river, green with algae and red with rust yet shimmering white in the moonlight. At any other time the camp would have been busy with expats. Live music up on the stage, half the notes off, but after a few drinks who would notice, and anyway the anarchic syncopation went well with the general feel of the place. A great big random horrorfest, like bags of plasma being thrown against the wall, yellow splatter after yellow splatter, the desperate chit-chat of people about to head upcountry the next day for six months under the stars, nothing but the racket of the insects for company. I'd seen it empty month after month as the war had gone on. There'd been a sudden drop when the mining people left, right after the generals started their rowing, then a brief pickup when the war made the headlines and everyone needed to have a crew down here, which was the time the agency sent me, then a steady decline. And now it was almost empty. Two tables taken, a couple of soldiers and civilian staff from the UN mission. I sat down by myself and ordered a burger; I ate it hastily, and when I'd finished I walked over to the bar. I ordered the most expensive drink on the menu, a cocktail made with rum and champagne and guava juice, and I left a big tip.

'So,' the barman said, 'your first time here?'

I was glad he didn't remember me. 'Kind of. I'm hoping to meet up with a friend of mine.' I showed him Ricardo's picture.

'Oh yeah,' he said. 'He was here last week. He was so here last week. Drinks all round every night. Big man. From Portugal, yeah.'

'From Spain.'

'Yeah.'

'Did he say where he was going?'

'Oh yeah. He went up to Kauling, told everyone about it.'

'Kauling,' I said. 'That's not a good place to go. Do you know when he left?'

The barman counted on his fingers. 'Thursday.'

That had been five days ago. With a bit of luck I might discover what was going on. But Kauling was hard to get to. Permits, controls. Still, I'd come this far. I ordered another cocktail.

'What's your name?' the barman said.

'Jon.'

'OK, John.' I could hear the H.

The barman poured me a double measure of rum and

filled the glass to the rim with champagne. A little confusion with the Hs couldn't do any harm.

My phone went off later that evening. It was a London number I didn't recognize. A voice like a foghorn at the other end.

'Bridget Mersey here. We've been trying to get hold of you.' It was a bad line, but I could tell she was unhappy.

'Oh.'

'Your regular check-up. We passed by today.'

'So who were the two men who dropped by my house last Friday morning, trying to take a blood sample?'

Nurse Mersey either hadn't heard me or pretended she hadn't. 'May I remind you,' she said, sounding as if she was reading something off a prompt card, 'that under the terms of the Public Health Amendment Act you are required to be available at all times for any testing and examinations that may be deemed necessary.'

'I'm sorry, I can't hear you, I'm losing the line,' I said, and rang off.

I turned on my TV. There were familiar pictures playing on BBC World, the same old archive shots of The Land Of, then an aerial shot of Charing Cross station, excitement and agitation. The case had been confirmed. She was on life support at St Thomas's. Vital functions hanging in the balance. Still no clues on how she had contracted it. But then the picture went blurry and there was a lot of white noise. It was just as well I was gone, but I was sure Nurse Mersey wouldn't give up easily. They'd be breaking down the door to the flat next, and then they'd trace me and there'd be a request sent to the embassy and then they'd probably do a démarche to the authorities and then I'd be in trouble. I needed to get to Kauling fast.

XII.

The boat was a patched-up old thing with a torn tarp and a wonky engine that kept stuttering, just like that launch in the Gulf of Guinea, but the tarp was even more torn and the engine sounded even more wonky. It was dark, but there was nothing to see anyway. I lay under the tarp cursing the heat and worrying every time I felt a little bump under the frail old hull. I could hear gurgling and a watery groan every now and again, and the voice of the man at the wheel, and every time I was worried he'd say the engine had given up the ghost. The boat had left the capital at nightfall and was supposed to keep going until mid-morning. It was more barge than boat, a giant pirogue some twenty metres long. Wooden struts across and something like a wheelhouse at the back with the tarp behind and a couple of ancient outboards, the whole thing stuffed to overflowing with bags of food aid sorghum, and nothing to do, nothing to see, no lights on the riverbanks, nothing but the reflection of the moon, a pale orange disc mired in the black water. There was a smell, that same decomposing smell I'd noticed on the Ethiopian side of the border, rot and putrefaction, impossible to tell where it was coming from, it shouldn't have been there, there was nothing out there after all, nothing on these banks at all other than dry scrubs and stones, no trees no forest no fields, nothing, though in the moonlight once or twice I thought I could see something fleeting and white, like sheets blowing past fast, and hear the sound of hooves.

At daybreak the barge got into a little settlement downstream, shacks by the river, a couple of hangars to store the food aid, an army outpost, and I made sure I stayed well out of sight, cap drawn down sunglasses on, pretending I was something to do with the food distribution people, then I got on another lorry. The trip was costing me an arm and a leg. I thought of Jonathan and the people at head office, sitting on whatever they knew and doing f-all.

It started as a gentle constriction in my stomach and turned into a sour spasm, spread until my whole body was tingling with anger, hot shivers running down my arms and the back of my neck, until I could think of nothing else, David a scrape of lumpy tar, nothing but a glassless watch left, and it was the bastards back in London who should be down here sorting things out.

The sun rose angry on the shadeless landscape. There were no rich red soils and handsome menageries here. I'd heard about the Badlands but had never managed to go in all my time down by the White River. Everything we put in our reports was hearsay, no journalist had ever managed to get a permit.

For a day and much of the night the lorry climbed up from the river. Heat and dust and riverbeds filled only with vultures and sand, the landscape like the back of a horned lizard. Zigzag canyons, a column of smoke on the horizon once and the driver saying 'Not good' and stepping on the accelerator so fast the rocks made the axles creak and my teeth slam as the chassis came down hard.

A roadblock or two. I said I worked for an NGO and here I didn't worry about showing my passport; they were freelancers anyway, one could tell though the rate was harder to guess, twenty fifty a hundred. At the second roadblock the guy kept standing and staring when the driver had given him my fifty, until I put in an additional fifty. They didn't get much traffic on this route. At this rate I'd have to sell the flat when I got back.

Late in the afternoon of the second day we got to Kauling, a plateau at the top of a steep climb through one of the zigzag canyons. A sullen place, sculpted by an angry god. Rocks like forsaken baubles strewn about or shards from a giant vase smashed in rage. The ground a dark volcanic abrasion. The air so thin it had you gasping. All but ochres and greys dropped from the palette. The leaves of the handful of wispy trees bleached and pale like weathered lichen. A dragon-tail range towering on one side, dark brown hills cleft with erosion running off in waves on the other side. Whirlwinds of sand forming and dissolving without warning. It was dramatic, if you liked that sort of thing. An army barracks stood on an outcrop just outside the town, technicals with men in *chèche*s standing on the platforms going in and out, auxiliaries, a huge cloud of dust behind them. And some peacekeepers, a forward base, a platoon or a small company probably, with a big blue flag flying from one of the watchtowers. It was reassuring, and it was a complication. I'd have to show my passport, and there'd be questions.

I stood out here like a heron in a flock of starlings. No milling crowds in the streets, no market. Fear and a big dollop of dust, and when it got into your face it was like a swarm of metallic midges coming at you. I wrapped my *chèche* up high.

Off the main street there was a small NGO compound, an Italian doctor doing vaccinations and some local staff. I asked if I could stay with them for a day or two. 'I'm looking for a friend,' I said.

'What does he look like?' the doctor asked. 'Not many people passing through here, and no one without a permit.'

I showed him Ricardo's picture.

'Oh yes. He was here till last week. He went up into the Jebel.' He shook his head. 'No one goes up into the Jebel. No one comes back from the Jebel.'

'What was he going to do in the Jebel?'

'Research, anthropology,' the doctor said, seeming surprised. 'I thought you knew.'

'Of course. We haven't seen him in a while. His family are a bit worried.'

'Oh, that's funny. Carlos showed us pictures of his family. He used my satphone to talk to them before he went up into the mountains.'

'Carlos,' I said, 'is a very complex individual.'

The doctor let me stay in his compound; I slept in a hammock in the courtyard and paid my share of the expenses. Fufu for breakfast and fufu for lunch and fufu for dinner. The water boiled from a borehole, a mile down and still a scummy trickle, and shooting after the sun went down, the rebels coming down from the Jebel to show off and the auxiliaries spraying bullets around, a stupid game of blindfold chicken. At night I dreamed I was up in the Jebel, the donkey paths vertiginous, no eagles soaring here, pricking my fingers on the points of the tallest zigzag peaks, their summits like the points of a rusty saw, drip drip, the vultures rising from their thrones. Let's get it over and done with, you little prick, the phoney in the NHS overalls squealed, the accent Irish but not quite, and perched there on the outermost wall was a cottage. You don't mind, do you, I said as I pushed at the open door. No, make yourself at home – a disembodied voice, it might have been David's – and of course every wall every surface was covered in symbols and runes. The fire, when it came, was almost a mercy; I knew I'd wake up.

But when I woke up, things were no better. The rough rope of the hammock cut into my back and a whirlwind of dust was descending on the little courtyard, clogging my nostrils and biting my eyes. I took shelter in the dispensary, and wrapped the *chèche* around my head and looked into a little dull mirror on the wall by the light of my phone, and I barely recognized myself; the *chèche* was done creditably, my face dark in the shadows. The next morning I checked my bag; a fine black sand was sedimented everywhere, inside my bunched-up socks and between the bristles of my toothbrush and between the pages of David's red notebook, every little fold full of ground-down volcano. I turned the pages, and I washed my face and put the *chèche* back on, and I walked to the highest point of the village, a great knobbly mass of basalt on the track leading out into the dragon's tooth mountains, and there they were, the mountains in David's notebook, the serrations a perfect match. Though what it meant I had no idea.

I tried to find out where Ricardo had gone. I showed his picture around in the street. A daft thing to do, the men from the army base were bound to find out, but now I'd come this far I wasn't going to sit around. Nobody knew, though, the Jebel, the Jebel, they all said, which could mean anywhere, and this was the Jebel anyway, the dry bloody heart of it. So I waited and waited, and then one morning came a rumble of diesel engines in the street outside the compound and shouted commands. I thought of running. There was nowhere to run; the mud walls of the compound were too high to scale, and already they'd come in. But it wasn't the army, it was four peacekeepers in flak jackets, a Norwegian captain, a Rwandan sergeant and two privates.

'Good morning,' the captain said. 'I heard there was a new face in town.'

'I wasn't planning to stay.'

'None of us do.'

He didn't ask to see my passport. He seemed a decent guy, so I told him I was looking for a friend who'd gone missing. And I told him I didn't have a permit.

'We don't report to the governor,' he said. 'But you're a bit foolhardy.' Then he invited me for a drink at the base before supper.

They gave me a flak jacket later that day and took me to the base. There was an open-air mess under a sheet of corrugated iron and a few plastic chairs, a fridge in the corner filled with beer.

'So who's this friend of yours?' the captain asked. I showed him a picture.

'He's called Ricardo,' I said, 'but apparently he's been calling himself Carlos up here.'

'Ah yes. Carlos. He was here for a few days last week. Another one without a permit. I'd say you were both crazy if I didn't know better.' He screwed up his eyes. 'And we'll have to bail you out when the auxiliaries catch up with you. Which they will. I wouldn't stay here much longer, if I were you. We can arrange a ride down to the river for you. Only next week though.'

'Thank you. I really need to find my friend.' I told him about The Land Of. And I told him about David, though I didn't go into much detail. He was interested in the note-book. I took it out and showed him the sketches.

'Yes, that's the Jebel. And what's this?' he said, pointing to David's scribbles, the phrase that kept recurring in some undecipherable rune-like script next to some of the drawings.

'I don't know,' I said. 'It seems to be the same word over and over.'

'It's a name. Khai Manni.'

And the clanging of pots in the mess kitchen stopped, the hungry rasping of insects in the spindly trees outside the base. Only silence remained and the constant whisper of a thousand little sandpaper vortices of dust grinding into the black rock.

XIII.

'I've been in this country three years now,' the captain said. 'Started out on the big base in the plains. A different planet. Three canteens to choose from. Movie nights once a week. You could go jogging round the base perimeter. Easy to get out to Addis. Not an easy posting. You know this country, right. Tough. But bearable. Most of the time, it was about interposition. The generals. A nasty business. You were there. But I think we prevented the worst. Then a year ago something else came up. I was in charge of a rapid reaction company. I got a call to go upcountry. We were focused on the country round the White River back then. Much smaller footprint. The call was about an attack on a village. Place I'd never heard of. A long trip by 4x4. It was horrible when we got there. I'd never seen anything like it. They'd crucified half the men. Most of the women were gone. And a lot of the children. Body parts everywhere. The smell. As a soldier you're trained to deal with things. But not this. I had some Ethiopians with me. Good soldiers. They were in tears. Ethiopian soldiers. They'd been on the front line with Eritrea. They'd seen things. Never anything like this.'

The captain looked up into the distance. The Zigzag Mountains were turning a light shade of pink. Campari pink. Watermelon pink. There was no Campari here, though, and no watermelon.

'We tried to pursue them, but they were gone. From the tracks we could tell they had trucks, plenty of trucks. And they had taken the cattle. Driven the cattle right out into the Badlands with them. The crazy thing is, we never found them. Followed the tracks as far as we could. But we were too late. The wind is always shifting the sands out there. And then the sand runs out. There's only rock. No tracks. We never even found the cattle. We got a mission helicopter to do a flyover. Nothing.' The captain took another beer from the fridge.

'I remember hearing about that raid,' I said. I was embarrassed. At the time I had been sitting by the White River filing stories about the generals and their quarrels. I should have been talking to the captain, back then. But I'd been talking to the other hacks down at the camp by the river instead. They had been fishing the headless bodies of ministers out of the river downstream from the steamer. We could only take in so much.

'There were a few more raids after that,' the captain said. 'Always the same pattern. A village attacked. Always out of reach, always a long way from our bases. The men killed. Nasty stuff. The women and children gone. The cattle stolen.

We always got there too late. You know the mission doesn't have enough choppers. And this never got prioritized. We had to keep a lid on things down by the river. So we always had to go the slow way. Once or twice we managed to interview survivors. They talked about men with *chèches*. Technicals, a few old lorries. And some kind of a leader, riding a horse. Nothing unusual. You know the kind. There's a name that comes up in some of the intel. Chai Munny, or Khai Manni. Something like that. Some reports said he was from Chad. Some from Nigeria. From Cameroon. From Libya. There was nothing on him. For a while nothing much happened. We got drawn back into the mess with the generals. Monitoring ceasefires. Protecting civilian sites. Keeping the whole thing down by the White River from blowing up completely. Until a couple of months ago. It's four in the morning, I'm sleeping in my container down in the camp. And my phone goes off. It's another attack, a big one. You've heard of Tiérida, I suppose?'

I had. 'I'd left by then,' I said. 'They'd sent me to The Land Of. I was medevacked out.'

'Oh,' the captain said, but he wasn't listening. He was back in the moment, that morning at four, a couple of months ago.

The Zigzag Mountains were shimmering in grey and purple now. Like a row of amethyst teeth about to snap.

One of the Rwandans came up to the captain and said, 'Curfew is starting soon, sir,' but the captain just said, 'Yes, yes, sergeant, I am aware.' His mind was elsewhere.

'I mean,' he continued, 'who could attack Tiérida and get away with it? Not some little village in the sticks. A town of twenty thousand. But they did. The army garrison, what's left of it, overrun. So we go. We manage to get a chopper this time. The huts are still burning when we get there. They must have come as the sun was going down. As people were eating their dinner. Cooking pots scattered. People cut up like meat. And they must have grabbed what they could. Fuel, money, trucks, all the guns from the army post. What they did to the soldiers...'

The captain was silent for a while.

'We manage to talk to a few people who lived,' he went on. 'The same story as with the other ones. Technicals, men in *chèches*. A leader riding a horse. It could only be Khai Manni. This time I really need air support. It goes the whole chain up to New York. I'm lucky. They give me two Mi-24s. The only ones the mission has. They've always had to stay down by the White River. Just in case. But this is big. So we go off after them. Easy to see the tracks. A big cloud of dust on the horizon. With the choppers we catch up quickly. They're heading towards the Jebel. Trucks full of civilians, the women and children they'd taken in Tiérida, pickups, a few guys on horses riding out in front. The choppers fire a few warning shots. They keep going. But some of the lorries fall behind. The ones with the civilians. So now it's only the bandits. They start firing at the choppers with the guns on the technicals. So the choppers take out the technicals. All within the rules of engagement. Till there's only the men on horseback left. They're riding hard. They're trying to get somewhere in the Jebel. Probably a hideout. But the choppers are right above them. They're riding up this steep rocky slope. Like a tabletop, at thirty degrees. It's the only way into the Jebel. You've been there. You had to go past it to get here. So they're riding up this slope, cliffs on both sides, nowhere else to go. They're shooting at the choppers, so one of the choppers puts down a ring of fire around them. There's only one of them left, the leader, you can tell he's the leader. And I know it's Khai Manni. He's still riding, but his horse gets scared, starts acting funny, he has to get off. So he's standing there in the middle of this huge slope of rock, doesn't have anywhere to run, cliffs on both sides, and he keeps shooting at the chopper with an AK. The chopper has to shoot back, hits the guy, he falls down on the rocks. We bring the chopper down right next to him. I get out. It's hot like a cooking plate on that rock. I walk over to the guy, my feet burning like on coals. He's lying there, a big pile of dirty white cloth, gown, *chèche*, his weapon next to him, the stock all splintered, it's taken a direct hit. It would have been better to get him alive, The Hague and all that. But I'll tell you one thing, I'm glad he's out of action. Strange thing is, I can't see any blood. When you've been hit by a few rounds from an Mi-24 cannon, that's strange. So I tug at the robes lying there in a pile. And there's nothing there.'

He stopped and looked at me. It was almost dark now. The Rwandans had lit a couple of gaslights.

The sergeant walked up to the captain. 'Curfew time, sir,' he said.

'Yes, yes,' the captain said. 'We're almost done.'

I was taking it in, trying to make sense of the story. 'I'm sorry,' I said. 'I don't understand. What do you mean, nothing there?'

The captain looked at me a little impatiently. 'I mean exactly that. There was nothing there. Thin air. Just a pile of dirty fabric and a shot-up weapon. I didn't say anything. They filed it as "Suspect evades detention by the rapid reaction company." And they transferred me up here, let me set up the forward base. Said it was a promotion.'

'It doesn't sound like a promotion.'

'There's more. I'd been up here a couple of months. Always trying to expand the radius. Let people know we have a presence. So one day we organize a patrol. Up the wadi that rises behind the village.' He pointed in the direction of the Zigzag Mountains. It was dark now, but you could see them in a pale moonlight shimmer like paper cut-outs. 'There's a famous waterfall up there. Before all this started it was a bit of a trekking destination. More for the adventurous type, but still. And when the war came, the Jebel went off limits. I mean, Kauling is bad enough. But anywhere outside, forget it. Even the auxiliaries don't go far out. They make a show of it, driving around in their technicals, out of sight. Just round the first bend, big cloud of dust, very impressive. But it's a facade. They're scared to go any further. So I've been pushing things a bit. Safe and secure environment, all that. I like to think it helps.

'No one had been up the wadi for a long time. So we take one of the Rwandan platoons, two of the APCs. It's hard going. Not really a road. Not even a track. Just a ledge along the edge of the stream. But beautiful. You wouldn't think so, but there's water at the bottom of the wadi. Even at this time of year. If it wasn't for all the bad stuff happening this place could be an oasis. We go up the wadi in the APCs, slowly. Probably no more than five kilometres an hour. Steep walls on both sides. Not a place you want to be caught out in without armour. But no one shoots at us, so that's good. We're making our point. Then we come to this place where there's another little gorge opening up into the big one. Too small for a vehicle. A crack in the rock face, twenty metres high. A narrow slit of sunshine coming in at the top. But I look at the map and I see it's where the waterfall is.

'I'm thinking, I can't go past here without checking out the waterfall. So I tell the drivers to stop. I ask one of the Rwandan teams to escort me up to the waterfall. "Please don't ask us to come," they say. But I'm their commanding officer. "Why?" I ask. "Not a good place to go," they say. They're apologizing, but they beg me not to order them. I've never seen anything like it. You don't beg your commanding officer not to give an order. They know this can get them taken off the force. And they're very good soldiers. But now they're so scared they simply stand there begging. I ask them again – "Why do you not want to come?" They look at each other, embarrassed. "Bad things there," one of them says, but that's all I can get out of them. So I decide to go by myself. Completely against protocol. But out here you can't always do things by the book. I leave the Rwandans behind. It's cool inside the gorge. There are rocks all along the bottom, and another little stream below the rocks. I can hear a gurgling noise from deep inside the gorge. For five minutes, maybe ten, I climb over the rocks up the gorge. I know that if anything happens to me in there, no one will hear me. But I have to see the waterfall. At last I get to the head of the gorge.'

The Rwandan sergeant came up once again to the captain. 'Sir, we will not be able to go out after this.'

'Yes, you're right, sergeant,' the captain said. He turned to me. 'Any later than this and we won't be able to go out even with the APCs. And I cannot let you out in the street on your own. It's my responsibility. I suggest you stay here for the night, if that's OK. I'll call the doctor to let him know.' He picked up his satphone.

'Now,' he said, when he'd called the doctor. 'Imagine the bluest blue you have ever seen. Like the watercolour blocks you had in school. Or a bar of really blue transparent soap. But liquid. A big pool, about this big.' He looked around the courtyard we were sitting in. 'And the cliffs narrowing to the top. That's what was at the end of the gorge. A column of water going vertically down into it. Like a column of glass. With a shaft of sunlight at the centre. Completely vertical. I don't know how that's possible, but that's what I saw. It made me think of home. I have a little island at home, you know, on a lake, with a cabin on it. A little jetty, with a rowing boat.

Great for fishing trout. I sit on the jetty. I don't even need a fishing rod. Only a line and some bait. I let my legs dangle in the cool blue water. That's what I'm thinking of, at the top of that gorge.

'I step all the way up to the edge of the pool. It's surrounded by huge boulders, and when you stand on one of them you can look straight down to the bottom through that crystal blue. So I stand on the boulder, looking straight down, and I see my reflection. The helmet a dark blue, my flak jacket, my face a pale bluish white. Then I see another reflection next to mine. A white robe, a white *chèche*. And where the face should be, nothing. Clear transparent blue, the rocks at the bottom of the pool. I turn and there's no one there. I look down into the pool again and there's nothing there.'

The captain stopped. He wasn't looking at me now, or at anything. Just fixing a spot on the rough whitewashed wall across the courtyard.

Things in the village beyond the walls of the base had gone quiet. The wind had stopped. There came another sound, small arms fire, very close, just behind the walls of the compound, first one volley and then another. Then silence, then a riposte from the other side of the village and the sound of engines being started up.

'That's the auxiliaries coming,' the captain said calmly. 'They'll spray some bullets around, then it'll be quiet again. Most of the time no one gets hurt. People simply stay in their houses. And keep away from the outer walls.'

The shooting went on a bit. There was some shouting in

Arabic, and everything went quiet, as the captain had pre-dicted. A donkey started braying somewhere in the village, then the insects got back into their racket.

'I got back out of the gorge,' the captain went on, 'as quickly as I could. The Rwandans were relieved to see me alive. I asked them if they'd seen anyone. Of course they hadn't. We went up the wadi a few more kilometres, and we didn't see anything or anyone.'

I spent the night in a proper camp bed on the peacekeepers' base. In the morning I had a shower for the first time in days. No news from Ricardo. I said thank you to the captain. He said I could stay on with the peacekeepers as long as it took. I thanked him but declined. He told me to be on standby for when the auxiliaries came to pick me up. They'd rough me up a bit, he said, but they probably wouldn't kill me.

There were spent rounds among the sharp stones in the street and little boys with donkeys queuing for water at the village pump. I went back to the NGO compound. I took David's notebook out of my bag. The scribblings made a bit more sense now, though I couldn't decipher most of them. I didn't think David had ever made it to Kauling. He must have been relying on Ricardo for some of the Khai Manni stuff.

The news came the next day. Someone called it in to the governor down in the plains, who called it in to the peace-keepers. A passport found next to a large bloodstain, the red sand dyed black, on a mountain path high up above Kauling, halfway to the Zigzag Mountains. The captain showed the passport to me. Ricardo's. 'It's not looking good for your friend,' he said. 'I'm sending a patrol to check it out.'

'I'd like to come.'

'I'm sorry, that would be breaking every rule in the book. Our security people would be all over us if they found out.'

'I could help identify a body. Or belongings. I'll be the next of kin, if you like.'

The captain looked sceptical. 'I don't want to lose another visitor on my watch,' he said. But then he made me sign a disclaimer and they gave me body armour and a helmet and put me in one of the 4x4s going up into the Jebel.

For an hour or two we bumped up the stony tracks that weren't really tracks, crawling past boulders the size of ice cream vans, carving through dusty ravines like roller coasters. The peaks of the Zigzag Mountains kept coming in and out of view, brooding like a coterie of spiteful gods. 'Nothing ever gets closer here,' the Rwandan sergeant who was driving said when I asked him if we were getting any closer. 'Everything keeps moving further away.' We were probably only ten clicks from the village, but it felt like we'd been driving all day.

I couldn't imagine what Ricardo had thought he was doing coming out here: it's not that there was nothing out here, it was that the landscape seemed to annihilate everything.

Eventually the Rwandan corporal in the passenger seat said something to his sergeant, pointing at his GPS. 'OK, now comes the difficult bit,' the sergeant said.

We left the cars perched on a ledge on the side of a canyon. The drop was so steep you couldn't see what lay at the bottom.

'Up here,' the sergeant said, and started climbing the slope above the ledge. There was no path, only a stony tangent leading nowhere.

'Who would be out walking in these parts? There's nothing here.'

'They come for wild honey.' The sergeant pointed at little clusters of thorny dried-out shrubs scattered across the slope. 'It's a honey-gatherer who called.'

The Rwandans spread out across the slope. I walked with the sergeant, looking at the ground for the spot where the passport was found. I kept thinking there was someone else beside me, casting a shadow on the brittle orange ground, but it was probably just the heat biting into my eyes.

'Here,' one of the Rwandans called out, and we walked over the shard-like stones to where he was standing. He pointed down. I saw a dark patch, dry now, the colour of tobacco or old beetroot, spread out in an irregular shape a couple of metres across. 'Look,' the soldier said. He pulled what looked like a piece of cloth out from behind a rock.

'Can I see that?' I said. It was a hat. It looked blackish-grey, but close up I noticed that one of the corners was khaki. The rest of it was drenched in blood now dried and bleached. I could make out the writing above the rim, PARQUE NACIONAL CANAIMA, and the stylized outline of a table mountain. Ricardo had worn one exactly like it in The Land Of. I looked at the inside of the hat. Some letters were scribbled on the ragged old label. *RS*. Ricardo's initials. 'This was Ricardo's,' I said.

They kept looking. There was a cotton scarf, blue and white, like one I'd seen Ricardo wear. And that was all.

The Rwandans took some pictures. 'He lost at least three or four litres,' the Rwandan sergeant said. 'No one survives that.'

'Who or what could have done this?'

'Nothing that lives round here,' the sergeant said. 'No lions or leopards here. Maybe painted dogs. But they don't attack people.'

'It doesn't make sense,' I said. 'Why wouldn't there be a body?'

'Many things don't make sense round here. We'd better go.'

I took a last look at the dark patch on the ground. As we went slowly down the steep slope I again had the impression that someone else was walking beside me. I didn't say anything to the Rwandans, but I could tell they were worried from the way they were glancing around, fingers firmly on their trigger guards.

'I'm very sorry,' the Norwegian captain said when we got back to the base. 'There's not much room for doubt.'

'But there's no body.'

'Yes, but if there had been, an animal might have dragged it off.'

'But there's no animal big enough in the Jebel for that.'

'There's a lot we don't know about the Jebel,' the captain said.

I went back to the NGO compound and gathered together my stuff. There was commotion in the street outside. The auxiliaries. They didn't knock before coming in. They spoke from behind their *chèche*s in the Touareg manner and they kept pointing their guns around. 'Who are you? What you doing here? Where your permit?' I played dumb for a while and then they started using their rifle butts and it was only the captain and a couple of platoons of Rwandans that saved me. There was a stand-off. 'The SRSG will sort this out with the minister,' the captain said to the chief of the auxiliaries, who wasn't happy. The captain wasn't happy either when he took me back to his base in the back of an APC with its machine gun trained on the auxiliaries. But he didn't hold it against me. 'I'm really sorry about your friend,' he said. 'But he was pretty reckless. Not unlike yourself.'

They got me out of Kauling in a mission helicopter, down to a bigger base in the plains, and then by plane on to the capital. I got a bollocking from the SRSG at mission HQ, then I got a bollocking from the British ambassador, then they took me to the airport. No one asked to see my visa, though the embassy and the mission were there to make sure I didn't get roughed up even more by the army before they put me on the plane.

XIV.

At Heathrow when I got off the overnight flight from Addis they were doing temperature and eyeball controls on all incoming passengers. There'd been two more cases when I was away. A chemistry teacher collapsing in front of her class in Basildon: at first they'd thought it was the fumes from the experiment she was doing but then someone had checked her eyes, then they'd taken her temperature: forty-one, rising, which I didn't even know was possible, though I'd probably been there. And some geezer on the underground, got on at Tottenham Court Road and never got off, not under his own steam anyway.

I didn't beep, though my passport did. The people from the Kent force must have fed it into the system in the meantime.

The border force officer looked puzzled. 'When did you leave the country, sir?'

'Last week.'

'Oh.' He picked up his phone to consult some superior. 'Have you been to The Land Of?'

'Not recently.'

'You should be reporting at least once a week.'

'Reporting to whom?'

'It doesn't say in the system,' he said.

And then I was in.

At home, everything was in its place from when I'd left, the armchair toppled, the kitchen a mess, the glass scrunching under my feet in the hallway. I left everything as it was and went to Palavers End to pick up Wystan. The floodwaters had risen even further. The cottage was surrounded by a shallow lake, only the driveway standing out. 'I'm absolutely fine,' my mother protested. 'This cottage has stood here since the seventeenth century, and it'll be standing here when I'm gone, and anyway I've got my wellies ready. The palaver's anything but finished.' It was something of a catchphrase for her: palaver's over, end of the palaver, et cetera. It's why she'd called the cottage Palaver's End, more as a joke, and as a birthday present one year I'd put the name next to the front door in cast-iron letters, though the apostrophe had soon fallen off. The ground floor was still dry, but she'd moved a lot of stuff upstairs to her bedroom.

'Promise you'll call me when things get really bad,' I said as I left. 'And before you do that, call 999.'

'There'll be strictly no need,' she said, standing in the open door, grey water lapping the gravel outside the house, scarecrow trees black and rootless dotting the paddy-like meadows.

Wystan was neither happy nor unhappy to be coming home with me. More than anything he seemed confused. When we got to my flat he sat in the car and I had to nudge him to get out. 'Come on, boy, it's not so bad,' I said. But he could feel my worry. I thought about what might happen if the men with the needles came back. 'Let's go to the police station,' I said to him. 'We have something to report.' He looked dubious.

Wystan was right: down at the local nick they said they couldn't take a statement from me. A code that came up when they put my name in the system. Way beyond their pay grade. And who would I need to talk to about that? I asked. Well, that would be the Home Office, they said.

I picked Wystan up from outside the Sainsbury's where I'd tied him to the bike rack. I thought the streets looked emptier as I walked down the high street towards the meadows by the river. I might have been imagining things. But there'd been another suspected case, first one outside London, in Manchester. A pinprick, a nurse who'd worked in a treatment centre down in The Land Of.

The river had burst its banks, and some of the pubs on the riverfront had water up to the bar. It had been raining hard every day since I'd left for the White River. I thought about moving in with my mother for a while, but the last thing I wanted was to put her in any danger. I thought about calling a friend, asking to stay over on their couch for a few weeks.

But there was Wystan. And I didn't have any friends, when it came to that. All those years of pounding red foreign soil. I'd drink with whoever was there to drink with, by the rusty steamer in the rooftop bar of the Radisson overlooking the Gulf in a shack by the pool watching giant red and yellow lizards dashing on flip-flop feet down the flower beds. Et cetera. Whoever had been there to share a Skol a Tusker a gin and tonic with and compare notes. The usual superficial bragging talk. And every once in a while, a squeeze under a net – 'You'd better stay over for the curfew' – or a weekend in Dakar, big hotel by the beach, windsurfing and round-the-clock buffets and DO NOT DISTURB. Then she'd be off on the rotation to Dhaka and that would be it. Or promoted back to Paris, producer of current affairs. We'd teased Ricardo about the girl from France Inter. But it had been nothing to do with Ricardo. *'T'es trop mignonne tu sais'* said with a terrible English accent, the sheets drenched with sweat while the backfire from the Mirages lit up the night sky over Bamako. None of that much use now.

I didn't like the thought of going back to my place. Nosferatu shadows rearing up on the living room walls at midnight. Every faulty screeching brake pad every pinking engine in first gear creeping stealthily round the corner enough to ramp things up, 999 pre-dialled on my phone ready to press call though I doubt they'd even come once they checked the address against their databases. Ready to jump out through the kitchen window, Wystan gently lowered out first. But what if they came in through the kitchen window? Still, I went home, walking up and down the street a couple of times before going in, checking every car parked in the vicinity, eyeing the bushes in the front garden. No one was there.

I gave Wystan his food, fat bloody chunks of animal insides in jelly, and started cleaning up the mess. They'd smashed one of the vases in the living room, one my mother had made, roughly glazed in cobalt blue with pockmarks like the moon. I gathered up the shards and put them in an old plastic ice cream tub and decided I'd never tell her. I got the hoover out to clean the carpet in the hallway, where there were little fragments of glass from the vial, and I had to shoo Wystan out of the way so he didn't get splinters in his paws, and I had to bend down to pick out a few bits that were partly stuck under the skirting board. One of them was bigger than the others, and it had a tiny number stamped on it. I put it in a Ziploc bag and kept it, just in case.

After that, I scanned the windows, the door, the back of the sofa. Had the wardrobe door been slightly ajar when I left, and what was that light draught I could feel? I had to call someone. I called Helen.

'Don't tell me there's another body.' She didn't sound as surprised as I'd expected.

'Not a body exactly.'

She didn't say anything for a while, then, 'Do you want to come over? I'm working from home today.' She texted me the address: 16 Coker Gardens, N6.

I was relieved to be getting away from my flat. But I

hadn't expected her to ask me over to her place. There'd be children's stuff, maybe. Husband paraphernalia. That shouldn't have bothered me, but it did.

I couldn't leave Wystan at home alone. Not that I seriously thought they'd kidnap a pet. WE HAVE YOUR DOG, in cut-out newspaper characters – A PINT OF YOUR BLOOD BY NOON TOMORROW OR YOU GET HIM BACK IN PIECES, with a picture of Wystan lugubrious and lost and the day's *Evening Standard*, the concrete block walls of someone's garage discernible in the shadows behind. But there was no telling what they'd do if they came back. When they came back. So I put the lead back on Wystan and shoved him in the car.

I could smell the colours from as far away as the North Circular. An infusion of flamingo pink. A little watered-down lilac running into Med blue all the way through the traffic jams and past the cash and carries. The smell got stronger as I went through Brent Cross: not unpleasant, but so strong I almost fainted.

Coker Gardens was everything I'd expected. Victorian villas with raised ground floors, big cars in the driveways. Sculpted hydrangeas. Number sixteen had a thick hedge, a remote-controlled gate, a recent burglar alarm, a security camera on the front facade. A brand-new Volvo SUV in the drive. No name on the buzzer.

Helen was wearing a simple white blouse, jeans and espadrilles. 'Oh dear,' she said. 'What happened to your face?'

'Bit of turbulence on the way back.'

'So you've been travelling.'

'The Zigzag Mountains.'

'The what?' she asked. Then Wystan waddled in. 'Oh, hello, and who's this?' she asked. She stroked his head.

'It's Wystan,' I said. 'I'm really sorry, I had to bring him along. He wouldn't be safe at home.'

The hallway of Helen's house was all muted elegance, pale blue with the mouldings offset in white, cement tiles, witch hazel branches in a vase that looked Japanese or expensive. 'Nice,' I said. She led me into the living room. It was chic in a respectable sort of way. Farrow & Ball hues and a glass coffee table with a base vaguely like the Forth railway bridge. Contemporary prints on the walls. A few political cartoons with dedications. Slick and presentable, with an undertone of dodgy politics. Like Helen herself. I preferred the room she'd had at university, in a college residence up the Woodstock Road. She hadn't had the same politics then. She'd had a view of playing fields. Hockey and blackbirds at dusk. The walls a little too thin. The bed a little too noisy. Posters pinned up on her walls: Frida Kahlo and Matisse. The books on her bedside table: Gabriel García Márquez, in Spanish, which impressed me at the time. A little gouache painting of El Che which she'd brought back from a gap year in Bolivia. That also impressed me.

Helen's living room now looked like something out of an interior design journal. 'It makes me want to do a profile,' I said.

She laughed, but it was a nervous laugh. 'I want to show you something,' she said. She went to a console in the corner of the living room. Faded gilt, lightly chipped, conch shell motif, inlaid top, the real thing, obviously an heirloom on her husband's side. She opened a drawer and took out a padded A4 envelope. 'Perhaps you could have a look at this.'

I opened the envelope. Inside was a little wooden mask, barely bigger than a Mars bar, crudely carved with little polished stones for eyes, feathers for eyebrows, the mouth a tight and narrow smile burnt into the wood like a black comma. And what looked like thorns stuck in a crest-like pattern in its head.

'It came in through the letterbox yesterday morning,' Helen said. 'I called the police, but they said there was nothing for them to investigate and I shouldn't worry. A prank, they said, or a mistake.'

'And what do you think?'

'It's probably just that. A prank or a mistake. But there's something about it. I feel a bit, you know, uneasy.'

'Of course. I understand.'

'With that Khai Manni business and all.'

'I'm sure it's nothing.'

'Do you know what it is?' she asked.

'I've never seen one before,' I lied. Helen put the mask back in the drawer.

A cluster of framed photographs stood on the console. Helen with various celebrities, probably taken when she was doing her interviews. Helen with the owner of her newspaper. And pictures of Helen with her husband. Helen with her husband and a young boy, all in shorts, bathed in white beach light, half an old wooden fishing boat rotting artfully in a corner of the photograph. Her husband in suit and tie, a series of official poses, royal standards in the background, gilded wallpapers. Her husband wearing abseiling gear and fatigues on what must have been a team-building exercise.

'Hang on,' I said. 'I didn't know you were married to—' He'd looked so different in that interview outside the Cabinet Office. 'It could never happen over here,' he'd said with the brash barrow-boy confidence they all had now, though in his case the barrow-boy style was clearly a veneer.

'Ah yes. He's off to some sort of a crisis meeting at Chevening. He won't be back till late.' I don't know why she told me this.

'And this,' I said, pointing to the boy in one of the photos. 'This must be your son.' A stupid thing to say. Not likely they were posing with a random nephew.

'Jeremy's, from his previous marriage. He's just started boarding.' I thought I heard at least a hint of something in her voice. A crack in the facade.

'Do you remember those phoney NHS people?' I said.

'Yes.' she said. 'They came to take your temperature. Weird, but maybe it was a misunderstanding. You know, databases mixed up.'

'There is no database. I'm a one-off. And they came back. They roughed me up and tried to put a jab in me. I barely managed to get away. Because of the minicab driver.'

'The minicab driver.' She looked sceptical. 'Have you been to the police?'

'They won't even take a statement from me. Some sort of an alert the Home Office have put on my name.'

'That's peculiar. It's not that I don't believe you, but can you prove any of this happened?'

'You don't believe me,' I said. 'But they dropped a vial when they tried to give me that jab.' I took out the Ziploc bag with the fragment of glass I'd found between the carpet and the skirting board.

'Interesting.' Helen briefly held the bag up against the light and put it back on the coffee table, then put her hand on my shoulder. It gave me a start, a little electric burst like one of those big fat flat batteries you use for experiments in school.

'I need to tell you about my trip last week,' I said.

'Those jagged mountains.'

'Zigzag Mountains.'

'Right,' she said. 'Coffee or tea?' She led me to the kitchen. It overlooked the garden. The borders just distempered enough to look impeccable, an old bench by the fence at the far end shaded by a bower, the branches and leaves lightly tousled. The fridge magnets spelled out nonsense. The mug she gave me had a Camp David logo on it.

Helen took me outside and we sat on the bench in the bower. I showed her the WhatsApp from Ricardo. I told her about the overland trip from Addis. The Big Six made her smile, briefly. I told her the story the Norwegian captain had told me. Khai Manni's robe and *chèche*, nothing there.

'You don't actually believe there was nothing there,' she said.

'I don't know, but the captain struck me as perfectly rational.' I told her the story about the waterfall. A cloud passed. When she bent over to pick up her mug I could see the points in her spine standing out in the back of her blouse. She had her hair doubled up with an elastic band. A few wisps of darkish brown hair spilled out from the nape of her neck.

It was getting cold. I could smell darker hues, graphite black, ground-up charcoal. Creosote. I shivered. Helen moved closer to me on the bench.

'Can you smell that, that burnt sort of smell?'

She said no, she couldn't smell anything, and she looked at me in a funny way.

'I'm sorry,' I said. 'All I've done is tell you these silly stories.'

'No, I needed to hear them. But Ricardo, did you find him?'

I told her how we'd gone to see the spot where Ricardo had disappeared, the bloodstain, his hat.

'You think he was on to something? Something to do with Khai Manni?'

'There are lots of coincidences.' I didn't tell her about the impression I'd had up on that slope, of someone walking beside me, someone other than the Rwandan peacekeepers.

'You must be worried,' she said. 'I mean, about the police.'

'The police? In what sense?'

'Well, everywhere you go,' she said, 'your friends seem to, you know.' I must have looked shocked, because she put her hand on my shoulder again and apologized. 'No, but that's not at all what I mean, I mean that you, you know.'

'It's all right. I guess it is what it looked like. But is that what you think?'

She was so close now I could feel her breath on my cheek. 'No,' she said, 'of course not. I'm very sorry about Ricardo.'

I nodded. Her face was only a few inches from mine. I could smell the scent of roses, pink and scarlet and hot.

'I've always wanted...' I didn't finish the sentence. Her lips were a deep carmine and she reminded me of someone and I couldn't put my finger on it and suddenly my headache was back, a rush of lead balls pounding my temples. 'I'm sorry,' I said, and I must have swayed because she moved as if to catch me, but I got a grip on myself. 'I feel such a fool. I'm sorry. I have these relapses.' I expected her to recoil, but she didn't move. She seemed to have become her old self again, and it almost scared me. 'That patch in your iris,' I said. 'It hasn't changed one bit.'

She took a sip from her mug. 'Did it bother you back then?'

'Bother, what do you mean, bother?'

I wanted to say it was one of the things I'd loved most about her. Like a tiny reef in the turquoise waters of a miniature lagoon. Like a world inside a world. But I didn't get round to it, because someone stepped out on to the patio from the kitchen.

'Well, I'm sorry to intrude.'

Before I even turned to look, I recognized the voice, mellifluous and matey in a vaguely fraudulent sort of way all at once. Helen's husband, the czar, permanent or principal secretary or national security adviser or whatever he was, Knight Grand Cross of something or other.

I could sense Helen shrinking back like one of those plants that close their leaves when you touch them. 'Oh, hello, darling,' she said, 'I thought you were still at Chevening.'

'Finished a day early because of the G7 meeting. Am I intruding?' He was smiling, but I thought I heard something sharp in his voice. Helen introduced me. 'Yes, I do believe I've seen your file,' he said.

'My file.' I didn't know my case was considered a matter of national security. 'I'd love to see my file.'

'Oh, I'm sure there's nothing in there you don't know already.'

I suppose he was trying to sound reassuring, or simply to fob me off; but there was something in the way he looked at me: knowing, and more than a little amused. Chances were the file contained any number of things I didn't know, and it was obvious I'd never get to see it.

A wind was coming up, a door slammed somewhere in their house, the azaleas started to shake. And there was a new smell in the air, sickly and cloying. Like something sweet that had gone off. 'I'd better go,' I said, and grabbed Wystan.

Helen didn't offer her cheek when she said goodbye at the door, and her eyes had clouded over. She looked like the thumbnail on the newspaper's website again. Slick and efficacious.

As I drove back down the North Circular I thought about the mask-like totem Helen had shown me. The last time I'd seen one like it I'd been standing in the circular ruins of a village somewhere in the borderlands between Chad and Sudan. I was talking to the sullen villagers and there was a little red bird singing in the wispy bushes, and the smell of smoke hung in the air like a bad memory. The huts were roofless, the straw singed off. I wasn't going to tell Helen about that.

I almost got run off the road by a convoy of ambulances and police cars coming up from behind, going south at speed. A helicopter flew overhead. One of the ambulances was a strange boxy thing the size of a big lorry.

On the way home, I stopped over at Sainsbury's to buy dog food. The aisles were empty, and a man stood outside the entrance with a placard. Tattered black suit, patchy white shirt but hair neatly parted. The placard didn't say THE END IS NIGH, it said THE DARKNESS IS COMING, and when I walked past him to my car bearing two carrier bags and a fifteen-kilo sack of dog biscuits he came up to me, waving the placard in my face.

'You should know, you've been to a very dark place, yes you have, you've seen the glacial fires burn, you've felt the icy furnaces, don't you deny it.' He had a strangely stilted posh accent and a voice like a newsreel from the 1930s. He was blocking my way now.

'Excuse me,' I said, and he sneered at me and put his face up close to mine, so close I could smell his bad breath.

'Dark dark dark,' he snarled, 'we're all going into the dark.'

I almost had to push the man out of the way to close the car door. He kept waving the placard at me as I backed out of my parking space. Wystan barked at him, but the man pulled his face into a ghastly contortion, teeth bared, the whites of his eyes stark in the lines that criss-crossed his face like parchment.

When I got home I did the usual checks. The furniture in its place. The curtains drawn, as I had left them. My laptop closed, no fingerprints on the shiny cover. The random stuff on my mantelpiece. The NHS badge they'd given me when I was discharged from the Very Dark Place, along with a doctor's coat and a stethoscope with a little engraved dedication, To Seb From The Team. And the pills, a few months of supplies, with a health warning: take them and you might feel a bit funny. Don't take them and, well, you might go a bit funny in the head, know what I mean.

White vans in the street, ghouls in the camellias. Chisel marks on the door. None today.

When I went to bed I realized I had left the little fragment of glass from the vial at Helen's place. My only bit of evidence gone. Nothing to prove it wasn't all in my mind, and perhaps that was just as well.

XV.

Knock knock. Dring dring. But it wasn't the fever bell ringing, just the doorbell, daylight shimmering through the wonky blinds I'd never got round to replacing, with all those years frittered away in the field. I got out of bed, almost stepped on Wystan, who had curled up by the window, ran to the living room, threw back the curtains. A white van with an NHS logo was parked opposite.

I picked Wystan up. He squealed like a pig about to be speared. I went back to the bedroom. Yanked up the blinds in a rush. The catch on the sash window was jammed.

There was a commotion outside my flat. A big dark shadow behind the frosted glass in the front door. I went to the kitchen. I tried the window in the kitchen, shoved it open, pushed Wystan through the window, leaning a little too far forward, almost going head first after him, dropped him on the roof of the shed at the back of the building. 'Go, boy, go,' I said, and I heard someone yanking at the knocker on my front door. I was about to jump, then came the voice of Nurse Mersey.

'I must remind you that you are required to keep yourself available at all times. At all times.' Her baritone echoed through the building.

I looked through the window at Wystan, whose expression was even sadder than usual. 'I'll come out to pick you up in a moment, boy,' I said.

'Come in, make yourself comfortable, make yourself a cup of tea even,' I said, opening the door to Nurse Mersey, and I rushed past her down the stairs, down the little alleyway that led round the back of the building. I clambered up onto the bins next to the shed and tried to lift Wystan down from his perch.

Nurse Mersey was still lecturing me on my obligations under the Public Health Amendment Act. I was sure half the street could hear her. When I made it back to the flat with Wystan she was standing in the kitchen, thermometer in hand, ready to point. 'You see, we're a bit busy right now,' she said. 'Can't afford to do a single visit for nothing.'

'Oh. You mean there are more cases like me? Survivors? I would have read about those, surely?'

'I'm not saying they're survivors.'

'Oh, what then? More suspected cases. Like that teacher or the bloke on the Underground.'

'I'm not authorized to disclose any such information.' Nurse Mersey pointed at my forehead. 'Thirty-seven point two,' she said. She shone a torch at my eyeballs and nodded to herself. 'But I shall have to make a note of the mental health issues I detected when I entered your flat.' She took out a clipboard. 'Does it come over you frequently, this urge to escape? Is it triggered by hallucinations? Do you have psychotic episodes?' I was sure the neighbours could hear every word.

'None of these, but I was worried you might be those other people I tried to tell you about over the phone the other day. The fake NHS van. They tried to take blood from me by force.'

Nurse Mersey went down whatever list she had in front of her on the clipboard. 'Paranoid delusional,' she said to herself, though it sounded as if she was giving orders in a parade ground.

'Do you really think the neighbours need to know?'

She didn't take any notice. 'You should continue to keep yourself available,' she said, and she packed her thermometer back into her little black case and left.

Nurse Mersey needn't have bothered pretending. Dr Bicknell was more forthcoming when I saw her later that day.

'Case fatality around 80%, from what we can tell by now. But I'm not telling you anything you don't know,' she said. I thought it funny she would use that phrase. I'd heard something similar not long before from Helen's husband. I wondered what she knew. And what she was keeping from me.

'So why did I make it?'

'We'd love to know that.' The doctor looked at the notes on her PC. She took her glasses off briefly. Without them she looked a little tired, and more kindly than not.

'Is there a file on me?'

She looked taken aback. 'Well, there's the file of case notes from when you were on the ward,' she said. 'That's quite voluminous. And there are the case notes I'm looking at now, and all your results.'

'Yes, of course. I meant, is there another file? Something people higher up would have access to?'

Dr Bicknell smiled uneasily. 'This isn't *The X Files*, you know.' She looked at her screen again. 'Have you still been noticing things? The smells, et cetera?'

'Well, yes.' I noticed she hadn't answered my question. I showed her the journal I'd started keeping.

'That's fascinating,' she said. 'Do you mind if I keep this for now?'

'Of course. Do you think there might be something to it?'

'Well, it's far too early to say. And you are the only case. Except for some anecdotes from The Land Of. But none of those are reliable.'

'Am I a freak?' I asked.

She looked shocked. 'Well, that's certainly not the word I would have chosen.'

They were putting up the headlines on the news stands when I came out of the station on my way home. The pinprick case had died. She'd lasted barely a week after getting home. The news websites were already on to something else: a car crashing headlong into a tram in Edinburgh. Unremarkable in itself, except that the driver had managed to extricate himself from his car and start vomiting blood onto Princes Street. 'Like a bloody fountain,' at least one eyewitness was quoted as saying, and his eyes when the paramedics got to him apparently yellow like antique pieces of ivory. The pathologists were still doing tests, but the media had already drawn their own conclusions. The driver had been a newsagent from Leith, hadn't been outside Scotland or travelled abroad in years. There were bound to be more where that one came from.

'I'm a lucky bastard,' I said to Wystan when I got home, but he wasn't interested. On the doormat in my hallway was a letter he'd mauled. It had probably been put in one of the neighbours' letterboxes downstairs and they'd shoved it under my door. 'Not good, Wystan,' I said. A Spanish stamp with Wystan's tooth marks in it. MUNICIPALIDAD DE CÓRDOBA, REGISTRO CIVIL, the little transparent window with the sender's details said. Now that's funny, I thought, until I remembered that Ricardo was from Cordoba.

My Spanish was rusty, but I figured it out. An inquest, a coroner thing, *in absentia*. Although the body had been absent, the only witness needed to be there. I don't know why they'd decided to call me as a witness. No one had seen a body. They could have asked the peacekeepers. But I couldn't refuse. I owed it to him.

'Wellies by the gatepost,' my mother shouted at me from over the water. She was standing on the threshold of Palavers End, a hundred metres away. I should have known I was pushing it. It was only a few weeks since I'd got out of the isolation ward, and I kept shuttling Wystan to and from the cottage. The paddock was one big grey mirror now, dented only by occasional black branches and fence posts, the driveway covered in a few inches of oily water. I looked behind the old gatepost by the road. The wellies were in a plastic bag among the branches of an old gorse bush. 'No wellies for you, boy,' I said to Wystan. I picked him up like a baby and waded across the causeway that used to be the drive.

'I'm sorry. This'll be a short one.'

'Ah yes, I've heard that one before,' she said, but she was probably happy to have Wystan for company.

'You really should move, you know. You could stay in my flat till the waters go down.'

'I'm fine.'

'What about Wystan? He won't be able to go walkies.'

'Oh, there's enough of a ledge,' she said, and she pointed to a line of brickwork visible below the water around the base of the cottage, where the flower beds used to be.

'I'm not keen on ledges.'

'We'll be all right.'

I waded back along the causeway. The rain had started again, big drops like a leaking mains pipe, and a gentle current tugged at my feet. I put the wellies back in the plastic bag and drove through the rain to Heathrow. The gutters and drains were full along the M4, and little lakes had started to form on the outer carriageway, slowing the traffic into two lanes.

It was a good thing I'd left early, since there was a bit of hassle at Heathrow when I showed my passport.

'Excuse me, sir.'

'What now?'

'Oh, nothing, sir, I'll just need to talk to my supervisor.'

Half an hour in a windowless cubicle with nothing but customs notices on the walls. The neon light like a drab supermarket.

When the supervisor came, I showed him the letter from the council in Cordoba. 'It's in Spanish,' he said with a grim face.

'Of course it's in Spanish. It's what they speak in Cordoba.'

Another twenty minutes while he was on the phone to the Home Office.

'It's not the Kent force at all, is it?' I said while I was waiting with the underling. 'It's something else.' The underling stood in the corner and looked at stuff on his phone.

When the supervisor got back, he merely said, 'Here you go, sir,' without apology or explanation.

I only just made the flight.

I took a bus from the airport in Malaga. It was forty degrees and it wasn't even summer; the landscape parched, olive trees to the horizon in neat little rows in the dust. I was staying in a little hotel in the old town and lugged my bag through the narrow alleyways dodging tour groups and student couples high on it all, Lorca Tárrega Albéniz, Recuerdos de la Alhambra and Ribera del Duero. It felt sad: the place throbbed with life and light and I was there for a funeral without a body.

My room was dark, with a small window facing out onto rooftops, a jumble of ochre angles. In the distance I could make out the stone towers of a church, conical like a heretic's hat.

I had the evening to myself so I walked down to the river, across the Roman bridge. Some flamenco event was on at a fairground outside town. Flocks of girls in red and black dresses, caballeros with greased-back black hair, riding trousers and shiny pizza-cutter spurs. Arpeggiated guitar chords tumbling through the air. The heat like a thousand shards of glass. Carriages circling the outside of the fair, with women in ruffled outfits fanning themselves. I got a glass of sangria at one of the stalls and wandered round the stages. Everyone seemed to be dancing. There were troupes of kids with castanets and portly women with red flowers in their pinned-up hair. Guitars on every corner doing *rasgueado*. I went into a tent to escape the heat, but it was like a greenhouse. Girls whirled like dervishes up on the stage.

A rush of random images. Rough wooden rafters under the white plastic sheeting. Gravel under my feet. Shouts and laughter and cries, life and death. The furnace burning hard and yellow in the night. I had to get out, and I tumbled and swayed. Perhaps I'd had more than one glass of sangria. A pint of turbulent blood. *La cólera, en la sangre.* Something Helen had explained to me, once, back then, open window, blackbird trilling, hockey sticks clanging, to do with one of the books on her bedside table, in Spanish the disease is *el cólera*, but then there's anger. *La cólera.* And passion. A birthmark on her back, a long way down. 'Ah,' I'd said, then I'd forgotten about it, and now it came back, the shape of a tiny little zigzag island. It was hard to be certain in the heat. I thought I saw a familiar face smiling at me through the haze and the rippling arpeggios. No, it couldn't be. I fell over a chair or two. '*Es el calor,*' I said, '*es el calor, perdón.*' They were polite, thought me yet another drunken foreigner, and I wanted to say no, no, I'm different, I have it hardwired in my blood now, but in no time at all they had a first aid crew there and carried me to a tent with a cooling fan and dabbed my forehead with icy water, *gracias gracias*.

Somehow I made it back to my hotel. As I stumbled along I had to beat back the walls as the street corners crowded in on me. The angles and vanishing lines were all screwed up, no longer a question of perspective but a matter of life and death. The columns of the Mezquita swayed like El Greco saints – *where's this vanishing point now vanishing to? and whoa, those two lines will never meet.* The goalposts kept shifting and shadows kept jumping out at me from the shadows, Oh sorry, I said, running four-square into a pack of young Americans there like quarterbacks, but at least they were sober and threw me back into the flow of things. When

I got back to the hotel they all seemed to be waiting for me, but it was probably only the receptionist in triplicate. 'A message for you,' she said, and handed me a black-rimmed envelope. The black-rimmed envelope contained a black-rimmed card.

'It's not for me, is it?' I said, but I don't think she got the joke, because she kept nodding earnestly.

'*Sí, sí, señor*, is for you, yes.'

I scanned the invite. A memorial service for Ricardo. To take place in the church of San Rodrigo Calderón, shortly after the inquest. That much I read. Then, having fought my way up to my room, defying the stairs' every effort to confound me, I passed out.

The municipal building where the inquest was to be held had an inscription chiselled into the limestone facade by the entrance. EN LA CAPILLA ESTOY Y CONDENADO, I started reading. Some happy Andalusian poet to get the punters in the mood.

A man in a black suit with a municipal badge on his lapel came out and addressed me in a deferential voice: '*Sr de Souza, por aquí.*' He led me through a cavernous reception hall dimly lit by a huge cast-iron chandelier like a soot-coloured octopus. Old wooden benches like pews along the walls. Up a stone staircase winding like a conch shell, down a long dark corridor laid with hollowed-out slabs like tombstones.

The registrar's hall panelled in wood dark as ebony. A

man in a black robe presiding. A few rows of seats, mostly empty, a handful of older people in black, family no doubt. A Guardia Civil officer in uniform. In the far corner of the room, two youngish men who didn't seem to fit in. They were wearing polo shirts and chinos, they had their sunglasses up on their heads, and they seemed to be checking their phones a bit too much for the circumstances.

My Spanish wasn't good enough to follow everything, but I caught the gist. A long recitation of the known facts of Ricardo's life. After an hour or two they called me to speak into a microphone. They asked me through an interpreter how long I'd known Ricardo. When I'd last seen him. If I thought the WhatsApp had really been from him. If I thought he'd actually gone through Kauling. What I knew about Khai Manni. Yes, I said, and yes, and yes. I told them what I'd heard from the barman in the camp by the White River. And from the captain up in Kauling. I had the impression the two men in polo shirts and chinos were listening when I said what I knew about Khai Manni. But I might have been imagining it.

'This knocking,' they said, 'tell us about it.'

'Like this,' I went, and I remembered exactly what Ricardo had done, in the departure lounge as we were waiting for the plane, and I knocked on the dark wooden surface of the table in front of me, once, twice, three times. The knocking echoed and bounced off the panelling and I thought a chill went round the room and the presiding officer was silent for what seemed like forever. 'Thank you,' he said after a while, and with that my bit was done. He concluded by reading out a long statement in legal Spanish. I understood something to the effect of unlawful killing, with an element of misadventure. Something about the Guardia Civil conducting an investigation. And that was it. There was some sobbing on the benches in front.

The two young guys in polo shirts had walked out as soon as the registrar finished reading his statement.

I left with everybody else. The family shook my hand. 'I'm so sorry,' I said. They spilled into the street. The sunlight hurt my eyes. It was midday. An acrid smell floated in the air, like an electrical fire slowly eating its way through a box of old wiring. I walked through the old town with the family. I assumed they were family.

The church was the one I could see from my hotel room, conical auto-da-fé towers on the edge of town, the river flowing past lazy and low in its bed below the roughly cut stones. The nave was a gloom of shadows and gold, its Romanesque pillars painted with fading murals of saints and processions and trials of faith. There were more people now, a few rows colourful with folk Ricardo's age who must have come down from Madrid, the local crowd all in sombre black. One could tell they were waiting for proceedings to be over and done with so they could go to the fair. There was a picture of Ricardo with a black ribbon next to the altar. Readings, bits of the Bible and Lope de Vega and Lorca.

I wondered what would happen if the doors swung

open and Ricardo walked in, shouting 'I got away again'. He didn't. For the first time I wondered if I had something to do with it all. Perhaps I should have stayed away. Let that WhatsApp be. Gone on a safari with Mette instead and found the Big Six.

Someone was reading a poem by Góngora. The Madrid crowd, if that's what they were, started giggling.

The old town was busy with revellers getting ready for the fair, a swirl of red and black fabric and black hats and riding boots. Street performers waited to pounce outside the Mezquita. A mime artist walked alongside me for a while, pulling his made-up face into cartoon glumness. I didn't give him any change and he turned round, giving me the finger. The air in the alleyways smelled of woodsmoke and charcoal.

When I got back to the hotel, the woman at reception looked at me apprehensively. 'It's OK,' I said. 'No sangria today.' She smiled uneasily.

Lying on the bed in my room, I flicked from channel to channel. The Charing Cross case had died. Definitely a home-grown case. They were putting people with remote thermometers and pen torches in all major stations and checking antecedents for every traveller arriving in the UK. Helen's husband popped up in some crisis centre on an army base somewhere, saying they had it all under control, everything was just a precaution. I thought of Helen, the awkwardness when her husband came into the garden.

I wondered what she had told him about us. I thought of Mette, the stud in her nose her shoulders sunburnt and lightly freckled her legs tanned and smooth, a scar she'd shown me on her thigh that she'd said she got from one of the ostriches in Georgia, and when she'd laughed her laughter like the midsummer sun lightly filtered through the branches of a pine tree shading a little spot of the Baltic.

I sent a text message to Helen asking if she was OK. She didn't answer. I lay slumbering, for a few hours maybe, or just for ten minutes. At one point I drifted off and dreamed of the Big Six. A hunting dream: all six going after me at full throttle, lions bouncing from rocky pinnacle to rocky pinnacle and leopards grinning like toothy Cheshire cats from branch to branch, and the earth shaking all the while from the stampede snapping at my heels, until I finally found refuge in a little hut at the centre of the reserve where Danish was spoken. Not for long though.

Around midnight something knocked on my window. Three knocks, evenly spaced. I could hear them coming in my dream, a knocking on the flimsy door of the hut even as I was learning the basics. I reached out and groped around me, wanting to say something comforting, but Mette wasn't there. The sheets were sweaty, the red eye of the smoke alarm blinking. At first I thought it was the door. I put on the chain and peered out and I fleetingly thought the fake NHS people might have come after me, hire car in Malaga and large dark glasses and garish Rip Curl T-shirt, shadowing me all that time, invisible through the old town, but no, there was no one there. I went to the window. I tried to open it but it had a catch, the kind you could only tip. I couldn't see anyone immediately outside, but then I heard a voice. Someone standing right up against the wall to the side of the window. I could only make out a dark outline, and what looked like the visor of a baseball cap pulled down low.

'Hello, Seb,' Nikki said.

It couldn't have been Nikki, but it was: I knew it was her, just as I knew I'd never be a blood donor again.

'Bloody hell. Is this some kind of a joke you're playing on me?'

I tried to shine the light from my phone out at Nikki behind the window, but all it did was light up the terracotta tiles on the roof. She was staying well out of sight in the shadows.

'There's no joke involved. If only there was.'

'I think you should stay away from me. For your own good. Look at what happened to Ricardo. I suppose you know.'

'I was at the memorial today,' Nikki said. 'You can be sure I don't want to end up like Ricardo.'

I pictured her standing at the back of the church, wearing a wig and a baseball cap. Or a black mantilla pulled down over her face. It all seemed a bit over the top.

'And you know about David, I suppose,' I said.

'The broad outlines. Poor David.'

'I suppose you're going to tell me what's going on. Why

you were suddenly gone in the shanty town. You know I was looking for you. We were fucking desperate.'

'I know. And I will. But not here. It's not safe.'

'Where then?'

'Over here. They're probably listening.'

I walked to the side of the window frame to put my ear as close as I could to the opening. I could see the shadow bending over to get closer to me.

'Meet me at one,' Nikki said. 'Make sure you don't come before that. I'll be waiting in a car. By the Puente de Villamediana. Not before one.'

One in the morning or one in the afternoon, I wanted to call after her, but a roof tile or two cracked and she was gone.

I looked at my watch. It was ten past midnight. I googled the Puente de Villamediana. It was a little upstream on the Guadalquivir, not far outside town. Medieval, strategic in the Civil War.

I got dressed and went downstairs. I couldn't take any chances.

As I went through the maze of alleyways, I glanced behind me. It didn't look like anyone was following. The Plaza de las Tendillas was still bustling. I got a taxi and asked the driver to take me to a place called Alcolea. Just before Alcolea I asked him to stop. 'I'll walk from here,' I said. The driver probably thought I was crazy, or about to do something very stupid.

I was early. Half an hour to go. I walked along the empty country road running parallel to the Guadalquivir. Eucalyptus trees along the side of the road, street lights every fifty metres, crisply cut-out circles of light like landing zones for something in the darkness. Giant geckos with heads like blown-up diamonds stuck halfway up the poles. A rusty old road sign up ahead pointing right said PTE DE VLLAM'ANA, with a historic monuments logo. I had ten minutes to spare. I went as far as the turning. A little side road, roughly paved, wound off through the trees. Insects chirped. A plaintive bird cried. It might have been a nightjar, but I'd never heard a nightjar before so I couldn't be sure. A car's engine far away on the main road, coming closer.

I looked at my watch. Five to one. I could see the head-lights approaching in the distance, coming from the di-rection of Cordoba. I stepped into the shadows between the eucalyptus trees. Something crunched under my feet, a carapace or shell. The car slowed down as it approached the turning. A pickup, mud-splashed white, the windows too dark to see anyone inside. Agricultural gear on the platform. It went slowly past but didn't turn, then accelerated before fading in the distance.

I waited until one o'clock. No other car came. I walked through the darkness towards the bridge. I could see the water of the Guadalquivir shimmering between the skinny trunks of the eucalyptus trees. The dark bulky shape of a car parked down by the bridge. So she'd been there all the time.

The explosion ripped through the darkness with a cartoon flash, jagged zigzag orange and white, the eucalyptus leaves briefly lit up and shaking. Stuff raining down among the branches. A hubcap, the plastic casing of a door mirror. Flames shooting up from what remained of the car, all the windows blown out. I tried to get closer. There was a second explosion. A shower of hot black bits of metal and PVC. I wanted to yank at the handle on the driver's door and reach inside, but everything was twisted and mangled and hot like burning coals, the fire trying to draw me in, flames singeing my arms, smoke biting deep into my lungs, and nothing to grasp in there except the flames dancing, stuff melting crackling burning. A siren in the distance, coming nearer. Blue lights in the night behind the eucalyptus trees, a fire engine and an ambulance bumping down the little road to the bridge. It took them a while to put out the fire and I just sat there on a rock by the river in the shambles of the rising sun, the skin coming off my lower arms. I'd failed again.

Two

Enter Divers Spirits

XVI.

I don't know if it was a relapse, scientifically speaking. A pallid-looking monkey sat on the riverbank. Or perhaps it was a flying fox. A very fruity bat. Drilling rig muzzle and claws, leather copter wings, the whole shebang. It looked at me with what I thought was unnatural interest, then it jumped and stuck itself to a branch and swung yodelling across the water. The willows weren't weeping. They were howling and raging with wild abandon against the fading of what little light there was, a little red light blinking to salute the end of days. I had to take a boat to get across the great zoonotic stream, and things were loosening up out there, a mid-Atlantic rift and drift, species shimmying and shifting and slipping about in the seabed scree. The monkey bat was still there when I landed on the other side. Circling like a guardian angel, zooming in and out to size me up and measure the species gap. The final strides before launch. One-two-three and impact. *Ca va ça va*, I said, I'm a member of the National Union of Journalists, but that didn't cut much ice. It hit me with a big smack between cell wall and spleen, blood and lies all over the pretty pink horizon, then they took me in for testing, NHS tattoos all over the shop. I'm not political, I said again, but it didn't matter any more because they had me in an armlock and the syringe up my vein. Two pit bull thugs, one stocky one an Old Etonian of sorts. The accents were fake, always had been, the Irish thing a scam, my blood pulsating through their little black machine. Knock knock. Who's there? Spoiler alert. It's nobody. Just the wind messing with your mind.

When I woke up, there was no river. It looked like they'd tried to DIY an isolation ward. Screens with extra plastic sellotaped around the edges. The doctors, three of them and a nurse, were viewing me through ski masks. Permeable fabric and bare skin showing everywhere. My arms hurt. There was some jelly-like substance on them, and when I moved my fingers it hurt. Something wasn't right about my skin, little scarlet ridges and weals. Oh right. It all came back, the Guadalquivir dark and the jagged orange of the blast searing the night. Perhaps I could have saved her, perhaps not.

'Two things, *señor*, to inform you,' one of the doctors said, and it came out muffled from behind his respirator: *foo fings fenmor foo iffom foo.* 'One, your arms will be OK. But a bit painful. We need to keep bandaging for a few days. Two, we need to wait for test result to come back. Nearest lab is in Madrid. OK, any questions, *vale.*' And with that they were gone and I noticed a little plaster on my upper arm and I wanted to yank it off because it was itching, but I couldn't move my arms, and then there was a nurse with plastic gloves up to her elbows taped firmly to the sleeves of her plastic overall, or maybe it was a he, I couldn't even see their eyes and they didn't say anything as they worked swiftly on my arms, putting down mesh dressing on my hands and forearms and rolling gauze around them like prosciutto around a breadstick. And then I found myself alone, though I could see the little red flashing light of a CCTV camera in a dark corner of the ceiling.

When I was in the Very Dark Place there was no CCTV. They had a glass eye at the end of my bed recording and transmitting me 24/7, and they had all kinds of sensors that measured every little blip of my struggling heart, every flutter of my eyelids, every gasping twitch and spasm of my lips, every split centigrade travelling up or down the graph. It hadn't actually been very dark in the Very Dark Place. It was lit up stark and bright like a football stadium. Like an operating table, every little needle and blade shining like a thousand crying suns, the liquids coursing through the drips like red-hot gold. It was only towards the end that I saw the light. For most of my time in the Very Dark Place I was somewhere else. I didn't know where I was. I got occasional glimpses, a flash of colour here, a little spike of pain, then the drugs would kick in again and I'd be on the slide. I couldn't describe the landscape at the end of the chute. The shapes were shifting and the rocks were wrapping themselves around my brain like putty. Something was lurking in the darkness but I couldn't figure out if it was very big or very small. My senses moved at snail's pace. Tick. Tock. It might have been a machine, infernal or divine or both. Waiting to go boom. But I felt like shit most of the time, even when I wasn't feeling anything, and that was most of the time.

Although I felt like shit after three days in the makeshift isolation ward of the Hospital de la Caridad in Cordoba, the same committee of doctors and nurses who'd convened when I was admitted came to tell me that no, I hadn't had a relapse, but yes, there was still something in my blood they couldn't identify, and no, I didn't have to stay in hospital but yes, the Spanish authorities strongly suggested I take the next plane back to the UK. 'All right,' I said.

'But first,' they said, 'the Guardia Civil want to have a word.'

I was becoming an expert at this. I could tell they'd let me go, because they wanted to be rid of me. Too much hassle to look after some dodgy foreigner who might or might not be infectious. The Guardia Civil station was a few roundabouts away from the hospital, a concrete block from the 1960s with razor wire around it. They kept their distance in the interview room. They'd kept their distance in the squad car too, a plastic screen behind the driver and no one next to me. At the station they sat across a U-shaped table from me. It felt more like a viva than an interview. The obvious questions. When had I last seen Nikki. How well did I know her. How could I be sure it had been her on the hotel roof that night. Why had I not called the police there and then. When had I noticed the car by the bridge over the Guadalquivir. I could tell they were suspicious. It was something to do with the burns. I didn't think they'd dealt with a lot of bomb-makers down here, but the burns on my forearms triggered something. Some atavistic copper's suspicion. 'I wanted to get her out,' I said. 'I didn't even touch the car, it was so hot.' And somehow they didn't believe me. If I'd really been there to set off the charge, I wanted to say, I would have landed in bits in the forest like the hubcap and the plastic fragments from the mirrors. But I didn't. I sat it out, they conferred for a while, then they let me go.

The weather was turning. A few fat drops of rain came down, each descending slowly as if suspended from a yo-yo before exploding frame by frame on the dusty pavement. The air was cooler and clearer and it smelled of Easter. If I'd believed in all that I would have said it smelled of hope and rebirth and spring flowers in a meadow, but at the end of the day I just felt a little less like shit, and that was something.

They put me in a municipal van, three rows of seats and I was all on my own, and there was a Guardia Civil car in front and one behind as they drove me down the motorway to Malaga and I don't think it was for my comfort and convenience. They made sure I got to the gate and they smiled and saluted and I said *gracias*, but no one shook my hand, and they'd put me in a window seat and kept the other seats in my row empty.

I must have picked up the scent somewhere over the Bay of Biscay. Vegetable notes at first, mushed cucumber, courgette with white growths sprouting from the pockmarked spokes. I thought somebody had rotten lettuce in their sandwich, and then the smell went away, but as the plane flew over Brittany it came back and I saw the green cliffs receding into the Channel and now it wasn't the smell of compost, it was the smell of putrefying flesh, the same smell I'd noticed before I went to David's place the first time, getting stronger as the plane came in over the Downs, and when it touched down at Gatwick it was as if a pail of decomposing animal innards had been emptied down the aisle of the plane, though no one else in the rows around me seemed to notice: sunburnt suburban couples back from their timeshares look-ing bored; the flight attendant checking her fingernails. 'Can you smell that?' I asked her as I stepped out of the plane once it had reached its mooring, and she put on a forced smile and said, 'Goodbye, sir,' and 'Thank you, sir,' then I had to move on because the other passengers were pushing from behind and anyway a policeman was waiting by the little door in the jetway with the stairs down to the tarmac. 'All right,' I said. 'Just a few questions we'd like to ask you,' said the policeman, a uniformed sergeant, and I could tell he knew bugger all and there was no point asking as he led me down the stairs with a constable and they put me in the back of a van and I noticed they were both wearing gloves. They drove me round the cargo bits and the parts where they practise putting out a blaze on the hull of an old 707 and the bits where they take dodgy animals for quarantine purposes, then next to the bits where they take the dodgy animals they stopped outside a prefab with bars on the windows, the kind where they take the dodgy people, and they took me inside and put me in an interview room, and I made a mental note to choose another mode of travel if ever I had to leave the country again.

I wasn't surprised when DS Kennan walked in. I couldn't tell from his face if he'd found anything to charge me with. His face was completely devoid of expression. Like the wax figure of an undertaker in a cheap horror flick.

'So,' he said. 'Wherever you go. You could say you have a bit of a gift.'

He leafed through a file. A scanned letter was on top, with writing in Spanish. Pictures of the wreckage by the river. No picture of any body. The wreckage barely recognizable as a car. Twisted black things, springs, lumpy shapes that could have been body parts but were probably plastic seat bits cooked to a splodge.

'You know you're getting some serious name recognition. Like, here's another body. Oh, then that de Souza fellow can't be far away. Or: watch out, that de Souza bloke's in town. And everyone goes *run for it*.' DS Kennan was not smiling. 'I'm not smiling,' he said, 'because this might be a murder inquiry.'

'Which body are we talking about?'

DS Kennan frowned. 'We're being cocky are we, eh. Taking

the mickey.' He looked at his watch. 'Disrespectful towards the interviewing officer at 2.37 p.m.' He didn't smile. 'You think I'm joking, don't you? But I'm not. When did you last see Nicola Penthurst?'

'But the Spanish police asked me about that.'

'I'm not the Spanish police.'

'I told them everything,' I said. 'Up on the roof of my hotel in Cordoba. It must have been eleven.'

'What was your relationship with Ms Penthurst?'

'We were colleagues.'

'You've worked in some dodgy places.'

'That's my job.'

'Except you haven't been working of late,' he said, 'have you?'

I didn't say anything.

'Plenty of places that would come in handy for somebody hoping to hone their bomb-making skills.'

'Why on earth would I want to put a bomb under Nikki's car?'

DS Kennan looked at me with expressionless eyes. 'That's what it's my job to find out. Did you have a romantic attachment to Ms Penthurst?'

I almost laughed out loud at the way he said *romantic attachment*, but I thought better of it. 'No,' I said. 'Nikki was just one of the boys.'

DS Kennan looked at me with one eyebrow raised. 'Just one of the boys,' he repeated and wrote something in his notebook. He looked back at his file.

'Am I being charged?' I asked.

'This thing you caught in Africa,' he said, 'I suppose it could do things to your mind, could it not?'

'I don't think anybody knows what it does.' I regretted this as soon as I said it.

'We could keep you in under the Terrorism Act.'

He made it sound like an afterthought, but I knew it was what he'd been building up to all this time. For a while I said nothing, to give him something to feel good about. I could have acted dismayed, made a big deal of it. Leaving aside the small detail of my being innocent, what's any of this got to do with terrorism, I could have said, but he would probably have come up with something about all forms of scheduled explosive substances falling within the remit of the Act, et cetera. I was sure he was bluffing anyway. And sure enough, he lobbed test balloons at me for another half hour. Why had I looked at Nikki's statements on her e-banking account? Why had I sent Nikki threatening messages by SMS? Et cetera.

'No,' I said. 'I didn't. None of the above.'

He pulled another photo from his file. A professional job, done with a police camera with one of those stilted tripod things and a circular flash, by the look of it. A little stone animal, black, serrated tail, tiny jaws in a big toothy smile. 'Found at the scene of the explosion.'

'Oh, I see.' I must have looked surprised.

'Suspect signals recognition,' DS Kennan said to himself, scribbling in his notebook.

When he closed his file I asked him when they'd stop harassing me. 'You haven't got a clue, have you?' I said.

'A clue. Is there something you want to tell me? Or do you want to go back to the cells?'

'This is all so much bigger than your little murder inquiries.'

'You don't know what you're talking about,' he said, but I could tell he was listening.

'If you could get your hands on that file they have on me, you could start to put together some of the pieces. Why do you think they've slapped a D-notice on all this?'

'You're delusional.'

DS Kennan got up and walked out. But he'd made his point: he really didn't have a clue. Not that I had much of a clue either, but at least I wasn't alone.

'It's great to be back, thank you for the warm welcome,' I said to the uniformed constable who deposited me at a back entrance to the main terminal after another long drive weaving around hangars and planes and refuelling trucks and all the bits the airport people wanted to keep out of sight and out of mind. He thrust my passport into my hand and pointed to a long queue leading up to passport control. 'What, couldn't you drop me off in the arrivals hall?' I said, but he was gone already.

The electronic gates were broken and they'd left me at the back end of a throng of passengers arriving from some-where far away and sunny, roasted and a little dazed and very smelly after a night flight in economy. 'I'll never fly again,' I said to the Border Force officer in her glass cage when she handed me my passport half an hour later, and she opened her mouth as if she was about to say something but then thought better of it and called up the next passenger. But I meant it: ferry, train or freighter, anything was better than this.

I missed Wystan's yapping and scratching at the door. I'd have to go and pick him up in the morning.

After locking the doors behind me, I turned off all the lights. I looked out at the street from behind the living room curtains. Nothing was moving in the sickly yellow light of the street lamps. A musty smell hung about the flat, like dead mice turning to mould in some dark corner. I could feel a headache coming on like a typhoon snapping everything in its wake, palm trees splintering like matchsticks, a thousand rice paddies up in the air in a fury of green and white slush. It grounded me on the couch and it wasn't just a headache, it was the full suite of sequel symptoms. Eyeballs brimming with pressure, ready to pop, neck muscles loaded like a catapult about to go, temperature crawling steadily towards forty and beyond. If I'd been a good boy I would have crawled to the kitchen to get the card with Nurse Mersey's number on it, Section Whatsit, sudden deterioration et cetera, but Nurse Mersey had driven off and I was about to fall off my couch into a very deep and dark hole.

XVII.

The hole wasn't labelled. Every time I fell through it the entrance looked different. At times it looked invitingly final. One way and be done with it. This time it looked like the flaking stucco pillars by the entrance to a Victorian police station. Blue light flickering reassurance in a little cast-iron lantern. Lions and griffins in a leering pose, pawing at me teasingly as I pass. A cross-eyed unicorn with sergeant's stripes on the back.

It's a bit of a climb down the hole. Zigzag hills around the circumference steeped in blood like jaws. All nine circles of it, and every time I get to a lower one there's a porter's lodge and a grumpy old man in a boatman's uniform asking for a tip, a penny for the old guy and *boom*. A desk and cage at the bottom of the pit. Officialdom presiding, in the shapely shape of Nurse Mersey. Except she's not a nurse, is she. She's top of her class at Porton Down. A most distinguished incubus, FRSC. Purely on the defensive side, of course. We'd never. No we'd never. International conventions and all that. It's what others do. No moral equivalence. But what if I took a peek behind the desk, the RMP patrol. You're allowed to aren't you, in a dream you can do anything before your chickens come home to roost.

And speaking of chickens, it's not long before the real cages start, glistening row upon row, chimeras and sweating macaques on drips. Dogs too. They've got shiny little metal tags with names etched on them, in a beautiful if childlike hand – John and Tom and Stéphane and Charles and Wystan, all the poets utterly dead these days. Not sure what they've done to the pooches though, they all look a bit worse for wear. And this one here, a fine mongrel specimen veering into lion or puma, or crab. They've sharpened his tooth. There's something about him, a thunder rumbling inside, a pathogen perhaps. But before I can have a word with him, Wystan, boy, they've vectorized you and weaponized you, there's Nurse Mersey bearing down on me like a warhead. I didn't really see anything did I. No I didn't, ma'am, honest, I say, and how could I.

It's an interview room I'm sitting in, a fine specimen too. The table clinical, the prospect a sweeping one, the uplands stretching to infinity, the scaffolds and jails. You're nothing, Nurse Mersey's voice a little tinny now, more schoolmistress than torturer, need to twist the dial a little to get back into frequency. You're nothing, she's got the right timbre now, an Abrams tank in full charge, We can keep you in as long as we like. But what about Wystan, I want to say, but it comes out as a woof, w–w–w–wooh–wooh–wooh–waah. Of course we can charge him, she says. Section Whatever, she says. The Chimera Clause. We can do whatever to whatever and whomever, human or canine, and anything in between. And yes, she says, the pooch has been charged. Wha–wha–wha–what's the charge, I woof, and she frowns. The viral charge, she says. We thought you knew, And she brings the gavel down, guilty as charged, then she starts tugging at her mask and there's nothing there but money no Manni and bang bang bang and knock knock knock.

A knocking on my front door: everybody's at it these days.

When I rolled over and got out of bed I could feel everything aching, every object every bloody Edwardian brick in the building every teabag in the kitchen an extension of my ache. Morning, daybreak, something filthy in the air, a rag and bone aroma. I didn't open the door. It was the postman, by the look of it through the frosted glass. A van sat outside, Royal Mail, but how could I tell it was either royal or mail? For all I knew it could have been a tattooed goon with a fake Irish accent. Black regimental daggers sprouting from black flowers and next thing you know you've got a needle down your neck. 'Got a parcel for a Mister dee Sotsa here,' the man said through the door, and there was nothing Irish about his accent. Anywhere in a broad arc between Wallington and Gravesend. How had he got in the downstairs door? Nobody had rung the outside bell. Or perhaps they had, and I'd been out of it, and somebody else had buzzed him in. If he was genuine, I could always pick it up later. He was. He pushed a little card under the door and went back down to his van. I waited and listened and peeked through the letterbox and popped one of the pills Dr Bicknell had prescribed and waited for some of the aching to subside, though it didn't; and eventually I had to go out. I had another appointment with Dr Bicknell.

'Oi, watch where you're going, mate,' a workman shouted at me when I got out of the lift. I'd stepped into a building site where before there had been a waiting room with a reception desk and a row of anonymous consulting rooms, nitro gloves and syringes and the view from the small window a washed-out Whistler if you liked that sort of thing, power and barges. They were hammering and sawing and soldering, putting up screens and airlocks and green lanes and red lanes and lanes that were one-way and no coming back. Getting ready for a massive scrum, by the looks of it. Who could blame them: there'd been more dodgy car crashes, people zoning out and bang, and on top of the expected fractures and things there'd be the most intricate pattern of internal haemorrhage, inexplicable by trauma, not to mention the eyeballs exquisitely jaundiced. Even Dr Bicknell's office looked different: disposable plastic sheets on everything, her PC covered with a protective screen, her keyboard encased in a transparent plastic glove.

'Everything's under control, is it?' I said when I sat down.

'These are just precautions.' She looked worried. She didn't normally look worried. 'How are you feeling?'

I told her I felt like I'd been dropped on the tracks at Clapham Junction at rush hour.

She looked even more worried. 'But there's nothing obviously wrong with you,' she said after she'd done a quick examination. 'It's consistent with the neurological sequels reported by survivors in The Land Of. It'll come and go. It's unpredictable.'

'It's coming, isn't it? A big wave. Hence all of this.' I gestured at the sound of drilling coming from the corridor behind me.

'The modelling isn't very conclusive yet.' She didn't sound convinced.

'The case fatality rates aren't getting any better, are they?'

She didn't answer my question. 'It might burn itself out,' she said. 'Or not.'

'I still don't understand why I survived.'

'Yes, yours has been an interesting case. Speaking of which, have you had more of those, shall we say, sensory experiences?'

I told her about the flight back from Spain. The burnt smell in the alleyways in Cordoba. The explosion after that. She typed rapidly, with two fingers, adding to her case notes. Was there, she asked when I had finished – and you could tell she was in awe of her own question, the import and portent of it – any sense that the unusual sensations, well, preceded events that in some way resembled them?

I hadn't thought about that.

'Hypothetically speaking,' she said, 'because that isn't possible, is it?'

'No, it isn't. Though when I think about it—'

'Yes?' Dr Bicknell fixated me with her scientist's eyes.

'It's possible.'

'Extraordinary,' she muttered; then she corrected herself: 'That's not possible though.' She went back to typing stuff on her PC.

'Surely there must be other cases.' I said.

'Nothing tangible. Just rumours from people who've worked in treatment centres in The Land Of. A mutation. Maybe. But no properly documented cases.'

I could see the *Lancet* piece taking shape in her mind. Intimations of bigger prizes, things that glitter. Gilt and red velvet in Stockholm. Not that she was motivated by any of that. And not that I minded. She'd saved my life, after all.

'There's something down there, isn't there?' I said.

'I can't say I know what you mean.'

'In The Land Of. If we'd been able to stay on, we might have found stuff.'

'I'm not sure "stuff" is a meaningful concept in epidemiology.' I was surprised at her tone.

'And that's probably what my file is about,' I said. 'If there is one.'

She didn't take the bait. She looked at the calendar on her PC. 'I suggest a slightly shorter interval for our next appointment.'

I remembered the journal I'd given her the last time I'd seen her. 'Should I continue that journal you asked me to keep?'

'Ah yes, that journal. We've got a bit of an issue there. There's a few things that disappeared from my office when they started the works round the ward. My laptop, some papers. And your journal.'

'They simply disappeared?'

'Yes, well,' she said. 'Probably just a mix-up.' She walked me to the lift. 'See you the week after next. And look after yourself.'

I wasn't sure why she added the bit about looking after myself. But from the way she said it I had a sense it wasn't only about doing my temperature charts and checking my eyeballs in the mirror every once in a while.

I hadn't thought the water could rise any further at Palavers End, but it had. The tarmac itself only barely showed on the road that wound through the paddocks by the riverside. There was nowhere to park, so I left the car with the warning lights flashing standing in the middle of the road.

The fields on either side were like rice paddies at high tide. Black clumps of shrub and trees sticking out like dark archipelagos. The bush where my mother had left the bag with the wellies was submerged except for a small crown of thorny twigs. The cottage stood across the rippling expanse of water like the wreck of a clumsy steamer marooned on a sandbank. If it wasn't for the neat line of willows emerging from the water a little further out, I wouldn't have known where the river was. My mother would have to leave any day now.

I called her on the fixed line but only got a busy signal. I called her on the mobile. She'd never liked the mobile, but this time she answered. She came over to me in a little flat-bottomed rowing boat I'd never seen before.

'Where did you get that?' I asked.

'It came drifting past last week. Got stuck in the rhododendron out by the compost bin. I managed to pull it in with a rake.'

'Oh,' I said.

She tied the boat to the boot scraper by the front door. The stone steps were almost submerged.

'A couple of inches more and you'll be swamped.'

'They're coming to take me away tomorrow,' she said. 'If it was up to me, I'd stay. But they've served me with an evacuation order. Uninhabitable, they said.'

Wystan was sitting on the threshold. He didn't look thrilled at the thought of going off with me.

'It's probably for the best,' I said. 'And you'll be looked after.'

'I can look after myself.'

'What will you do with the cottage when you're gone?'

'Well, it's not as if anyone's going to break in, is it now? I mean, who'd want to get soaked and break an ankle just to steal a few old trinkets?'

I put Wystan in the boat and my mother rowed us across

to the road and I waved goodbye. I didn't meet any other cars until I got back to the motorway. It looked like they had already evacuated a broad strip of land and houses along the river. My mother was probably among the last to leave.

When I got home I gave Wystan his lunch. I tried to call Jonathan at head office. He hadn't been replying to my messages on the mobile. He hadn't even been reading them. I don't know what I was trying to achieve. I didn't actually think he'd offer me any work. Least of all after what had happened in Spain.

'Hello, Carol,' I said when his secretary answered the phone. 'I know Jonathan's really busy, but if he could spare a couple of minutes.'

'He's been taken ill,' Carol said, sounding spooked.

'Oh, I'm sorry. Just normally ill, or ill-ill?'

'He's really ill. They came to the office yesterday to take him away.'

'I'm very sorry to hear it,' I said. 'Do wish him a good recovery when you speak to him.'

I sat staring at my phone. Sirens sounded in the distance, rising and falling. Lots of sirens. I decided to call Helen. She picked up the phone immediately. And it was Helen who suggested we meet.

The train into town was almost empty. It reeked of piss overlaid with something darker. It wasn't offal, exactly, now, but a touch of processed meat starting to go off. Or pâté. With little red specks of cooked liver and chewy white bits of sinew. It didn't come from inside the carriage. It came from somewhere outside. Another little charge every time the doors slid open, Raynes Park Earlsfield Vauxhall. Something off about the prospect from the train. The playing fields in Raynes Park, something missing, the goalposts or the linesman's hut, I couldn't tell. I thought about what Dr Bicknell had said: a mutation, perhaps. The rest was clearly speculation, and probably a load of tosh: it's impossible, she had said herself. And yet. Dr Bicknell didn't strike me as the kind who'd fall for esoteric nonsense.

A dozen people at most got off the train at Waterloo, keeping their distance, eyeing each other suspiciously. I was going to take the Tube to Leicester Square, but when I went down the stairs the smell got too strong. As if it came from deep inside the guts of the earth. So I walked instead. Angry rain showers on and off. Hardly anyone on the bridge. There'd been a raft of new cases when I was in Spain. Out of nowhere, not obviously imported. Several dead already, a few still on an isolation ward. And the cafe was empty. Not a good place to meet. Too ostentatious. There wouldn't be much of a crowd to hide in, all the cameras along the street were idling, the algorithms bored.

The waitress didn't look too happy when I walked in. She handed me the menu with the tips of her fingers and cringed when I sneezed. Not a sound in the cafe apart from the occasional clinking of spoons in the kitchen. The cakes behind the glass counter pink and cold like Viennese debutantes who'd missed the last bus home. It's all right, I wanted to say, I've already had it, I'm done. I didn't say anything though. I knew what would ensue, panic, screeching tyres, the street blocked off at both ends, the slamming of ambulance doors. A false alarm again, but I was sure to have violated one of Nurse Mersey's Sections.

Helen was half an hour late, but she made up for it. There was rose hip and there was hibiscus and there was cherry blossom and there was something I couldn't put my finger on even though I seemed to know all the floral aromas now, the auras, the beautiful intimations. She hesitated when I got up to say hello.

'It's all right,' I said out loud, and I knew the waitress would hear it in the perfect silence of the cafe, no chatter and no traffic noise from outside. 'I'm the one person in the country you definitely can't catch it from, and I'm the one person who can't catch it.'

Helen laughed, nervously.

The thing I couldn't put my finger on was something like a memory. A slope on a clifftop in spring, a warm breeze, the sound of waves crashing and carpets of blue and yellow flowers undulating down to the jagged edge of things. I didn't remember ever going for a walk on a clifftop with Helen. Maybe it wasn't a memory.

'Cordoba,' she said. 'You were there, weren't you?' I couldn't tell what she was thinking, but I could tell now why she'd wanted to meet in a public place, and I didn't blame her.

'I always seem to be there,' I said. 'How is the czar?'

'I don't see much of him. He's been a little busy of late. What happened in Cordoba?'

'I don't know. Someone blew up Nikki's car before I could get to her.'

'Are you a suspect?' she asked, and her aura darkened, the petals flushing to a deep purple, the smell of storm clouds pregnant with floodwater.

'Obviously.'

The waitress had been pretending to be busy rearranging cakes behind the glass, but now she was staring at us, her mouth open.

'Who do you think is doing all this? And who have they been running from?'

'I don't know,' I said. 'I keep thinking about Khai Manni.'

Helen frowned. 'You don't seriously think that, do you?'

'I don't know what to think.' I told her about the picture of the little stone crocodile DS Kennan had shown me at the airport when I got back from Cordoba.

'That's weird. But people do bring back knick-knacks from exotic trips, don't they?'

'That might be it,' I said, though I wasn't at all convinced. 'I still haven't found out who sent me that mask thing.'

'Some prankster. You're a public figure, so you probably get a lot of this kind of crap.'

Helen shrugged. 'Anyway,' she said, 'I'm sorry about the profile. I would have published it, but everyone's a little on edge.'

'The D-notice.'

'There is that,' she said. 'But there's also this.' She pulled a piece of paper from her handbag. It had what sounded like the name of a chemical compound scribbled on it. 'I had to google it too. It's a tranquillizer.'

'And?'

'That fragment of glass you left at my place the other day. It had a batch number on it. Got a colleague on the news desk who traced it. They also found the consignee. Company called Glenniston Life and Health.'

'Never heard of them. What do you think I should do?'

Helen put the piece of paper with the name of the compound on it back in her handbag. 'I think you should be careful.'

'Perhaps you could ask your husband to look into it.'

Helen looked at her empty cup. 'I'm not sure he'd be in a position to help. Anyway, how are you doing, healthwise?'

'My doctor thinks that when I caught it, it might have come with some rare mutation.'

'And is that good or bad?'

'It's neither good nor bad,' I said. 'You know how I told you I can smell things.'

'Yes, you've mentioned that.'

'She seems to think there's something to it. It's not just about colours and auras and stuff like that. She seems to think there's more. As in, smelling things before they happen. Or something to that effect.'

Helen frowned. 'That's taking it a bit far, surely.'

'I'm not sure what to think myself.'

The waitress brought Helen's coffee. She slammed down the cup on the edge of the tabletop, in such a rush to get away that half the coffee spilled into the saucer.

'But can you?' Helen asked, and she looked at me so intensely it scared me a little.

'I'm smelling things where there aren't any.'

Helen raised her eyebrows. 'Our son had that once when he fell on his nose in the school playground.'

Yes, but... I wanted to say, but then the waitress came up to our table, still keeping her distance. 'I'm afraid we're closing,' she said, and I could tell she was relieved to be rid of us.

The rain was starting again as we walked down Greek Street. Harsh cold drops that blackened the pavement when they burst.

'Listen,' Helen said, 'there's something I picked up.' A car crept past, a Jaguar with blacked-out windows, so slowly I thought it was eavesdropping. Helen stopped. The car went on. 'It might be a good idea if you went away for a while.'

'What do you mean, went away for a while?'

'Look, I really can't say more. Just trust me. Something I heard.'

Leicester Square looked tacky and forlorn, the movie hoardings flashing garishly to themselves. The stairs to the Tube station were blocked by a handwritten sign, *Closed for flooding*.

'I've got to go,' Helen said, and to my surprise she drew me close and held me for what seemed like a very long moment.

Her skin smelled warm and comforting and familiar. Like a flowering meadow on the Downs, or a National Trust gift shop on a balmy afternoon in June. And there were darker undertones too, like thunder flashing from a cluster of black cloud on the edge of the painting: the peasants resting after bringing in the hay and everyone eager for the dance, but out of the corner of the sky something evil falls.

Suddenly Helen gave a start. 'Oh no,' she said. 'Don't turn around. There's a guy who works with my husband. One of his security people. I think he saw us.' I turned around. A youngish man in a short coat stood across the road holding a Foyles bag, looking at us with a mocking expression. He turned and walked off as soon as I spotted him. I wanted to say something to Helen, but the shutters had gone back up now, like the first time I'd met her again, at Kew. 'It was nice to see you, Seb,' she said, and the light in her eyes had gone out, and the aura that had hung around her shifted, rose hip cherry blossom hibiscus fading rapidly like the ink from a Hiroshige, pastel flags swaying lightly in the breeze or carnations wilting.

I walked back to Waterloo. Pumps belched down on the flooded embankment below Charing Cross station; a dredging barge was moored under the bridge, the current pushing hard against its chains. The sky convulsed with thick black clouds looking to vomit their load. No one was on the footbridge with me as I walked across, but I couldn't help feeling I had company. As if there were two of us, a shadow walking beside me. Just my mind playing tricks. But then I heard her.

She must have stepped out from behind one of the pillars, and I didn't want to look straight at her because I was afraid of what I would see. But I recognized her voice right away.

'Let's get this straight,' she said. 'I'm dead.'

I did look at her then, and I had never seen anyone as pale before, and it wasn't just the black of her sunglasses contrasting with the white of her face. The freckles were like specks of bleached coral in a dying sea.

'It might be better,' she said, 'not to look at the dead.' Her hand rested on my shoulder, and it felt very light and very cold.

'Why all this?'

'I think you're beginning to figure that out for yourself.'

'How many more times are you planning to die?'

'That's enough dying for now,' Nikki said, 'but you might want to look after yourself.'

'Why?'

'Something we came across in The Land Of. Something we weren't supposed to see.'

'Is this about Khai Manni?'

'Khai Manni doesn't exist,' she said. 'I thought you'd worked that out by now.'

'But what about those stone animals? The crocodiles they found in David's hut, and in Cordoba.'

'We got those on the first tour. Something to keep the police wondering.'

A train went past on the railway bridge, empty. 'What is it you came across in The Land Of?' I asked.

Nikki stopped and looked back towards Charing Cross. 'Stuff,' she said. 'Awkward stuff.'

'How awkward? Is it to do with a mutation?'

'There is that. But that's not all.'

A jogger came up behind us, all black in Lycra with a hood like a balaclava, and I thought, this is a strange place to go for a run, and a strange day. Nikki had disappeared. Blended in with the struts of the bridge or jumped over the side. I hadn't seen her go. The jogger went past. I thought there was something funny in the way he looked at me. I walked on. He disappeared down the steps to the South Bank at the end of the bridge.

And Nikki was back, walking beside me, looking straight ahead. 'It didn't just appear out of thin air,' she said.

'What didn't appear out of thin air?'

'Maybe you need to go and see for yourself.'

Two policemen on bikes appeared, coming across the bridge from the other side, and with their helmets and black face masks they looked like something out of Star Wars, and Nikki was gone again, and when the policemen went past me I shivered and they were like dark riders dragging something in their wake, something cold. I looked around me, then I went down the stairs, and Nikki didn't come back.

They'd closed off most of the entrances to Waterloo Station, funnelling everyone through a checkpoint at the top of the main stairs. Someone in a high-vis jacket with a face mask pointed a thermometer at my face and then a torch; 'Thirty-five,' he said. 'White. Well, you're all right, mate.' Behind me someone beeped and suddenly five figures in full spacesuits jumped out from behind a little screen in the archway of the entrance and I just managed to slip through onto the concourse before they closed the station completely.

My train was probably the last one out that day. Rain streaking down the windows over the crudely etched tags, washing all colour from the city. Cloudbursts so fast and thick that entire streets looked blanked out.

The train stopped at Earlsfield and there was a cryptic announcement over the tannoy and everyone had to get off. I wanted to ask the guard when the next train would be in, but he was sitting in his little brick hut on the platform with the door closed and when I knocked on the window he shook his head and waved me away with something like terror in his eyes. I thought of the policemen standing by the little roundabout outside the hotel, in The Land Of. They'd had the same look of terror. Or perhaps it was the face masks. I did a quick search on my phone. Glenniston Life and Health was some sort of public-private thing with subsidiaries in everything from bioscience to public health support to contingency management, whatever that meant. Headquartered in St James's Square and with research centres all over the place. The main life science campus was in Wiltshire, but when I tried to google the address it came up with garbled green patches on the map. Street View showed a wire-mesh gate at the end of the road, a guard hut, a couple of vans. Guards with their faces blotted out. Dark brown splodges that could have been dogs. I wouldn't have much luck getting anywhere close to Glenniston.

It was quiet inside the flat when I got home. Too quiet. Not a sound, no scratching no friendly bark no tapping of paws on the sisal carpet in the hallway. 'Wystan, boy,' I called, and I went from room to room and there was no sign of him, but the rug by the coffee table in the living room looked like it had been disturbed. A big damp patch on the carpet next to the sofa. A glass I'd left on the coffee table the night before was lying on its side.

I took a vase from the mantelpiece. The neighbours were probably used to the sound of disturbances coming from my flat by now, what with Nurse Mersey's calls and the goons and all, but the sound of the glass fracturing into a hundred little crystals when I threw it against the wall must have made an impression on someone. I took a few deep breaths and checked the flat once more. The windows were all closed.

I went out into the staircase and rang the neighbour's bell to ask if he'd seen or heard anything, but nobody answered. A software analyst in the City. We'd never really talked, and since I'd got back from the Very Dark Place I had the impression he'd been making sure to avoid meeting me on the stairs.

I locked the door behind me and walked down the road and round the corner and up the high street to the police station. The lion's heads and unicorns on the stucco columns by the entrance were looking a bit off colour. The front room was empty. I waited. There was coughing in the back room. I waited a bit more. I noticed a little bell in the corner of the counter. The kind Santa Claus would wield, throning by his crate of garishly wrapped gifts in the atrium of the shopping centre down the road. I rang it and it made a light tinkling sound and I got distracted and behind the trees I could see a sledge carving through the snow at the bottom of the valley and reindeer tossing their heads and I could feel the crisp winter air forming crystals in my nostrils.

'Hello, sir,' the sergeant said. He was wearing a mask and waving his hand from side to side in front of my face. I must have drifted off thinking about the reindeer. 'What can I do for you?' he asked impatiently, and I already knew I was wasting my time.

'I'd like to report the kidnapping of a dog.'

'I'm sorry, could you repeat that? I didn't catch the last bit.'

I stepped closer to the counter. 'The kidnapping of my dog.'

'You've lost your dog, have you?' he said. 'I'm afraid that's not a police matter.' I could hear a suppressed laugh from the back room.

'Well, he was stolen from my flat.'

The sergeant took a piece of paper and started writing. 'Stolen dog,' he called out to whoever was listening in the back room. 'Is he valuable, your dog?'

'Well, he is to me.'

'That's not what I meant,' the sergeant said. 'Is he some

sort of a prize whippet? Kennel Club champion? Is he a prized possession?'

'He's a mongrel. A bit of spaniel in him, a bit of sheepdog. You can't be too sure.'

'Well, like I told you, sir. Not a police matter. And I'll have you know we're being restricted to essential public order duties.'

'But somebody broke into my flat. I think it might be linked to the people who tried to take my blood.'

'Sir, I'd strongly suggest you leave before we put you in a cell,' the sergeant said, and that was that, and I walked out past the lions and unicorns and into the high street and the rain was starting up again. Big fat globules of black water were forcing themselves on the earth with nowhere to go and the waters kept rising and rising. The shops the scruffy front gardens the traffic lights all in black and white. A storm was sweeping in from over the Atlantic.

I felt a dizziness coming on when I got back to the flat and I had to steady myself against the wall. I went to swallow some pills. I wasn't sure they were the right ones, but it didn't seem to matter much. I didn't want to think about what they might do to Wystan. Whoever had taken him wasn't exactly going to gift him to a more loving and caring home, though there would have been a case for that.

I was expecting a ransom note on the coffee table. Instead I found a little folded piece of paper in the pocket of my coat. The piece of paper had an address on it. *Lotissement*

No. 454, Boulevard du 8 juin. I thought of the ghost on the bridge. A cold hand on my shoulder. I must have been stunned, because I hadn't noticed the piece of paper being slipped into my pocket.

I tried to google the address, but most of The Land Of was a grey-green mash. The resolution as crude as a tray of frozen peas. Lotissement No. 454. The Boulevard du 8 juin fizzled out in a part of the island that didn't seem to have any roads on it. I could picture it and I couldn't. Lotissement No. 454 didn't sound like the kind of place where all the big questions would be answered: why David and Ricardo and Nikki kept dying on me; what all that Glenniston crap was about. I thought about calling Helen: want the story of a lifetime? It was the daftest thought I'd had yet. The crazy stuff was all mine, I had it all to myself. And anyway there wasn't much I could do for Wystan by staying in London.

Three

Getting to Atlantis

XVIII.

The island was there and then it wasn't as the boat went up and down on the swell, now you see it now you don't and all the while you're trying to hold back from puking. The white cliffs fading behind thick grey curtains of rain. The glorious green turned to porridge. Somewhere in that jagged polygon Wystan was yapping. The ferries were grounded, but this wasn't a ferry. It was a trawler, and the waves tossed it up and down like a child at a trampoline party, but this was no party. It had cost me a couple of thousand quid, and the two trawlermen thought I was crazy and it's likely that I was, and they must have been desperate to take my money. The sole season a bit slow right now. I thought they were crazy. 'You're sure you're not afraid?' they'd asked, and I'd said something like 'All my friends are dead anyway,' and they didn't try any more small talk after that.

I'd come down to Folkestone by train the day before, and I'd met them round a few corners through a bloke I'd spoken to in a pub on the harbour front that evening, just going about his business with a pint and the sports pages of the *Sun*, but he had the look of the sea about him. 'Know anyone who's going out on the Channel tomorrow?' I asked. 'I'm doing a report for one of the Sunday supplements.' He did, and I showed them my NUJ card, and I gave them Helen's email address, in case they had any questions. They didn't. The money was cash in hand. And who was to say it was illegal. I had my passport on me, after all, and in this direction there was nothing to worry about. Least of all when everybody else was grounded. Border force coast guard police, everybody and anybody in their right mind. The storm having its way with things.

The weather was getting heavier. Hell emptied of its fiends, all the little tinpot jokers out to chuck their slingshots about. The trawler came crashing down in the troughs between the five-metre waves like an angry fist. The masts and stays shook like blades of grass, cages and trays dancing madly against their anchorings. Every time the hull of the trawler smacked down on the boiling water it let out a deep metallic groan. I'd had the trawlermen tether me to the wheelhouse and I saw flounders flying through the angry waterlogged air and dive back into a vertical wall of water risen on the other side of the boat and I had to duck because the sea was throwing up a ballet of flotsam like a toddler in a tantrum, 2CV fenders and shell cases and wine crates and something that looked like the snout of a big red bus rising briefly from the depths before being swallowed again, and once or twice I thought I spotted a periscope piercing the surface at a right angle to the boat and I thought it couldn't be but then I saw a ragged old ensign cutting through the foam, the dark-red cross bleeding gloriously into the scrappy white, the sun wheel turning and clawing into itself. And then it was gone, and there were octopuses and sad-looking moonfish hurtling sidelong across the foam and shattered lobster pots, and the fish looked fried and chips of ice were raining from the overhang. There was a singing in the air like whale song, but it was only rusty sheets of metal straining against their rivets and pistons choking on the void.

I don't know how many hours passed. Drowning thoughts were rushing me like hungry sharks, but then the continent appeared out of nowhere without warning, angular and grey. A neon supermarket sign, LES TROIS MOUSQUETAIRES, right on the seafront, and the quay so close I could have touched the weathered old stones with my hand if I hadn't been tied to the wheelhouse. The ugly concrete slabs of a housing estate shimmering in and out of view through the drifting rain. No one around. It wasn't the grandest way to land in France. Some decayed hole among the dunes, Wimerant or Ouisserant or Outrancé or something of the sort, I didn't catch the name as the trawlermen cursed to each other – 'Bloody useless, we're at least ten miles off' – but to me it was all the same. There'd be a train station somewhere and though my hair was wet and I was neither living nor dead there'd be a train, eventually, to Charles de Gaulle.

All the direct flights from Paris had been suspended, so I had a ten-hour stopover in Dakar. I stretched out across four or five plastic bucket seats by an empty gate. It was painful, but the pain kept me from thinking about Wystan or where I was going. The neon lights flickered their sickly yellow haze around the terminal. Beetles crawled over my legs and mosquitoes kept buzzing me like drones. There weren't a lot of people travelling. The flight to The Land Of was supposed to leave early in the morning, but it kept getting delayed.

It was mid-afternoon when the flight was finally called. I had to walk out to the plane, an old Fokker Friendship operated by an outfit called Air Equateur. I was the only passenger. A spare wheel stashed in a net behind the cockpit. The door rattling noisily in its frame as the Fokker lifted off. Row upon row of empty seats, the hostess with her face mask not managing to hide the fear in her eyes. She was wearing rubber gloves. The plane turned over the black waters of the Gulf of Guinea. Little flashing lights from the oil rigs. But that was another world altogether. Quarantine among the drillheads. Three months of boxed meals and purity, but then where did you go? Up here my nostrils were flaring like a dog on a scent. Charcoal and dust. Burnt things and fevers. The smell of a body count, growing. I looked at the hostess, but she sat on her little foldable seat fixing her gaze on the end of the aisle, arms clasped around herself.

Touchdown at dusk, and the airport every bit as crummy as when I'd last landed, with David and Ricardo and Nikki. The hostess staying well back from the open door as if a wave of pestilence was waiting to flood into the plane. A single health inspector stood on the tarmac with his thermometer and torch. I didn't beep and my eyes were pure egg-white. '*Raison de votre visite,*' the lone policeman in the terminal building said. '*Je suis journaliste,*' I replied, and he looked sceptical, but he stamped a visa in my passport and took his CFA francs.

Everything was covered in a white chlorine crust now. I'd had no one to arrange a car for me this time. A minibus was waiting, the driver in face mask and gloves. He hadn't been expecting any passengers. '*J'espère qu'il y aura un bateau,*' I said. '*Ah,*' he said, '*il y a toujours un bateau. C'est tout ce qu'il y a. Ils ont besoin pour sortir les corps de l'île.*' I was hoping there wouldn't be a boat, when he said that, but there was, a little inshore launch like the one I'd taken the last time I came, with the others. The plastic seats looked dirty. Yellow water sloshed about in the bottom. I'd been here before, but it was worse now. Everything coming back, and more. The boatman wore a Batman mask and a black raincoat and what looked like ski gloves. He was alone. The little red light in the wheelhouse was on from the beginning. The engine coughing like a chain-smoker on his last gasp. The water of the Gulf of Guinea greasy and black. Specks of foam like spit on the cresting waves. Not a storm but a nervous swaying. The jittery heavens blowing hot and cold. The crossing longer than I remembered. I wondered what would happen if the boatman started spitting blood. The engine would go coughing on for a while, then it would stutter and stop. I didn't have any signal on my phone.

The streets were empty. The trash mountains bigger. The city itself like a rubbish dump with random growths of concrete and wood. Olive-green water marks and rot down the sides of the occasional tower blocks. The shacks blending with the trash mountains. A camouflage landscape, khaki and grey, goo-green and brown.

I didn't stay in the mirage overlooking the lagoon this time. No one was paying for me. I stayed in a cheap guest house down the wrong end of the unfinished highway, a stretch of tarmac strewn with concrete blocks like a dirty appendix. The guest house had a fence made of cement blocks with cut-out shapes around a garden of sorts, but the garden looked like everything else. A random mix of scattered things. Old plastic bags like ragged ghosts in the thorns. An old gnome gone green from the rains. Something with a tubular snout and a thick ribbed tail digging in what might have passed for a flower bed.

The owner was wearing a clown mask. It had a big opening inside the garish red-and-white mouth and couldn't have been much use as protection. It made him look like the killer in a slasher movie. The room had a wooden bed frame with a torn net hanging from four wooden poles round the outside and a small TV in the corner. Something was buzzing wearily in one of the darker corners of the room. '*Magnifique*,' I said, and I gave the owner his twenty dollars for the night.

There was a bright moon outside and the curtains only covered half the window. I tried to tuck the net in. It didn't even reach down to the mattress. I thought of Helen as I lay sweating on the dirty sheets with a little high-pitched humming sound in my ear, and perhaps I should have tried to swat it because even though I couldn't go back to the Very Dark Place I didn't really want to go down with a fever, and the aircon was stuttering ineffectually. But I was too tired and somewhere in the distance I could make out a whiff of roses, sweet and scarlet and orange and mauve. The back of Helen's neck soft and smooth and pale. The zigzag island on her back.

But it wasn't Helen I dreamed of. I dreamed of Khai Manni, on horseback with his scythe. Down the wadi he came, crushing everything under his hooves. Huts in flames down the sidings, cars popping wall-to-wall. Hubcaps and bloodied *chèche*s doing cartwheels. At first I thought I had company, four of us astride, but when I turned to look they were all gone. Didn't you hear the knock, Khai Manni was saying. His voice was like the wind like insects rustling in the thorns like the red rock being sanded down by time. Khai Manni was wearing a mask. An animal visage, a fruit bat maybe or a lemur, circular eyes glinting red and gold and a great zoonotic grin. It was chilly in the zigzag hills and hot like hell. That knocking, again, and this time it could only be for me. A village at the end of the road. The mud huts baking in the doomsday sun. A little boy in an alleyway playing with a box of happy pathogens. GLENNISTON'S FINEST HUMBUGS on the label. Stick men going down the high street. Is this what it's like then on the other side, I wanted to ask, but Khai Manni had read my thoughts. The other side, he laughed. This is the other side. And then he took off his mask.

The traffic had picked up again when I went out the next morning. The cut-out windows of the makeshift buses were frazzled and raw. I wasn't worried about the yellow in people's eyes now, but I couldn't see them anyway because everyone was wearing masks. All the presidents, Nixon Reagan Pompidou De Gaulle. Mobutu in leopard print. The odd demon or two. Heidi with blonde plastic tresses, black holes for eyes. A scooter taxi with Robespierre and Marie Antoinette hanging on for dear life. I couldn't imagine where they'd got them all. A container washed overboard en route for Rio, five tonnes of plastic carnival revelry, very convenient except they were useless. I'd told the taxi driver to take me to Lotissement No. 454 on the Boulevard du 8 juin and he'd looked at me in a funny way, or at least I thought he had because all I could see in his face was plastic tusks and painted bristles. I didn't think they even knew what a wild boar was in these parts. He drove through the centre of the city, past the locomotive with the makeshift lean-tos and the mounds of garbage like silt and sediment and the roundabout, the road leading off to the shanty town, the last place I'd ever seen Nikki alive. As it were. Then he went through a part of the city I didn't remember, bush and shrubland with shacks in the bushes, and the sea visible in specks of silver grey through the bushes and the mangrove thickets behind that, and I could feel him tensing up and I thought it was strange there weren't more people in this part of town. It was scruffy and unkempt like the rest of the island, but by comparison with the centre of town it looked bucolic. The sky light blue. Seagulls tumbling about like froth. A smell of sand and salt and holidays by the beach.

The taxi driver hit the brakes abruptly. '*Ici et pas plus loin,*' he said: it was as far as he was willing to go.

'*Pourquoi?*' I asked.

'*C'est pas bon,*' he said, '*pas bon du tout.*' He was fidgeting in his seat and I thought he'd pull a gun on me.

'OK,' I said, and I paid him and got out.

The taxi reversed in a rush behind me and turned and sped off. The road fizzled out among the brush and the palm trees and the rolling sands. I walked a little further and it wasn't much of a boulevard and it didn't look like there were any lots, though here and there some old brickwork in stumps showed up among the frizzy yellow grass. The sound of waves a little further on, a promise of a beach. Butterflies tumbling about the white blossoms of trees I couldn't place.

Then without any warning the smell of death. They came out in twos and threes from the bushes in rags, random symbols drawn in their faces with the orange sand, stumbling forward with their arms outstretched. They saw me but perhaps they didn't, and I saw their shelters hidden among the branches, scraps of plastic, shopping bags cut open and spread across the branches, bodies lying and crouching, faeces and flies. They came up and they touched me with their scabby hands and they spat at me and I wasn't afraid. A boy with a thick crust of blood under his eyes walked next to me and he wasn't looking at me because he wasn't looking any more. I didn't know what they wanted. They were beyond helping and they knew it but still they had their rage and they were going to pass the damn thing to everyone foolish enough to wander out into the mangrove. '*Je suis passé par là*,' I said, I've been there, and they didn't seem to hear me and I walked on through their tattered ranks and maybe they understood and the boy with the crust of blood under his eyes stopped and stood there in the sun with the flies buzzing round his head and all the others went back into the scrawny shadows.

The mangrove opened up and in the breach there was a little beach, the sand a blinding white, the sea a dark shade of turquoise, the shore of the mainland just visible in the distance under the flicker of the heat, a thin green rim. A tern-like bird with a long black tail skimming the water. I'd almost forgotten why I had come. I walked on, the mangrove to my right, the sun hammering down at a right angle. The Boulevard du 8 juin was little more than a couple of worn ruts in the orange soil and stagnant puddles from the rains. A rusty fence cutting through the bushes, a half-open wire-mesh gate across the track. A chain dangling from one side of the gate. It looked recent, the metal still shiny, though someone seemed to have snapped it with bolt cutters. A bit of the chain and a padlock lay in a puddle on the ground.

I walked through the gate. A cluster of buildings stood in a clearing in the mangrove. An old hangar, a wide strip of chipped cement with trees like giant spider plants growing out of the cracks. An old concrete jetty reaching a few hundred metres out into the lagoon with a tower-like thing at the end, strutted metal half-tilting like a tragic scarecrow. A broad slipway going into the water, covered in algae and muck. A couple of preening black birds, legs too short to be waders and too long to be songbirds.

The hangar had large sliding doors with the flaking remnants of writing on them, Aéropostal with an *e* missing at the end, some sort of staging post for flying boats on their way down to the Central African colonies. At the side of the building was a door, its blue paint peeling but a crude lock fixed recently and broken into even more recently, another shiny padlock on the tarnished cement floor. Inside was broken glass, a musty corridor. Rats at the end of the corridor briefly baring their zigzag teeth at me before running. Storerooms on one side, crates of something and metal cylinders, the kind used for industrial gases, then an opening on the other side to the hangar itself.

It was the size of a large gym, a few rays of dirty sunshine coming in through the Bauhaus windows around the frieze below the corrugated iron roof. The roof had been done up not long ago, though everything else about the building had the neglected look of the tropics. The hangar was filled with things. Tentlike structures with transparent covers, some knocked over. Metal bars also still shiny, though the humidity was starting to encroach. Bed frames inside the tents, and tables and drips. Broken glass on the cement floors, smashed test tubes. And along the wall at the far end, shiny metal structures like fridges or ovens, except they were cages. Most of them were empty, the doors ajar, but something was buzzing in one of them, at eye level, a swarm of fat blue flies. There were tufts of black fur inside and bones and dark shiny things crawling over the bones. It should have made me sick but it didn't. I recognized the smell. A nice bouquet over the Bay of Biscay that nobody else could smell. In a corner of the hangar a makeshift office lay scattered in its component parts, the legs of a metal desk glowing with a scientific sheen but dented. A smell of burning, but I couldn't see any fire or smoke. More broken glass. A filing cabinet. Not the first thing you'd expect to find out here. Most of the compartments emptied out. A couple of hanging folders lying in a puddle of dirty water under the desk, left behind by whoever had hastily cleared the place out. Text and graphs, case notes and temperature curves. Aymeric Macondé, age thirty-three, et cetera. I took pictures of the case notes with my phone and threw the files back in the slush. Bits of a PC lay on the ground by the desk, a fan and twisted metal frame and CPU. At a quick glance it might have looked like it had been smashed, but it hadn't. An expert dissection. The hard drive extracted. But left to look tangled and random. Next to the office was a fridge, but it hadn't been used to keep drinks in. Twenty shelves or more, and racks for storing vials. A biohazard sign on the door. The shelves had been emptied in one go, the vials smashed on the floor. The cement was stained dark in places. The whole place should have been sealed tight with a security perimeter round it.

There was a humming sound outside. I took some more pictures with my phone and walked back over the shattered glass onto the cracked cement ramp. A helicopter was circling above the hangar. It looked like a Lynx, but with the glare I couldn't tell for sure, and it kept its altitude. I couldn't make out its markings. Perhaps it didn't have any markings. It stood still for a minute, then dipped its nose and headed out to sea. It probably wasn't a good idea for me to stick around, and I'd seen as much as I would.

I walked back past the jetty and along the track running through the mangrove. Jeering laughter rang out above my head in a quickfire staccato volley. A single mango tree, with a gallery of baboons on one of the lower branches. They were making monkey gestures and monkey noises and cackling monkey laughs and they were looking at me. One had something coming out of its side, a dangling thing like a cable. It was the end of a drip, transparent plastic tubing visible under a caking of goo. Some of the baboons had shorn square patches in their fur. They looked in a bad way but they were laughing at me. I walked on down the sandy ruts of the Boulevard du 8 juin. Something hit my shoulder. It was a fruit, or a nut in its shell. The baboons were bouncing up and down on their branch now, having the time of their lives, leaves shaking, twigs raining down, the racket so loud it startled a flight of orange and blue guinea finches out of the undergrowth.

The people in the mangrove didn't get up when I walked back past them towards the road. They barely turned their heads. There was a humming and a beating of little wings about them that I hadn't noticed when I first went past, and a slow, low sucking noise. When I got back on to a proper road the sun was starting to go down and little lights were coming on all over the shanty towns and people were starting to light their stoves and there was smoke in the air but it wasn't what I smelled. What I smelled was a mix of human sweat and something musky and animal. The smell of whatever had been in those cages. It stayed with me for a while as I watched the masked ball sweep past in the busy rush hour streets, girls in shiny tight-fitting dresses with Catwoman masks and men in string vests with ice hockey masks and any number of medics, Doctor Mumbo here and Doctor Jumbo there; a funerary procession, two, three, I lost count, it didn't make sense, the funny smiling manga masks and Sonic the Hedgehog and then all the wailing the women ululating the men beating their breasts, the bodies carried by a dozen of them sewn into colourful dyed shrouds.

I got a taxi and tried to go to the palace but this time I couldn't get past the first roadblock, guards with skull-print masks drawn up to their eyes brandishing their guns at me. '*Ces gens dans la brousse*,' I asked the taxi driver, 'those people in the bush, Boulevard du 8 juin, who are they?' and the driver slammed on the brakes and turned to me and took off his mask, a she-lion or a puma. In the lights from the lorries and vans going past I could see his eyes. They were bloodshot and the white was infused with yellow, and thick pearls of sweat shone like crystals on his forehead every time the headlights crossed his face. '*Personne ne peut parler de ça, OK*,' he said, nobody's allowed to talk about that. '*Personne ne peut aller là-bas, personne.*' He put his mask back on, and he was probably expecting me to get out of the car then and run, but I didn't. 'I can't catch it,' I said, in English, and I don't know if he understood, and I didn't know if it was true, but in any case I had nothing to lose.

At the guest house the owner was sitting on the wall by the dusty yard. He had his clown mask on and didn't say anything as I arrived, the mask slowly swivelling, ex-pressionless, to follow me inside. 'What's that burnt smell?' I asked him, and he didn't understand. He'd probably left a chicken roasting in the oven. '*Poulet DG cramé*,' I said with a smile, but the clown face kept grinning at me with its blood-steeped lips.

I went to my room and lay on the dirty bed with the scrappy bits of netting swaying in the breeze from the stut-tering air con and took out my phone and looked at the pic-tures of the case notes from the old hangar. They were about four pages each, all in the same neat template, subjective, objective, assessment, temperature chart. Aymeric Macondé's notes started with *Subject Admitted* and then a date, a few months earlier, and a big box with *Observations*, every fever-ish rambling taken down and transcribed, with times. 'I've seen your file,' Helen's husband had said, and I wondered if this was what mine looked like. I began to feel sick, as if someone was drawing a rough wooden spatula through the inside of my stomach, and I had to run to the bathroom and throw myself on the sink and retch, and I didn't notice the insect sitting on the cracked old porcelain tray below the mirror, some big crusading thing with chitin outgrowths all over its head and back and rows of little twitching legs. It lifted off and flew past me into a dark corner of the bath-room, brushing my shoulder with its filigree wings. I wanted a drink to forget what I'd read but there was nowhere to go, so I crawled back under the torn mosquito net and turned off the light and once or twice I heard a whirring noise from the bathroom like a plastic wind-up toy. I didn't really get any sleep; fragments from the case notes kept coming back in dark swirls, subject this and subject that profuse bleeding delirious thirty-eight rising thirty-nine five and maybe stuff was missing from the case notes because none of them re-ferred to any treatment or plan, but maybe that was just me as a layperson not getting it.

Sometime in the early hours I heard voices, footsteps going past my door. I got dressed and went out into the hall. The voices came from a narrow staircase at the end of the hall. They led up onto the flat roof on the second floor of the building. The moon full and lurid like a blood orange and a cloudless sky. The owner was standing by the balustrade with his family. Minnie Mouse and two little mice who might have been rats. They were pointing into the distance, beyond palm trees in jagged outline and bungalows and the handful of taller buildings. A plume of smoke billowed into the darkness, the bottom part lit up from below in a dirty orange flicker. It didn't look real. Like stage effects at a concert, or the backdrop to a music video from the 1980s.

'*C'est où ça?*' I asked, trying to work out what they were looking at.

The owner didn't turn his head. '*Ah, quelque part vers le vieux-port,*' he said. 'Nobody lives down that way.'

I watched the spectacle a little longer, veins of angry yellow and carmine shooting up into the orange glow. It was miles away and it had to be big. Then I went back to my room and tried to sleep. The fever bell went and the fake NHS thugs came to take me away. They were wearing shiny black gloves straight out of another nightmare and ice hockey masks, grinning skulls and shark's teeth stencilled on and little black apertures like bullet holes for eyes. Glenniston Life and Death HC. They played me without mercy, and I couldn't make out the coach's face, though from time to time I heard her voice thundering across the rink. Give it to that puck, boys, hit him hard. Section three and seventy, she boomed. On closer inspection she turned out to be squatting astride a '32 Latécoère floatplane. Get in, she barked, and I objected meekly and she slapped a fifty-seven para five on it and I had no idea what that was and she was not about to explain. No dancing out of line there, she screamed again. She powered up the Latécoère, five hundred horses throbbing into flight, the ascent vertiginous and when they fell there was such a splash. The Bay of Biscay unremarkable but for all the monsters, slick as sirens, bile pumping from blowholes. Khai Manni's shadow over the Sahel, an outline of tunic and *chèche* and tommy gun, zigzag mountains steeped in zigzag flames. The Gulf of Guinea a riddle of fevers and platforms and swamps, little fires flickering on rusty derricks. The staging post of the Aéropostale all shiny and lit up, a handy stepping stone for the species jump. I saw it now for what it was, the tower at the end of the pier, burning brightly to welcome friend and foe, beast and man. BIENVENUE À ----- it said, and still they wouldn't let me see where I was. A sweeping arc above the mangrove. Crabs goggling and manatees going belly up to see the shiny plane thing circling in to land. *Bienvenue* to the pleasure dome, the cages all shiny and slick, the Bauhaus windows there to tease me with a promise of daylight. Here's yours, the goon said, phoney shamrock growing from his nostrils and ears, his badge glowing in the darkness, N, H, S, clearly home-made like the little red bus he'd come on, and already the door had snapped shut on me and something was licking my face, Hello boy, yes you with the creasy face and the stilted diction I keep your every bit of doggerel on my bedside table, in my locket my amulet my shrine. Now why, he said with a voice weary from centuries of knowing me, gravelly and profound, now why would anyone call their dog *Wystan*—

A trickle of blood on my cheek. Something amiss with the coagulation. Or perhaps the mosquitoes here had given up, like everyone and everything else. I didn't want to go down with malaria. There were worse things than malaria, and I'd been there, but still, how careless.

I went out into the garden, where the owner had set up breakfast on a rickety little table, a croissant in a wrapper, baked some months ago in Dakar, and a plastic cup with scalding hot coffee. *'C'était quoi, hier soir,'* I asked, 'that thing we saw from the roof?'

'Ah ça,' the owner said. He was wearing a different mask today, a magician probably, pale white cheeks with black question marks on them and high curved eyebrows, the apertures black and pointless and dead. 'Just a warehouse that burnt down,' he said, 'out in the bush. *Personne de blessé.'*

'Ah bon,' I said. The croissant tasted like something out of the paper dispenser in an airport loo. But the coffee gave me a kick. *'Ah il est bon, votre café.'* I couldn't tell what the owner made of that, the eyes gaping and the question marks standing there on his papier mâché cheeks, questioning something or someone.

'Monsieur, you're wanted for questioning,' a man said, coming through the garden gate. He was wearing a dark blue uniform and a dark blue beret, big shiny pentagonal badges on his lapels and a profuse constellation on his epaulettes, huge pointy stars that looked like the pattern on gift wrap. His mask was in character, a stern moustachioed face that probably came in a pack with a sheriff's star and Stetson and plastic revolver, pif paf.

I thought it was a joke and kept sipping my coffee, but suddenly the sheriff had two of his minions on me. They were wearing white and black storm trooper masks and had long black truncheons that persuaded me they meant business. They put me in the back of an old Mitsubishi pickup and we rode through the streets, the masked ball swirling about us like so much garish puppetry, and they took me to an old fort on the other side of the island, star-shaped like the pentagons on the sheriff's lapels, a collection of broken-down scout cars in the courtyard with trees sprouting out of the hatches.

They didn't take me to an interview room. They took me up a tight narrow helix of a spiral staircase, the walls humid and cool, and when we got to the top there was a glorious view of the Gulf of Guinea on one side, turned towards the ocean, tankers moored in the distant haze like half-erased pencil drawings and derricks like little pins sticking out from a roughly sanded plank. And on the other side, the city a random motley of green and grey. '*Tu vois la fumée, là,*' the sheriff said, and he pointed to a spot in the mangrove not far away on the edge of town. A few pale wisps of smoke still hung in the air above the green clumps. I tried to figure out where I was, see if I could make out the old floatplane depot and the mangrove forest, but I had no time to find my bearings because just then the two storm troopers grabbed me by the shoulders and twisted my arms behind my back, and they pushed me roughly along the battlements till we came to a little opening in the wall, and I realized the fort was built right on the waterline, the waves breaking below against a medley of rocks. A rusty little footbridge some fifty metres above the sea, the railings broken in places, leading across to a squat round tower with a collapsed roof and fallen masonry piled up at its base. Swallows racing in the hot air, a species I'd never seen before, black bodies and white heads like darting little wraiths. I thought they were going to take me to the tower and lock me up. The only foreigner in town, and maskless. They were bound to find some by-law, some obscure *arrêté* or *règlement* or directive or *ordonnance* I'd broken, and I'd get out in a few days with a black eye or two and a couple of hundred dollars poorer.

But they didn't take me to the tower and they didn't lock me up. Not there and not then. They took me to a bit of the bridge where the rusty railings had collapsed, and the storm troopers pushed me down on my knees and I tried to push back but they'd clearly done this before, their own little interviewing routine, probably something they'd found on the internet, 'True Tales from a Black Site' et cetera, head and torso and arms into the void and the two of them sitting on the back of my knees, and it hurt so much I screamed and down below me the waters of the Gulf were glistening and shallow, a metre or two of water; it made me think of the flooded meadows around my mother's house and Wystan yapping somewhere on that jagged island in some filthy kennel or cellar and Helen Beaumont wherever she was in her posh house with its Farrow & Ball pastels and the hyacinths all glorious and fragrant, but right now all I could smell was death and more death and the waves of the Gulf like the creases in Helen Beaumont's blouse. I had to get back, and I didn't even know what the jumped-up sheriff wanted from me.

'*Il est où?*' the jumped-up sheriff was screaming at me, and I panted 'Where's who,' breathless, and my stomach doubled up and compressed and contorted and when I opened my eyes I could see along the coast, the mangrove and a strip of white sand upside down and then a horizontal line swaying, no, the swaying was me, and something like a slim black hook pointing down into the sky at the end of it, and the pale whitish blue below the ruffled mangrove tops with wisps of smoke floating in it; and that's probably when the penny dropped. '*Il est où,*' the jumped-up sheriff was still yelling, and again I asked, '*Mais qui?*' and it came out as a feeble squeak, but the sheriff or his minions must have heard it because they yelled as one, '*Mais Khai Manni, bien sûr.*'

The sea went from cresting turquoise to viscous sepia, the mangrove seemed to curl in on itself darkly and char, the swallows flapped gloomily about me like bats.

'Khai Manni doesn't exist,' I tried to say, but they probably didn't hear me.

'We know you went to the *aérogare* yesterday,' the sheriff said, in English. 'We know you work for Khai Manni, you tell us where we find Khai Manni.'

'But he doesn't exist,' I said again, a little louder now.

They simply pushed me a little further over the edge and I saw myself going headlong in one skull-crushing dive into the inky broth, and I flailed about with my arms and managed briefly to pull myself up and twist sideways, enough to see the jumped-up sheriff leaning over the railings, his mask like a grimace, and I thought there was somebody else with him, looking over his shoulder, a man in a suit with a surgical mask, and I only briefly glimpsed the top of his face: he was white and had straight short grey hair and old-fashioned glasses. But then they pushed me even further over the edge until I was hanging upside down like a bat in its roost flapping against the blackened wall.

XIX.

I'm not sure about the order of events any more. It might have been the bat-like roosting that burst a few vessels, grilled a few neurons, compressed soft bits that weren't for compressing. Or it might have been the roughing-up that probably followed, down in the dungeons, tunnels reaching out far under the Gulf of Guinea, hewn into the rock centuries ago by slaves, and now the launches plied their trade on the happy waves above, President *Lakamba* or *Lumumba* or whatever was left of it. The undersea galleries generously appointed to accommodate whoever dared call the mounds of garbage by the roadside by their name. Or the occasional foreign misfit like me. They must have been proud of it, their own national security crypt. I remember the rock walls sweating, brine dripping through cracks in the ceiling, cries and whispers in the gloom. A voice that sounded just like Ricardo behind the walls of rock, a little blurred by the seaweed but otherwise in good nick. And mermaids weeping behind their snorkelling masks.

None of it seemed very sequential, and none of it made much sense. Transport in some official conveyance or other with wire mesh on the windows across the dusky town, bonfires in the empty marketplaces where they sold little rodents on sticks. The masque in the moonlight. Catwoman dancing with Death. Cackling laughter echoing across the lagoon. Nocturnal rites. Cement bags for coffins. And another grilling at Heathrow when I got back. Nurse Mersey stern and unforgiving. It was strangely terrifying to see people without masks.

But I couldn't be sure of any of this. Perhaps they'd taken me straight to the airport and the rest was the fever singing. And I hadn't been taking my pills. No telling what that might do to the narrative. Something the doctors had said when I left the Very Dark Place. Never forget to take the pills. If you do, call this number without delay. So perhaps there were no national security crypts, no dripping vaults beneath the waves. But I had a nagging feeling I'd seen that white face again with the surgical mask, wherever it was they took me, after the dangling act at the fort. Always in the background fleetingly, keeping out of sight as they yelled their questions at me, *Où est Khai Manni*, how much he pay you, you take us to him. We know he pay you to burn the Aéropostale, to cause trouble, you lead us to him, we see you, we got pictures, and on his phone he played a little clip, me shielding my eyes from the sun as I look up into the sky at the chopper from the forecourt of the Aéropostale hangar, and even though I hadn't really slept for days and was feeling lousy from the slapping about I couldn't help thinking, what, a Lynx, they're showing me footage from a Lynx, here, in this part of Africa, how likely is that, the only choppers they have in this part of the world are clapped-out old Russian machines; if indeed it was a Lynx. But they had the footage, and yes it was suspicious. And also a whispered question in English, a different voice now, mixed in so I wouldn't notice perhaps. What exactly had I seen, in the hangar. What had Nikki and Ricardo and David told me. What did I know. The questioning tight and precise though the horn-rimmed glasses looked passé. And another voice: You out walking the old dog, were you? Nurse Mersey asked. Oh. The sequencing a mess.

And in between – or was it? – a flight. They must have put me on the plane in a daze, my veins full of some weird crap, just enough that I'd be awake by the time the plane landed in Paris. I was alone on the plane, and it was sitting on the tarmac, and I looked out of the porthole and saw a big white truck with AÉROPORTS DE PARIS on it, and the flight attendant at the front of the plane was frowning but not keen to come too close to me and that might have been the black eye or it might have been everything else. I stumbled out and walked straight into the arms of two health inspectors with thermometers and torches and of course I didn't beep, cold-blooded bastard, and behind their masks they looked almost disappointed. I felt in my pocket for my phone and it was there, but when I tried to switch it on nothing happened, the battery must have gone dead or perhaps it had taken too many knocks in the dungeons. The train through the tunnel was down so I had to take a coach up to Dunkirk and buy a passage on an old freight ferry, the kind I didn't think existed any more, two-thirds empty because who wanted to take any chances, rails on the lorry deck and you had to squeeze past the lorries to get on, clouds of black fumes, and there should have been a nasty smell of engine oil and diesel yet oddly enough I couldn't smell a thing, and I got fish and chips in the cafe, soggy with oil but again I couldn't smell anything and most of the taste was gone. I didn't think about it then because the whole thing was listing absurdly all the way over to Folkestone. The irony of it, I thought, if that was to be it for me, having stayed undrowned thus far.

The cliffs were off-white that day and a little under the weather. We passed Dover and I looked up to where the castle should have been, but it wasn't there, only chalk and weeds. At customs, a tired-looking man with a thermometer who didn't even bother to point. When the man from Border Force ran my passport through the system he gulped and ran it again and then he called his supervisor and his supervisor called me to his office with two armed officers standing behind him and said, 'You never left the country,' and shook his head.

'I suppose the system must have failed to register when I left,' I said.

'When did you leave?'

'About a week ago.'

'How?'

'Oh, one of the ferries,' I said.

'Which one?

'I don't remember. P&O, Stena, I don't know.'

'Why didn't you fly?' he asked, and he leafed through my passport, looking at all the stamps from The Land Of.

'I like the sea.'

There were phone calls from the back office, then I waited and then I was out. Two hours of waiting on a cold platform and when the train came it was an ancient thing with a door for every row of seats and ribbed cloth upholstery patched a dozen times over, the kind they must have taken out of service decades ago. Halfway up to London some kids appeared from one of the other carriages and started punching out the bulkhead lights at the end of the train. I thought about getting up and walking up to them saying, If you knew what I've had and I spat at you, then what? But I couldn't be bothered, and the train rolled on in darkness through the suburbs with the feral cackle of the kids underlaid by the bumping of the train over the sleepers.

When I got home I found a little plastic bottle with pills on the kitchen table. Ah yes. It all came back, though I couldn't find the little laminated card with the emergency numbers on it. And even if I had found it, I wouldn't have called. I took a handful and washed them down with scotch. The pills probably didn't mix well with alcohol, but what did I care. I lay flat on my back with a black eye and a slew of haematomas down my back like a prize Friesian, on my sofa in my flat with the bills mounting up and no traffic outside. Police cars on the prowl, most of the shops shuttered. The dog bowl in the kitchen untouched. I should have gone to the police to report it all. Well, where would you like to start, sir? Ah yes, the fire. And what was his name again? Oh yes. Ky, how do you spell that? Money, as in Money. Right. Ah yes, sir, it's coming back to me now sir, you're the nutcase with the lost dog. Oh yes. That's me. Are you taking any medication, sir? Well, yes. Oh yes. Oh, I see.

I plugged my phone in the charger and it slowly came back to life. I went straight into the photo archive, but there was nothing. Everything wiped squeegee-clean. Pictures of Wystan's face in a sad crease, all the pictures I'd ever taken of the slanting steamer in the White River, vistas of The Land Of. And all those patient records I'd photographed in the hangar before it burnt down, all gone. But there were a couple of missed calls from Nurse Mersey, one of them with an angry voicemail attached. Emails about unpaid bills. I deleted all of them.

A squealing of sirens in the distance gave me a start. I scrolled through the news. They'd adopted pretty much the same protocols as in The Land Of. Move in hard, shut everything down, tape everything off. Fatality rates hadn't come down, though. A lone WhatsApp pinging, from Helen, saying *Can you call me?*

'I don't think you want to be seen talking to me,' I said when she answered the phone.

'Nonsense. And anyway, no one is watching. You need to tell me all about your trip.'

I didn't remember telling Helen about my trip. Perhaps a report had crossed her husband's desk and he'd talked. It made me wonder how far I could trust her. 'Any time,' I said.

'That's great. Meanwhile, I got a little note from the producer of *Sunday Newshour*. There's interest in having you on the show.'

'Interest?' *Sunday Newshour* was a big deal. Everyone watched *Sunday Newshour*. Viewing figures a couple of million plus.

'I think they'd like to feature you as the lead story in one of their next shows. Give you a chance to tell your side of the story. Get some of this weird stuff out there. Make sure people don't forget Nikki. And David and Ricardo, of course.' I looked outside. The rain had stopped. A bit of sunlight leaked out from behind the clouds.

'I'm in.'

'Super,' Helen said. 'I'll pass your number on to the producers.'

I went for a walk by the river. I glanced around from time to time for little white vans, goons in bushes. The streets were empty, but it didn't feel right to be walking dogless. Although Wystan was useless, for all practical purposes, he'd always given me an illusion of something, security, company, whatever. I found the river, or perhaps the river found me. The water gnawing at the towpath. A steamer askew in the paddock below Richmond Hill. I'd seen it beaching on live TV, a pack of sozzled bankers disembarking in a daze, and now it sat there, paddles green with duckweed and slime, gulls and corvids circling its thin black funnel. The top of the dyke around the edge of the paddock just clear of the lapping water. The top of Richmond Hill vague with clouds, the Star and Garter all gone. Or maybe I'd remembered it all wrong. I walked around the side of the paddock to Petersham Road, down the leafy bit leading into town, past the old Odeon and Richmond Bridge. A black Mercedes van, darkened windows, went past, slowed down. I stopped. The van accelerated again, had probably braked for one of the foot-deep puddles that had formed all along the side of the road. There was trash floating on the oily black water seeping into Richmond Green. Sandbags lay around the cast-iron railings of some of the grander houses, water pumps chugging.

They called me as I was walking past Kew, some assistant producer called Mick or Mike with a Scottish name and accent, bright and cheery, would I want to be on *Newshour* that coming Sunday, they were doing a special. I'd be the first-hand eyewitness and all that. 'From the Martyrs in the Mangrove to Surviving in Surbiton'. Something to that effect. 'Yes, yes, whatever,' I said to Mike. I just wanted to get home. The rain clouds were piling up dirty and inevitable like something out of a Spanish baroque painting, the ground was shaky under my feet: with all that sogginess it was only a matter of time before something gave way. 'Yes,

yes,' I said to Mick. 'I'll be there, but now I need to run home, the sky's coming down.'

I don't know what he made of me, the chirpy fellow from the BBC, and presumably he'd been warned about me, but he told me a time and a place and I made a mental note, though really I wanted to get a bus home and all the lines were down, flooded underpasses and bits of Kingston town centre underwater, so I sploshed through puddles that were lakes and waded across streets like wadis, because I needed more of the pills and I needed them fast and I couldn't work out how I'd managed all this time without them.

I regretted agreeing to the *Sunday Newshour* thing almost as soon I rudely put the phone down on Mike or Mick, but I was stuck with it. I thought I'd tell Dr Bicknell about it. I knew nothing about Dr Bicknell, had met her for the first time, consciously, when I'd exited the Very Dark Place a month earlier, yet she was my confessor, almost, and confidante: nothing was out of bounds, since everything came down to that thing from The Land Of. She'd never judge, but she knew how to listen. And did I have stuff to report. I wondered what she'd make of the fact that I seemed to have lost my sense of smell.

First I'd have to get there, though. They'd changed the train timetables, cut down the number of services into town. Staff down to essentials. Someone flipping from passenger to patient on every other train. And every time it happened the entire carriage had to go into decontamination. It made the maintenance of anything resembling a regular service impossible. Shareholders were getting stroppy. Every little trip into town a roll of the dice. So I was late, very late, but I knew Dr Bicknell would be waiting for mem as she always was.

'Dr Caroline Bicknell, you say.' The woman at the departmental reception seemed to be clueless and new. They'd finished their building works. Perspex and rubber everywhere, green and red zones and arrows and everyone twitchy. People peering out suspiciously from behind their masks.

'Yes, Dr Caroline Bicknell,' I said. 'Consultant, head of department, professor of virology. Et cetera. The reason I'm here, and probably the reason you're here.' I didn't have time for this crap. I've been the other side and back, I wanted to say, way before just about anybody else. I'm the alpha team of patients. The very crème. I didn't. I waited meekly.

Even so, she looked offended. I couldn't see her mouth, but her eyebrows did the talking. She had purple plastic nail extensions with Egyptian runes on them. 'There's no need to get objectionable, sir,' she hissed. She turned to a colleague in the booth next to hers. 'A Dr Bicknell, he says, appointment, getting quite rude and all, oh right, cheers then.' Then, turning back to me: 'Sir, Dr Bicknell is on a long-term training assignment.'

'That's very peculiar,' I said.

'Was there anything else you wanted?'

I didn't answer. I was sure Dr Bicknell hadn't taken a leave of absence for training purposes.

At Waterloo, I had to wait for an hour for a train. An issue with the driver. The rain hammering down on the station roof like a steel band. Little waterfalls crashing down from the platform edges onto the tracks. The train had only two carriages, and I had them all to myself.

XX.

I lay awake most of the night worrying about *Sunday Newshour*. Helen would be watching, and all the jerks at head office. Every time a car went down a gear in the street I jumped. Every little creaking of the stairs, every hungry snout or beak foraging among the bins was a fuse to trigger my nerves. I'd put the wooden wedge under the door, scattered some old Coke cans in the hallway. Taken down some of the pictures in the living room and attached picture cord to the nails, stretched it out across to the coffee table like the criss-cross beams of a movement sensor. I didn't have a clue who I thought was after me, but boy would they make a racket if they tried.

The little sleep I got was shot through with dreams like shrapnel. The lagoon lit up with garish glowing garlands. Red, white and blue, all ready for the dance. Helen's hand as she walked with me warm and cold like leather, long kid gloves up to her elbows in the Viennese fashion. Fanfares and marching bands, up and down The Mall all decked out with flags, the Boulevard du Wotsit. The owner of it all squatting on the windowsill. I introduced myself gingerly, but all I got was a haughty wave along the lines of We don't audience with individuals wot travel by trawler. The couples waltzing, the monkeys clapping, the baby-faced bats all in a flap, painting zigzag tumbles in the sky like dizzy fireflies. I saw the Zigzag Mountains in the distance, though no atlas transcribed them. Where do I look then? Under Z for Zanzibar and Zinder and Zaïre, and I did, but there was Ziggowat and Zihouar but no Zigzag. And everyone spun into pirouettes, Mickey and his Minnie, Goofy and his Goofette. Triage in a jumble. A Gallic gunboat firing pop-pop-pop into the continent and all its crew beyond repair. The yellow flag of quarantine run up opposite Little Popo and Great Bassam. Lesser Wallop and Greater Wallop. A bloody shambles from coast to coast. Waltzing on water. Black-shirted and white. Tattoos identical from head to toe. Daggers spinning out of petals in a whirl. The wind's a bit on the sharp end today, I said to Helen. But Helen was gone. Gone, they were all gone, under the sea and under the hills, all gone but for the black-clad army dancing debonair upon the waves, a void where the masks should be though no one seemed to mind. And in their midst their leader like Venus rising from the waves, Etonian debris in a three-piece suit. In each eye a monocle spinning, top hat, Baron Samedi mask. But then the mask was gone and nothing was there, nothing and the hint of a *chèche* blowing in the wind. Are you Khai Manni, I cried into the void, and it was Nikki's voice that came back: No, aren't you?

The rain woke me, hammering pippa-poppa-ploof against the windowpanes as if trying to find a way in. I was lying on the sofa with the whisky bottle beside me, empty, and a scattering of pills. I remembered taking some of the pills and drinking whisky from the bottle, though I still couldn't remember what the pills were for. I remembered I had to be at the studio by ten, ready for make-up and a chat with the producer, and I looked at my watch. Ten to nine. I stuffed the NHS badge and lanyard into my pocket. A nice touch, if they asked me about my time in the Very Dark Place. I forgot to shave and I couldn't find my only tie and I ran into the picture cord on the way out and fell over and stepped on the Coke cans and almost cut my foot. I yanked at the front door till I remembered I'd shoved the wooden wedge underneath the night before. The Uber driver looked at me with alarm in the rear-view mirror and I looked at his eyes and I saw yellow, and I wondered how long he had to live. A week or a month, depending on the care he'd get once they took him in. I could have said something, but it wouldn't have made any difference.

I must have looked a right mess when I arrived at Broadcasting House. Wet like a dog because I'd forgotten to bring an umbrella. I thought of Wystan, wherever he was. I asked for Mick or Mike at reception and waited for five minutes on a black leather sofa next to some giant ficus trees in terracotta pots while the security guard walked past repeatedly throwing suspicious looks at me and the ficus kept shifting in and out of focus, but then Mike or Mick arrived. 'I'm Mike,' he said with a breezy smile, and things started to come together. They gave me a cup of bitter black coffee in a little room next to the studio and the woman who did my make-up joked that the stubble made me look like Brad Pitt with a hangover, and I thought she probably said that to everyone, minus the hangover.

'They'll be playing a documentary first,' Mick said. 'It's about The Land Of. And then Ralph will go straight into the live interview, if that's all right.'

'That's fine,' I said. Ralph was Ralph Chatteris and he had a CBE and he was a national treasure and I was starting to feel at home, almost, though I'd never really done TV. The hangover was starting to dissipate. I'd tell them everything that had happened in The Land Of, the knocking in the middle of the night, and then there were none, my stint in the Very Dark Place that was always lit up, the weird stuff later, Glenniston, the hangar in the mangrove, the lynx, the case notes: Aymeric Macondé.

'Will there be a little glass table?' I asked Mike, 'You see, I'd like to show the knocking.' I gave four little knocks on the surface of the dresser.

'Uh yes, I do think there's a glass table in the studio,' Mick said, and he gave me a funny look, though he'd done his homework and couldn't have been all that surprised.

A countdown started on a digital clock on the wall.

'Ten minutes to go,' Mike said. 'You might want to go in. Ralph will be on in a minute.' He got up and showed me down a narrow corridor till we came to a double set of doors, sound-insulated, with a little red light outside and an LED panel that said Sun Nwshr, 1100–1200. The brightness inside the room was like the time I was holed up in the Very Dark Place. Or the walk across the hillside where they'd found Ricardo's blood, in the Zigzag Mountains. A thousand suns brightly burning and all that. With the lights on me at full blast I couldn't make out much of the studio. A little stage of sorts, an armchair on one side, the presenter's, and two armchairs on my side. I stepped down off the stage to get out of the clinical glare of the lights. I'd been expecting an audience but there was no one there, just a vast empty studio with a concrete floor.

'Where's the audience?' I asked, stepping back onto the platform with the blinding lights.

'New regulations,' Mike said. 'There isn't one.'

'But there's another guest,' I said, pointing at the third armchair. Mick smiled at me but didn't say anything and then Ralph Chatteris appeared from behind the backdrop with its swishing logos and screens, and he came up to me and shook my hand, saying, 'So happy you could make it, Sebastian, really appreciate it,' then someone else stepped up from out of the shadows, a familiar face, and sat in the chair next to mine, slick and suave, Helen's husband the czar, his suit a subtle shade of mid-blue, luminescent like napalm, the creases in the legs of his trousers sharp as scalpels. A bit irregular, surely, to have a civil servant on a show like this, and anyway I thought I was the star, I wanted to say to Mike or Mick, but he was gone, everyone was gone except for Ralph Chatteris and the czar and the occasional cough from some flunkey out in the gloom where the audience should have been sitting. 'We're joined today by the man leading the government's response effort,' I heard Chatteris saying, far away, as if on fade but never quite disappearing, then his voice seemed to grow ever more distant, as if the studio was expanding infinitely and his armchair was moving backwards like an ejection seat in reverse, and when he introduced me, from whichever far-away galaxy he was now speaking from, it dawned on me that I was a prop, a bauble: a souvenir. Whatever this was, it was going belly up, and though the czar wasn't looking at me I could tell he was smirking and the smirk was meant for me, even as he was talking, and he talked a lot.

The whole thing was like a cosy fireside chat between Chatteris and the czar: one friendly pass after another, and the czar so smooth and suave and glib: The situation serious but the task force throwing everything at it: the kitchen sink and the army and the NHS, all of it, and every virologist still standing: more, and faster, than anybody else. And that in-cluded the Americans, even. Chatteris nodding approvingly. I was adrift by this point and largely off duty. With a jolt I realized Chatteris had turned to me.

'So, Sebastian – you're one of the very few people who have had it and come out alive. Tell us what it is like. What is it actually *like*, having *it*?'

'It's like,' I said, and I put in a little pause for effect, 'your body is on fire, like your bones are burning. And nothing can put it out. And you're not really there but you are. Enough to feel it. At least at first. The first week maybe. But you can't be too sure. You lose your sense of time. And eventually you blank out.'

Chatteris was nodding out there in the Pacific doldrums, a vigorous, understanding, empathetic sort of nod, and I could feel the audience rooting for me though I couldn't see them.

'The doctors, the nurses, they were absolutely brilliant,' I said. 'In fact everybody when I got back was absolutely amazing. I just want to say we're so incredibly lucky to have professionals like that.' And though there was no one in the audience I could sense a wave of feelgood rippling through them: bloody right we're lucky we are, envy of the world and all that. Even that supercilious bastard the husband and czar was nodding, mouthing a hearty hear, hear. But then things went off the rails.

'I understand you've also attracted the attention of some rather unsavoury characters since you got back,' Chatteris said. 'Is that something you'd like to share with us?'

'Well, to begin with it was only Nurse Mersey. And that was fine. She's been coming to check up on me, basically.'

'Nurse *Mersey*,' Chatteris repeated. 'How do you spell that?' I could sense the first intimation of a titter spreading up and down the country, the dads in PJs slurping their cornflakes in Milton Keynes and the hungover students in a flatshare in Morningside and even Jonathan: Jonathan, who'd never come to see me in the Very Dark Place, in his chic Thames-side loft, but no, Jonathan was out of the game. Jonathan was in a dark place of his own now.

'Nurse Mersey would come at irregular times. It's part of the protocol. I mean, I'm fine with that. But then these other guys showed up.'

'Let's get this straight,' Chatteris said, and I could sense him turning all precise and forensic. That was how he'd made it to the top of the pile, after all, by being forensic and precise: a handsome set of scalps on the belt of his neatly tailored trousers, ministers, dissolute princelings, bigwigs taken down by their hubris. But I wasn't expecting forensic nor precise. I was expecting sympathy. 'What you are saying is that this Nurse Mersey used to come to check up on you, after you were discharged from the isolation ward. Then some other people showed up.'

'Absolutely. At first I thought they were standing in for Nurse Mersey. But then they went at me with a syringe.'

'I see. So they attacked you with a syringe. Could you de-scribe them, these people who attacked you with a syringe?'

'Well, they were wearing NHS smocks. They came in a little NHS van, like Nurse Mersey—'

Beaumont sat up with a jolt, looking aghast. A little too theatrically, I thought. But then again I'd never really done TV. 'Really now. I think it's time to put paid to this nonsense. Frontline responders ambushing people in their homes. Whatever next.'

'No no,' I said hastily, 'of course not. They were fake. Even the guy's accent was fake.' I could feel the onset of a headache. Like one of those hydraulic spreading tools firefighters use to extract people from their crushed cars. Except the spreaders were inserted behind my temples and their jaws were expanding fast.

Chatteris wasn't letting go. 'So there was a man wearing a fake NHS smock, with a fake accent. And what were they trying to do to you?'

'I don't really know,' I heard myself say. 'At first I thought they were, you know, after my blood.'

'After your blood,' Chatteris repeated. His voice was neutral. But he was just giving out more rope.

'Well, I couldn't be sure.' My voice was feeble and a little shaky, faraway. I was no longer sure who was doing the talking. I wanted out. I wanted to call Helen and ask her why the hell she'd talked me into doing the interview. But Chatteris was sitting there looking at me patiently like a curious bloodhound, waiting for his answer. 'Afterwards I think they were out to, well, take me away,' I said. 'And then there was the Glenniston thing.'

'Glenniston,' Chatteris said. 'You mean the life science company.'

I was taken aback by that. I wasn't aware Glenniston was a company one was supposed to know. I hadn't, until I'd started researching them and I'd found precious little about them on the web. 'Well, if that's what you want to call them.' My voice came across feeble and defensive.

'Sir Jeremy,' Chatteris said, turning to Beaumont, 'perhaps you'd like to come in here. Glenniston – what's their role in a crisis like this?'

'Thank you, Ralph.' Beaumont was all serious and sincere. 'And yes, absolutely. Glenniston are one of a number of companies who have been playing a pivotal role in strengthening our biosecurity. They've been working hand in hand with the NHS to help protect our frontline responders, enhance our protocols, keep people safe. I have to say that without them we'd be facing a much bigger threat right now.'

Bullshit, I wanted to say, but I could see Chatteris nodding. I went all in.

'What I do know is they were linked to a tranquillizer I found in my flat after the fake NHS people tried to take me.'

Chatteris had his arms half-crossed, his right hand extended, his index and middle fingers pointing vaguely in my direction. 'They were linked,' he repeated, emphasizing the *linked*. He was in cross-examination mode. 'Linked by whom?'

Linked by Helen, Helen Beaumont, I wanted to say, but I couldn't, not in front of her husband and a few million strangers. Not in the glare of the studio lights.

'I saw a laboratory when I went back to The Land Of. Cages, animals, case notes. There was a Lynx. You see, it all points to Glenniston.'

'This is all very, er, interesting,' Chatteris said.

Even from where I was watching, hovering sky-high

above it all like a kite in a gyre, I could tell I was rubbish. I was there and I wasn't there. I could see myself from a spot on the ceiling, looking down, and what I saw was a drifting wreck, all at sea. And something else: Helen, sitting on a lone chair in that vast empty studio where the audience should have been sitting. Her face expressionless. Then the glimpse was gone. The lights all on me, or what was left. The fact was, I knew f-all about Glenniston. I didn't have shit. I heard them listening to me, like a distant murmur across the seas. Ranting about some deserted hangar and ragtag monkeys malingering. Some kooky gibberish about hanging upside down like a bat from the battlements, and the Lynx like a keen-eyed peregrine, turning and turning. And some drivel about a muta-something or other. A what? A mutation? A mutant, like a what, a turtle? Everyone squirming, Ralph Chatteris and each of the millions of voyeurs up and down the land. Helen's husband taking in the scene with an air of detached amusement. Having the time of his life, blow by bloody blow. Of course he knew, about Helen and me. Chatteris's voice receding even further. Like the scummy outcrop of the waterline on the beach drawing back, except it kept going further and further out, a distant demarcation on the horizon now, reefs and sea creatures exposed on the sloping wet flats running for miles, starfish flapping in agony and something big and glum and scaly raising a barnacled eyebrow.

Chatteris wasn't done yet. 'Now there's also the curious business of your three colleagues. They disappeared in The

Land Of. Then they reappeared. And then they each met a rather grisly end.'

How the audience were hanging upon his every word. Nothing they didn't know, but the way he put it. And his voice so trenchant and seductive.

'Shall we start with David Weston? Is it correct that you are helping police with their inquiries regarding a fire at his cottage on the Isle of Sheppey?'

'Um,' I murmured, and it was like the murmur of the sea beyond the horizon, and so much for the D-notice, I thought with what remained of my lucidity. I said something at that point about Wystan. 'They came to take my dog.'

'Take your, um, *dog*?' The way Chatteris masticated the word *dog*: masterful.

'Yes, yes,' I said, because I was unstoppable now. 'Kidnapped. They kidnapped Wystan.'

'Wys-*who*?' Chatteris was doing a victory lap. Here was one to tell his grandchildren about while pruning the roses outside his cottage in Stoke-le-Something. There was no one at home now. Questions like fragments lobbed from way behind the tideline out in the doldrums. Who did I think was behind my colleagues' disappearance?

Uh and *er*. 'Well, David,' I said, 'he was after Khai Manni. And Ricardo, too. The trail led to the Zigzag Mountains.'

Chatteris was full of pity now. 'The zigzag *what*? And Ky, how do you spell that?'

I spelled it out: I tried, honestly I did, but the alphabet failed me. 'A *K* perhaps, and a Y, or an H?'

And Chatteris in hot pursuit: 'What did he look like, this Ky Money?'

'Well,' I stammered, 'the thing is, he's always wearing a *chèche*.' And I was hoping they wouldn't ask me to spell that. 'But the thing is, *he doesn't have a face.*'

The *coup de grâce* after that came almost as a relief.

'Have you been on medication since you were discharged from the isolation ward?'

I don't know if I said anything, but I could sense something growing back behind the tideline, sultry beyond some distant tropic, the water massing sky-high, and when it came thundering in it swept over London Bridge and up the hill, King William Street, chuckling bones and rats and all that, and Helen's husband riding the Hokusai crest, surfing on a silver spoon.

I must have been quite a sight, exiting that studio, then making a beeline down the stairs, tumbling on the edge of vertigo, clinging to banisters and walls, Mick or Mike assisting solicitously. The security guard in reception averting his eyes with a cringe. I made for the nearest Tube station with the haste of a hunted animal running to its hole. I went north and then south: in the tunnels at least no one could have seen the show. I sent a WhatsApp to Helen, and immediately wished I hadn't, and I never got a reply.

XXI.

The M4 was almost empty. Hardly any traffic either way. The deer all emboldened grazing on the verges, not too bothered about zoonosis. This was a primate thing after all. Give and take a flying mammal or two. Squirrels popping up where they shouldn't, flashing their rude rodent health at me from the middle of the carriageway and back with bold athletic bounds into the bushes.

Flashing lights on the hard shoulder near Maidenhead. An SUV with its bloated nose half stuck in the bushes, an ambulance and a police car attending. The ambulance crew were pulling someone from the SUV and didn't even have proper PPE. Swimming goggles over raincoats, hoods up.

I got off the motorway shortly before Reading. Woodcote Mapledurham Checkendon, everyone holed up in their pretty houses down pretty lanes with pretty names. No one wanting to be caught out with a broken clutch cable right now: AA patrolman comes up, gets out his toolkit, torch clamped to the open bonnet lighting up his face from below and you realize; you see the yellow in his eyes and he starts coughing, et cetera, and before you know it there's goo all over your grille. Or a zombie column coming out from the trees: the ivory in their clouded-up doll eyes gone a stark shade of egg yolk, foaming at the mouth, the ambient drizzle boiling to steam as it hits their fevered bodies, and all they want is to ask you for a lift.

Every time I got closer to a bigger road there seemed to be flashing lights a little further down. ROAD CLOSED AHEAD signs, roadblocks on roundabouts. I turned the radio on, hoping to catch the traffic news, but all I got was Mahler on one station and a call-in on another: yeah, seems like the geezer had a complete meltdown, someone was saying, on live TV. Laughter in the studio. Like, cringe, I mean: poor bastard, they say it's the medication that got to him. I turned off the radio, zigzagged to avoid flooded bits of road, doing U-turns squeezed in among the hedgerows whenever the water got too deep. I seemed to be going in circles around a village called Four Ashes and I was worried about running low on petrol and suddenly there was a roadblock again, and this time I didn't see it in time to do a U-turn. An army Land Rover sideways, yellow signs, but this time the road itself was a dead end, a tall gate backed with green panels and razor wire and floodlights, the gate slightly ajar. I thought I could see a row of little white vans parked inside, the kind that kept showing up in my street, with a blue logo on the door, but I was probably imagining it. A redcap with a torch came up to the car. I fumbled in my pockets and pulled out the NHS badge and lanyard they'd given me when I got out of the Very Dark Place, and I put my window down.

'Lost, are we?' the soldier said.

'Yes,' I said, 'with all the flooding.'

'Where are you going?'

'Oxford. Got my shift coming up at the Radcliffe.' I held up the badge.

'Well, I'm sorry, doctor, but you'll have to turn around here. Just keep going straight and take the second left. That'll take you back to the M40.'

I did a three-point turn. Every once in a while there'd be blue strobing lights, and you couldn't tell if it was an ambulance or the police giving chase. Once or twice I was stopped, but I showed them my badge and that was enough, a good thing they didn't run the name through their computer, and eventually I got on to the M40 and from there it was easier, no more roadblocks or flashing lights. I got off the motorway at Lewknor and went south again. Somewhere outside Wallingford my phone started ringing. For some reason I expected it to be Helen. I pulled into a lay-by. It wasn't Helen. *Mette*, the phone said.

'Guess what?' Mette said, and there was sunshine in her voice and birdsong.

'Tell me you found the Big Six.'

She laughed. 'Guess what. I found the Big Six.'

'That's wonderful. What are they?'

'Wait, I need to count,' she said, and she laughed again. 'Maybe I'll send you a picture.'

'That would be nice.'

'And what about you? Did you find those friends you were looking for?'

'I did. But then I lost them again.'

'I'm really sorry to hear it,' she said. I heard water splashing at the other end. 'I'm back home. Will you come and visit me?'

I looked out of the window, all fogged up. 'I'd love to,' I said, and I knew I couldn't and wouldn't.

'I'll send you the address.'

The rain picked up again, drumming down with nowhere to go. Now more now less, as if someone was playing with a lever. I should have gone after the Big Six, back in Loching. I pictured myself walking down the beach on some cosy dune-ringed island in the Baltic, eating cherries and drinking akvavit from a little hip flask I'd share with Mette. Ha ha.

Epilogue

Palavers End

XXII.

The waters were where I'd left them. Lapping up against the bottom of the metal pole with the letterbox on it, the boat tied to a tree, half covered in branches with a foot of water in it but afloat. The water was just deep enough for the boat to scrape along over the meadow or path or whatever it was. The oars kept hitting things. When I got to Palavers End I had to get out and pull the boat over the gravel that lay around the submerged flower beds. I tied the painter to the boot scraper. The front door was locked. I didn't have a key.

I waded round to the back of the house. The kitchen door was also locked. I fished in the flooded flower beds for a rock. I wrapped my hand in my scarf and smashed in one of the little leaded panes in the door. My mother had left the key in the lock on the inside.

Apart from a shallow puddle by the door, the house was dry. The fridge was humming. For a moment I thought Helen was standing by the kitchen door. I had brought her once, for a weekend. My parents had still been living in town, my father was still alive. We walked along the towpath all day and had a picnic in the meadows and sat on the stone step outside the kitchen watching the sunset in the haze somewhere behind the bend in the river. But I was alone. The light playing tricks.

I looked in the fridge. Spinach turned to mush in the vegetable drawer; a lump of dodgy-looking butter. But I couldn't smell anything anyway. I looked in the larder. It had a stock of baked beans and sardines to last a few days. The kitchen taps still worked.

The rain started up again and I went through my mother's bookshelves: a lot of mid-century French and not much else besides. I took out a pile of Camus and Gide and Malraux and went to the kitchen and looked out at the river or the fields or whichever was which. Raindrops coming down hard. The current a little further out looked scary, and if the water rose any more it would get hard to cross back over to the road. It would also be more difficult to reach the cottage from the road. They'd come for me, eventually. But at least I'd see them coming, during the day at least.

Once or twice I thought I saw a car or an overturned yacht float past among the branches and the random junk going down the river to the sea. My phone pinged. A message from Mette. An address in Denmark, the Red Cottage, Læsø, and a photo, but nothing Danish in the picture. Spiky plants, grainy, the light bad, the soil red and African, and the muzzle of something with a big shaggy mane protruding from the vegetation, feline, canine, lupine or vulpine I couldn't tell, though it clearly had bite. *The big Six: Number six*, the message attached to the photo said, with a smiley face.

I put a chair in the open kitchen door and watched the flow, thick and dark like lava in fast forward, throwing ridges and ripples and welts. I could hear voices somewhere upriver, coming closer. A narrow canoe gliding past with three men in it in cagoules like ghouls with their knees up, a chanting that sounded monastic but was probably just a drinking song badly slurred. One of them threw a bottle in a wide arc over the water and it landed with a splash in my mother's flower beds. Laughter, fingers stuck up to the ash-coloured sky. Then they were gone.

A single thin ray of sunshine like a stiletto thrusting out through the clouds. More branches, plastic crates, the roof of a milk float, a red phone box though it can't have been. Far too heavy to float unless something or someone was messing with the laws of physics. There were snaking serpentines of red, white and blue bunting in the flow now, the zigzag of little forked tongues flapping on the waves. Bits of band-stands. Occasional logs drifting perilously. A keelboat still upright that must have been ripped from its mooring upriv-er. A ragged pennant fluttering on the mainstay, RYS. The shovel of a JCB. Things that should have sunk and yet were afloat. Little splattered bits that could have been anything, old footballs or tyres half-submerged or giant hedgehogs or teddy bears. And a ragged little mop-like thing bouncing in the waves, crooked pointy ears and black bead-like eyes paddling. Escaping from the pull of the stream, head bobbing eagerly like a mechanical toy. He waded up through the flower beds and stood shaking his motley fur, then he came up to me and put his head in my lap. I patted Wystan on the head and he wagged his crooked tail, and the rain briefly stopped. A bird flew past, a slim white bird that could have been a dove had it not been for the long pointy beak in which it carried a twig. Or a plastic straw, perhaps.

I rummaged in the cupboard in my mother's living room and found an old bottle of port. I poured myself a glass and dripped a few droplets on Wystan's head.

The rain started again. The current outside had got stronger and was tugging at the tips of my mother's roses. The water was starting to lap up onto the kitchen tiles. Not much, but enough to cover part of the floor with a thin layer of water. Half a thimble deep.

Around four in the afternoon there was a noise at the front of the house. A pebble or some other hard object thrown against the front door. Wystan ran to the door, barking. I got up and took a knife from the block in the kitchen. I turned the lock and opened the door with the knife at my side. There was no one to be seen. Just something sliding and writhing in the vegetation right up against the wall of the cottage, a rat or a vole. I closed the door. I heard Wystan shuffling behind me. False alarm, old boy, I said and turned around, but it wasn't Wystan. It was a homunculus in a black suit, compact like a sumo wrestler in miniature, water dripping from his bowler hat, his face without expression: not angry, not smiling, simply there. He must have come in through the kitchen door when I went to the front of the house. Before I could do anything he had lunged at me. He went for my right armpit. I couldn't see what it was. A syringe or a knife or something altogether more sinister. I was expecting pain, or numbness, but the man stepped back and looked at me, his eyes empty like a dead pigeon's. 'Served,' he hissed, then he turned around and walked off to the kitchen door and disappeared. I looked at my arm and saw nothing, only a plain white envelope which had fallen to the floor. Laid paper, a few drops of water on it and one of the corners starting to soak but otherwise immaculate, and my name neatly typed, *Esq*. I heard splashing outside the kitchen door and the sound of an outboard engine and when I went to the door a small motorboat with two black figures in it was plodding out through the violet light towards where the river used to be. Inside the envelope was a neatly folded sheet of paper and I saw a court stamp and the name of a fancy firm of solicitors and words that no longer meant anything to me, Glenniston and defamation et cetera. I wondered how I'd get to Læsø without crossing a border. I scrunched the writ up into a ball and hurled it out into the flow of empty bottles and milk cartons.

Sometime around eleven in the evening, the fridge stopped humming. I tried one of the light switches, but there was nothing. I went to the fuse box by the stairs. All the fuses were in. Probably a short circuit in the mains. I went up the stairs in the darkness, arms stretched out in front of me. I stayed up for an hour or two by the open window in my bedroom, listening for anything unusual, but only heard the pitter-patter of the rain, then I started to doze and at one point the rain stopped. The silence was absolute now and the clouds cleared a little and there was a silvery shimmer in the sky but no moon. A light breeze came in through the open window, and for a split second I thought I could smell again, roses, sweet and full and ripe like Turkish delight or the long hazy afternoon of a wedding party, not one's own. Then the smell was gone. I'd probably just imagined it.

I wasn't properly asleep when I heard the knocking, and at first I thought it was the rain again. Tap tap tap, it went; I tried to turn on the light and then remembered the mains had gone dead. I sat up and realized it was someone knocking on the bedroom door, and the door opened and it was Helen. Please don't knock, I said. Whatever else you do, don't knock. She didn't say anything. She was standing in the soft pale light coming in through the leaded rectangles of the window and her bare skin looked soft and smooth and very pale, it made me want to cry, and I tried to remember something and couldn't, but then she came over to my bed and I could feel her bare thighs against mine and her hair loose on my forehead and her breasts brushing against my chest, and I didn't try to remember then and I didn't cry. The clouds moved and covered up the moonlight again and the silver light was gone but I could see the flowers now, the rose petals straining scarlet and moist against my hands and the orchids angry happy streaks of violet and dusky pink and mauve, and Helen's breathing the only sound until the rain came back, tap tap pitter patter pit pat like bony fingers drumming softly against the windowpanes like rodents scurrying in the attic.

The knocking came at four in the morning. It woke me up, and then I was awake. The dream of Helen's body like an imprint on my sweaty sheets. It sounded like someone was tapping on the windowpanes. I went to the window and checked, and there was nothing there. I looked outside, in the corridor, and there was no one there. I went carefully down the stairs and listened for any sound, and there was nothing. I checked the front door. I looked in the living room. Wystan was stretched out on his side by the fireplace, his ribcage moving up and down like a bellows. I looked around for my mother's pottery but I couldn't see any; the shelves were all empty, the darkness playing tricks on me. I went into the kitchen and listened and there was no sound. It was cold, a chilly draught coming in through the pane of glass I'd had to smash to get in. The kitchen door was locked the way I had left it, the key on top of the fridge.

I took the key and unlocked the door and my feet got wet as I walked through the puddle inside the kitchen door. I stood on the threshold and saw an ocean at my feet. There was no wind and the flow had stopped and the water was flat and dead, the moon reflected still and shiny like a drop of quicksilver in a Petri dish. Skeletal trees on the horizon, somewhere across what once had been the Thames. An owl calling, so close it must have been sitting somewhere in the eaves. I walked around to the front of the house. The boat was lying immobile up against the hydrangeas. I felt for the painter on the boot scraper and undid the knot, and as I threw the rope into the boat and looked down into the water I saw my face rippling on the surface and next to it, clear and stark as day, white robes and *chèche* reflected and the moonlight casting about in vain for a face to light.

Acknowledgements, and apologies

No, he didn't (do it all by himself).

My unbounded gratitude goes to Nemonie Craven: my perfect reader, and the most resourceful and resilient of agents. Thank you: for getting it: 'diese sehr ernsten Scherze'.

And sincere thanks to Damian Lanigan and Neil Griffiths at Weatherglass: for taking a punt on this meander of a book. For their patience in pruning and clipping and straightening so the meander became a little less untamed. And to Sarah Terry for a thoughtful and thorough final edit.

Also: to Faber and Faber Ltd, for permission to use a quote from 'The Love Song of J. Alfred Prufrock' by T.S. Eliot as the epigraph to this book.

And finally: apologies, to TSE and WHA. I don't know the first thing about gods, but I'd like to think these two can take it on the chin.

THE UNDROWNED

TOBY VIEIRA

First published in 2025
by Weatherglass Books

Copyright © 2025 Toby Vieira

A CIP record for this book is published by the British Library

ISBN: 978-1-0687941-4-8

Cover design: Luke Bird
Typesetting: James Tookey

Printed in the U.K. by CMP Books, Poole

www.weatherglassbooks.com

Weatherglass
Books